TAKING
CHANCES

A WINDSOR FALLS NOVEL

Carolina Blue
PUBLISHING

Kimberley O'Malley

WHERE ROMANCE IS TRUE BLUE & RED HOT!

Published by Carolina Blue Publishing, LLC

Copyright 2017, Carolina Blue Publishing, LLC

ISBN: 978-1-946682-03-1

To the readers of romance novels everywhere. Thank you for being true to what you love, despite often being asked, "Why do you read those?" I was a reader of romance novels long before I became a writer of them.

Praise for
Kimberley O'Malley

"There was so much emotion in the story that you will definitely need to keep the box of tissues close by. I felt the heartache, joy, and love that the characters were feeling throughout the story. The author writes a beautiful story that kept me hooked until the end."

–Alpha Book Club

"Kimberley O'Malley really manages to captivate the reader with her words and descriptions. I felt their heartache and joy and loved the ups and downs."

–Texas Book Nook Blog

"Kimberley O'Malley has brought to life very multi-dimensional characters and given them a purpose. The world she has created is so vivid and really helps the reader feel like they are there with the characters. A strong and fast paced plot will keep you invested the entire way through."

–The Indie Express Blog

"Kimberley O'Malley has done an impeccable job of bringing to life some very compelling characters. There is plenty of drama laced throughout this wonderfully real novel and some heartache and emotional moments as well."

– Novel News Network

Chapter One

Katie Fitzgerald cursed under her breath as she ran across the gravel parking area in heels. Never a good idea. The thought had no more entered her head when there was a sickening snap. She stumbled sideways as the ridiculously high heel of her right shoe fell to the ground. Katie lost her balance and was about to join her heel in the dirt and gravel. The items in her arms scattered everywhere. The string of inventive curses that followed colored the air around her.

Strong arms reached her, picking her up as though she weighed no more than a feather and placing her back on her feet. "I thought nice, Southern ladies didn't know words like that," came an amused drawl from behind her.

Katie stood still and counted to ten in her head. Do not look up, she ordered herself. It didn't matter if she did, though. She already knew it was *him*. His voice alone was enough to send her female parts into a chorus of "Hallelujah", while she plotted his painful death in her head. Bending to pick up her broken heel, Katie spied a shiny pair of men's shoes next to her. Straightening, her gaze tracked up charcoal gray dress pants. A snowy white dress shirt and bold red tie covered his broad chest. It was him. Great.

This was exactly the last thing she needed. More crap in an otherwise already less than delightful day. And it was supposed to be an awesome day. Elizabeth and Sam, two of her oldest friends were getting married tomorrow. Katie was running late for the rehearsal. After years of separation and adversity, they had beaten the odds and were getting their happily ever after. Yep, a momentous day. But things were not going well so far. Despite being off last night, Katie ended up working. The critical care unit had gotten not one but two call outs. When staffing called, Katie couldn't say no. Even though she should have. So now she was sleep deprived on top of everything else.

Then, as she was ready to leave this morning, Ginny Nelson had stopped by to talk to her. Ginny was a big deal, the Director of Nursing for the entire medical center. One didn't say no to her. So, off she went to Ginny's office to talk about the upcoming Heart Health Awareness Day. This was an annual event that the medical center was very proud of. The community was invited to the hospital for a day of free programs and information to promote better heart health and awareness. Many departments of the hospital would be participating in this event. It was a way for the medical center, and its staff, to give back to the community.

Ginny had shocking news for her. Linda Foster, the event chairwoman, had been diagnosed with an aggressive form of breast cancer. She had taken an immediate leave of absence from work and all other duties to focus on her own health. Linda had been a mentor to Katie when she was a new nurse. And she was still one of the best nurses Katie had ever worked with. Ginny told her that Linda had personally recommended Katie to take her place. Katie had been both shocked and gratified. This was a big deal. And it would look very good on her applications for graduate school.

Ginny had gone on to assure Katie that everything was in place for the event, which was only a few weeks away. But there were many last-minute details to attend to. It would be on Katie to ensure that everything ran on schedule for the event.

Of course, Katie had said yes. Her head was still reeling with the implications when a quiet knock sounded at the door. And then *he* walked in. Dr. Flynn Reynolds, staff Cardiologist and personal nemesis.

Katie listened with growing horror as Ginny thanked Flynn for his willingness to be a part of the campaign. The other woman's lips were still moving, but Katie had stopped listening. Or maybe it was the buzzing in her ears. She and Flynn would be working together on the event? What? Why? But Katie had already agreed. And she wouldn't back down now. That would be cutting her nose off to spite her own face, as her dead Granny Dee would have said.

And here he was again. Katie straightened up to her full height, which at five feet nothing, wasn't saying much. She craned her neck to look at Flynn. His raven hair shone in the early evening sun. The piercing blue eyes didn't miss a thing. There was more than a foot of height difference between them; another of his faults as she saw it. Katie had gotten her mother's height in the sea of giants that was her family. The fourth of six kids and the oldest girl, Katie was by far the shortest. Her brothers were all over six feet, and even her younger sister, Riley, was five ten.

"We meet again, Katie," Flynn said in his smooth, lightly mocking tone.

As usual, she made up for her lack of height with attitude. "Don't you dare laugh at me, Dr. Reynolds. I am so not in the mood."

He didn't have the grace to even try to remove the smile from his handsome face. "Did you hear me laughing, Katie? And what's with the 'Dr. Reynolds'? You don't even call me that at work."

Katie chose not to answer that. How could she? She'd be giving him the upper hand if she explained that using his title kept a wall between them. No thanks. He was already too smooth. Too confident. Too damn gorgeous for her own good.

"As interesting as this chat has been, Flynn, I'm already late." She took one step forward and almost stumbled again. Drat! Being this close to him always made her mind go blank. But how could she have forgotten about her stupid heel?

Flynn reached out and grabbed Katie's arm to steady her. Again. But the touch of his fingers was anything but. Her arm tingled where he touched her, and liquid heat gathered low in her belly. Wrenching her arm away, Katie turned back to face him. "I'm fine, thank you." With as much dignity as she could gather, Katie limped back to her car. Luckily, she always kept a spare pair of flip flops in the back. She might not be winning any fashion awards, but she needed shoes.

She glanced at the thin, silver watch on her wrist. One minute until she was late. Katie turned and crashed into the solid wall that was Flynn. "Are you trying to make me even later than I already am?" That was when she noticed the large, bunch of colored ribbon in his hands.

"No. Trying to help. You dropped Elizabeth's bouquet."

Katie stared at him. "You know what that is?"

Flynn grinned down at her. "I have sisters, Katie. And they're all married. Let me help you. Please." He had at least stopped grinning at her.

She nodded, knowing he was right. She shifted the large box she was holding to his arms, grabbing the "bouquet" from his hand. "Thanks, Flynn. I need to get inside before they start without me." She took off as fast as the gravel and her flip flops would allow, muttering under her breath the whole way. Katie tried to ignore Flynn, who easily kept pace with her. But the sight, and scent, of him made that impossible. The man was sin on a stick.

Flynn jogged ahead and held the door open for her. She sailed into the banquet hall where Elizabeth and Sam would be holding their wedding reception the next day. She had spent most of the day here, helping her family to decorate for the festivities. She'd run home an hour before to take the world's fastest shower and make herself presentable. The lovely hotel would be the site of both the wedding ceremony and reception.

"You can set that down over there," she directed Flynn, pointing to a table against the wall.

Flynn did so before turning back to her. "You seem a little stressed. Are you okay?"

"I will be. All I have to do is get through the rehearsal and dinner." Katie grimaced at the sound of that. "Let me rephrase. I'm excited about the wedding, but I'm exhausted. Once the rehearsal dinner is over, I'm going up to my room and sleeping for twelve hours straight."

Flynn leaned in, peering at her. For one wild moment, she thought he was going to kiss her. Her heart pounded. "That would explain the dark circles under your eyes."

The eyes in question widened. "Wow. You really know how to flatter a girl. Thanks for that. Like I wasn't aware already." She turned her back on him and rushed out the side door. The rest of the wedding party was already assembled on the terrace, and all eyes turned to her. Her face reddened as she remembered she was wearing flip flops with her dress. Oh well. Nothing she could do about that now.

"Sorry I'm late," she murmured as she reached Elizabeth's side. Handing her the bouquet of ribbon from her bridal shower, Katie leaned in and kissed her on the cheek.

"No worries, Katie. We're waiting on Flynn as well."

"I'm here," Flynn called, joining the others on the terrace. He approached Elizabeth and Sam, hugging her and shaking his hand.

"So glad you could make it," Sam said dryly.

Katie grinned at Sam. Until recently, her friend had viewed Flynn as competition for Elizabeth's heart. The two might not be great friends yet, but Sam had been gracious enough to allow Flynn to act as one of his groomsmen. Flynn was the first new friend Elizabeth made after coming home last summer. Sam could never say no to Elizabeth. His love for her was glowing in his eyes for everyone to see.

Katie glanced around. Sure enough, all the players were in attendance. The minister raised his hand to get their attention.

"Good evening, everyone, and welcome. If you could take your places, we'll begin."

People began to murmur as they shuffled into place at the side of the terrace. The front row was reserved for family. Katie noticed her mother, Maggie, and Elizabeth's mother, Diane, were already seated there. Her father, Joseph, would be walking Elizabeth down the aisle.

Katie moved to the front of the line where the best man, Sam's friend Quinn Adams, waited. He glanced at her feet and laughed. "Don't ask," she hissed under her breath. Behind them was her oldest brother, Donovan, and his wife, Nora. Then came her youngest brother, Aidan, and Kelsey Williams, one of Elizabeth's co-workers. Bringing up the rear was the devil himself, Flynn Reynolds, with her younger sister, Riley. It could be worse, Katie thought. She could have been walking down the aisle with *him*.

Katie forced thoughts of Flynn from her mind and concentrated on the rehearsal. Everyone turned and watched as Elizabeth made her way to the front with Joe. Katie bit the inside of her lip to keep the threatening tears in check. She knew there wouldn't be a dry eye in the house tomorrow.

The minister waited until everyone was in place before speaking. "Remember your places. This is exactly where y'all will be tomorrow when I start. Elizabeth, you'll hand your bouquet to Katie." The bride smiled as she did so. "Now Joe, you'll hand Elizabeth off to her lucky groom. I'll say a few words about love, etc. The bride and groom will say their vows. I'll pronounce them husband and wife. Then Sam, you can kiss your bride." Sam unexpectedly swept up Elizabeth in his arms and kissed her. He did so until the minister tapped him on the shoulder. "I meant tomorrow, Sam."

"Just practicing," joked the groom to everyone's delight.

"Where was I? Oh right, so Sam kisses Elizabeth, and then they proceed back up the aisle. Everyone else follows in the order they came. Any questions?" He glanced around and saw that everyone was nodding. "Okay then, let's go have dinner."

The wedding party made its way into a private dining room. Waiters buzzed around bringing out salads to start the meal. After a few moments, Sam clanged his fork against a water glass to get everyone's attention. He rose, waiting until silence fell before speaking.

"Y'all know I'm not one for speeches, so I'll keep this short." A round of good-natured cheers came from the audience. "Very funny. Elizabeth and I would like to thank everyone for taking part in our wedding."

Sam turned to Elizabeth, seated next to him, and took her hand in his. His smile was for her alone. Katie noticed that both of their hands were trembling. He had eyes only for her, even as he continued his speech "As you all know, I have loved Elizabeth for a very long time. I never thought I would be standing here tonight, about to marry the woman of my dreams. My best friend. I am the luckiest man in the world. Having y'all here to share in this with us is the icing on the cake. Thank you." When he finished speaking, Sam pulled Elizabeth up from her chair and kissed her tenderly. A sigh rippled through the room.

Katie turned away from the couple and sniffed delicately. A handkerchief appeared from the side of her vision. "Here. I wouldn't want your mascara to run." The gentle tone of his voice was almost Katie's undoing. Sparring with Flynn she could handle. Kindness was another thing altogether.

"Thank you," she whispered as she dabbed under her eyes. She didn't look at him. Flynn was dangerous. He was everything she needed to avoid. Katie focused on her career and going to graduate school to become a nurse practitioner. Getting involved with someone like Flynn Reynolds would be a disaster. He was too handsome. Too wealthy. Too much temptation. No, she was better off continuing to avoid him as she had done since January, when he moved here from Atlanta.

"They make a nice couple. Especially when you consider what they overcame to get here today."

Katie nodded in agreement. "I wasn't sure we'd ever get Elizabeth back from California. But she and Sam reconnected, and here we are. Some people are lucky that way, I guess." She took a sip of water before glancing around the table. She would have to be sitting next to him at dinner. Katie had to be careful about her reactions to the handsome cardiologist. She was surrounded by her siblings. Like a school of sharks, they could smell blood in the water, so to speak.

Flynn raised a dark eyebrow. "Lucky?"

"Yes, lucky," she challenged. "Sure, they had a long road, filled with obstacles. But here they are, almost married. I'd say they were lucky."

Flynn looked at her but didn't respond. He turned his attention back to his salad.

"Unlucky for you, though. After all, you didn't hide your interest in Elizabeth last summer. I'm surprised you're even here today. And not home licking your wounds."

Katie grabbed her fork and took a bite of her salad. It looked amazing but tasted like sawdust. She should never have said that to Flynn. Even if it was true. The comment had been rude and uncalled for. But the thought of apologizing to him made her crazy.

"Been holding onto that one for a while now, Katie. I'm touched at your concern." This was not said in his usual joking tone, and Katie felt sick. She might have hurt his feelings. Damn. Now she would have to apologize.

She sat very straight and still, deliberately avoiding eye contact with Flynn. "I'm sorry," she choked out.

Flynn set down his fork. "What are you sorry for, Katie? For speaking your mind? Or for the hurt you believe I suffered?"

"Either. Both. I don't know." She twisted her linen napkin in her hands. She couldn't even apologize to him without Flynn making it difficult. "Fine. I'm sorry I was a shrew. Can we forget it now?"

"Certainly," agreed Flynn. He picked up his fork and took another bite of his salad as though nothing had happened. Katie watched the strong muscles of his jaw flex as he chewed. She flushed when he turned and caught her stare. Damn her red hair and fair skin.

Quinn asked her a question, and she focused her attention on him. The handsome firefighter was normally great company, but she had no idea what he had said to her. When the waiter came, she ordered a glass of white wine, hoping that would calm her nerves.

Flynn made her feel things she hadn't felt in a long time. And that was bad. She had no desire to feel those things again. He was confusing. She had never wanted to kill someone in one breath and have her way with him in the next. But that was Flynn. Normally, she was a level-headed critical care nurse who was confident and professional. But something about Flynn made her lose it. On a regular basis.

In a perfect world, she only had to deal with him at work. But now, it seemed they would be spending time together on a regular basis. At least until the health fair was over in a few weeks. Not to mention she would have to put up with him all weekend. Sighing, she took another large sip of her wine. She would ignore him as much as possible. But how did one ignore a man like Flynn?

"Penny for your thoughts," murmured the man in question.

So much for ignoring him. "They're not even worth that," she replied.

"Why don't you let me be the judge?"

Katie took another sip of her wine and a bite of salad before responding. "Okay then. You asked for it. I was thinking that dealing with you at work was taxing enough. Now here you are at a family wedding." She tried not to wince. Even for her, that came out a bit harsh.

Flynn didn't seem to notice. "And here I thought we were on our way to becoming friends, Katie." He raised his glass to take a sip, saluting her with it as he did. "Don't forget our new partnership."

"As if I could," she muttered half under her breath. It was a shame, really. She would have liked to be friends with him. She had lots of guy friends. Flynn was charming and funny. His patients, and their family members, loved him. And he was dedicated to them. She admired that about him. Being friends with him would mean that she wasn't attracted to him. But she was. Wildly.

"We work together, Flynn. We aren't friends."

"But we could be, Katie." He had lowered his voice and leaned in until his lips touched the sensitive skin of her ear.

She didn't answer him. She couldn't. The touch of his lips had short circuited her brain. Instead, she reached unsteadily for her wine glass. Finding it empty, she waved at a passing waiter and signaled for a refill.

"Cat got your tongue, Katie?"

"Knock it off," she hissed at Flynn under her breath. She turned to him, green eyes blazing. "I don't need you baiting me right now. I have enough on my mind."

Although she was thrilled for Sam and Elizabeth, Katie hated weddings. She didn't believe in happily ever after anymore. Not after having her own heart crushed. She spied Riley getting up from the table. Hoping she was going to the ladies' room, Katie joined her.

"Excuse me," she muttered to Flynn as she rose.

Flynn rose as well. His perfect Southern manners made it hard to not like him. He had obviously been raised right. She grabbed an unsuspecting Riley and dragged her towards the rest rooms.

Chapter Two

Flynn sipped his Scotch and watched as Katie stalked off. That was the only word that fit. He was playing with fire, and he knew it. He was getting under her skin. Good! He shouldn't be the only one affected. Katie had been a constant thorn in his side since the day they'd met. A hot thorn, but a pain nonetheless. She might be tiny, but she was curvy in all the right places. Even in shapeless scrubs, thoughts of Katie Fitzgerald kept him up at night.

But it was more than that, he mused. She was very bright and had a quick wit and razor-sharp tongue. Usually used on him. With her patients, though, she displayed an endless amount of compassion and professionalism. He never batted an eye at leaving a critically ill patient in her care.

Because of his friendship with Elizabeth, he and Katie had been thrown together at several Fitzgerald family events recently. The result was usually explosive. She might not want to admit it, but they shared a chemistry that was undeniable. As much as she intrigued him, he needed to keep his hands off. Even though he didn't want to. Flynn was cautious about mixing business with pleasure. And he was new to Windsor Falls. He and Sebastian Walker, his best friend, were building their cardiology practice at the hospital. He couldn't afford to do anything to screw that up. He knew that his outgoing personality had earned him a certain reputation. Sleeping with an ICU nurse, even one as desirable as Katie, wasn't a promising idea.

But his good intentions had nearly flown out the window when he first saw Katie in the parking lot tonight. He had run for a shower after work, which made him almost late for the rehearsal. He spotted Katie wrestling a box out of her car. The sight of her bright red, wavy hair cascading down her back had stopped him in his tracks. At work, she always wore it in a ponytail. Even now, his fingers itched to run through it. That of course would lead to other things he wanted to do to her. With her. He glanced at her brothers seated at the table. Better to keep those thoughts to himself this weekend.

Katie returned to the table as the main course was being served. As she slid into the chair next to him, Flynn could smell the subtle floral scent that surrounded her. He watched as she placed a napkin on her lap and ignored him. She might be hands off, but that didn't mean he couldn't rattle her cage a bit. This was going to be fun.

"It's a shame we aren't paired for the wedding, Katie."

Good manners won out, and she turned toward him. " Why's that, Flynn?" Her tone was bland.

"Because then you'd be on my arm walking down the aisle. I guess I'll have to settle for a dance. Or two."

She smiled at him politely. "And what makes you think I'll dance with you, Dr. Reynolds?"

"Because you burn as hot for me as I do for you, Katie." Flynn returned his attention to his steak and tried not to grin at the daggers he knew her eyes were shooting at him.

After a few bites, he turned to Katie's younger sister on his left. "Riley, we haven't had a chance to get to know each other. I work with Katie."

Riley smiled at Flynn. "Oh, I know who you are. She's mentioned you. Once or twice." Her dark eyes twinkled with humor.

Turning his head to glance at a fuming Katie, Flynn murmured, "Has she? That's very interesting. All good things I hope."

A bubble of laughter escaped from Riley before she could answer. "Well, I'm not sure that 'good' quite covers it, Flynn. You seem to get on her nerves quite a bit though."

"Just part of my charm," he answered. "Katie is quite taken with me actually. She won't admit it."

Katie had been swallowing a sip of wine and coughed at his comment. Flynn patted her on the back.

When she could breathe again, Katie glared at Flynn. "Taken with you? I don't think so. Annoyed by you? Yes. Driven to homicidal fantasies? Every day."

"See, Riley, she admitted to fantasizing about me." Katie glowered at him, which only amused Flynn more.

Riley's laughter floated on the air. "Well, who could blame her, Flynn? You are quite gorgeous." She swept her gaze over him.

"Pure luck, Riley. I have excellent genes. As do you. The Fitzgerald women are all very beautiful." Flynn kept a straight face as Katie muttered something that sounded like 'snake oil salesman.'"

The waiter came and removed their dinner plates. Flynn noted that Katie had barely touched her meal yet her wineglass was full again. He couldn't resist commenting. "You might want to slow down on the alcohol. Especially since you didn't eat your dinner."

Katie lifted her glass with a defiant gleam in her eye. "No need to worry. I'm not driving this evening. All I have to do is make it back to my room."

"Good to know." The thought of her sprawled across a bed was enough to make a witty comeback difficult. His thoughts wandered further down that road. In them, they were wearing a lot less clothing. Dangerous thoughts considering where he was.

Shifting his attention back to Riley, Flynn asked, "So what was it like growing up with Katie? I imagine she was quite a handful."

"Katie and I are the only girls, so we had to stick together. But she has a temper, Flynn."

"Oh, I'm aware of that, Riley. She tried to take off my head with a coffee mug last summer if you can imagine."

A furious Katie joined in the conversation. "Only because you kissed me, Flynn." Her eyes grew wide with horror as she realized what she'd said. Her hands flew to her mouth.

Riley wore a curious expression. "You kissed her, Flynn? Funny she didn't tell me that." Leaning in front of Flynn, Riley addressed her sister. "How was it, Katie? Not good I guess if you threw a mug at his head."

"I threw the mug because I was pissed at him. Not because the kiss wasn't good." A blush spread across her cheekbones.

"So, you did enjoy it, Katie? Glad to hear it. But 'good' seems a bit mild for that kiss." Flynn chuckled at her expression.

Riley raised her brow at that. "Care to tell, Flynn?"

He glanced at Katie. "Not when she's got sharp instruments in her reach. Besides, a gentleman never kisses and tells." The color rising in Katie's cheeks told Flynn all he needed to know. She wasn't as immune to him as she pretended.

"This conversation is ridiculous." Katie rose a bit unsteadily and made her way to Elizabeth. Flynn let her go. Best not to poke the bear, he thought.

*****

Katie sat down next to the bride-to-be and waited until the room stopped spinning. She folded her hands in her lap, hoping to anchor herself in some way. But the room kept tilting this way and that.

"Exactly how many glasses did you have, Katie? You always were a bit of a light weight."

Katie turned towards Sam's voice. At least she thought it was Sam. She had closed her eyes, trying to ease the sway. No such luck. "Not sure," she mumbled. "Probably too much unless we actually are on a ship. In which case I don't have my sea legs."

Elizabeth put her arm around Katie's shoulders. "If you were in my ER right now we'd be betting on your blood alcohol level. Off the top of my head and judging by your swaying, I'd go with over the legal limit."

Katie tried to focus on Elizabeth's face and then Sam's. Both were frowning at her. And they had every reason to be. Her brother, Connor, Elizabeth's first husband and Sam's best friend, was killed by a drunk driver. For obvious reasons, they took alcohol very seriously.

Katie squirmed a bit in her seat. "I only had a few glasses. I haven't slept since yesterday and haven't had time for a real meal."

"What about dinner?" Sam inquired.

"He's too pretty. And he smells like sin. I couldn't eat."

Riley joined them. "Pay up Elizabeth! You owe me twenty bucks. I told you she liked him."

Katie's fair skin flamed. "I do not like him. I'd have sex with him in a heartbeat, but I don't like him."

"Interesting. I'm not sure whether to be insulted or turned on."

Katie closed her eyes again. She wished the earth would open and swallow her whole. But even in her alcohol induced haze, she knew she wouldn't be that lucky.

"What makes you think we were talking about you? You're not the only man here." Still no sign of the floor shifting. Drat! She could use a little help from the universe about now.

"Well, you were sitting between Quinn and me. I had a fifty-fifty shot."

Katie opened her eyes and glared at Flynn. A devilish grin lit up his handsome face. The worst part was that everything she had said was true. But Flynn didn't need to know that.

Mustering as much dignity as she could, Katie stood up. She wobbled a bit but didn't fall. "Whatever. I'm assuming you've looked in a mirror, Flynn. You know you're hot. Every woman at Windsor Falls Regional has a crush on you for goodness sake."

"I never noticed."

She scoffed. "Right. I must have imagined the flirting with everyone with a pulse then." After smoothing a hand down her dress, Katie grabbed her purse. "I think I'll be heading upstairs now. I need a nap." She walked away, head held high and thankful for a graceful exit. Which was a great plan until she stumbled on her flip flops. She would have sprawled on the ground if Flynn hadn't been there to catch her. With one strong arm around her waist, he scooped her up and tossed her over his shoulder in a fireman lift.

"Hey," shouted an enraged Katie. "Put me down."

Flynn said goodnight to everyone then weaved his way amongst the tables, heading for the lobby. He didn't show any signs of slowing until he reached a bank of elevators. "Care to hit the button?"

Katie muttered another string of unladylike words. "I'd like to hit something right now. Please put me down. I'm fine to walk now."

"You sure proved that in the dining room." Instead of releasing her, Flynn shifted her weight and reached down to hit the button. "Never mind, I've got it."

Katie ground her teeth. "The blood is rushing to my head. Please put me down."

Flynn was saved from answering by the arrival of the elevator. An elderly, white-haired couple gasped as they exited the car. Of course. Because she hadn't been humiliated enough. Katie buried her head in his back.

Flynn murmured a "good evening" to the shocked couple before entering the elevator. He lowered Katie to the ground. "Which floor?"

Not bothering to answer, Katie stabbed the button for the third floor with more force than necessary. She turned her back on him and continued to fume in silence.

Flynn chuckled. "If you were a cartoon character, there's be steam coming out of your ears about now."

She whirled on him, a bit too fast, and wobbled. Flynn reached out a strong hand to steady her, which made her angrier. "What did you think you were doing back there? You don't pick someone up and throw them over your shoulder like that."

"Apparently, I do."

Katie stomped her foot, forgetting she was in flip flops. The effect was ruined. She took them off to prevent tripping again. "A civilized person doesn't do things like that, Flynn." She turned her back on him as the doors slid open soundlessly. Hoping to leave him in her dust, Katie walked off the elevator. All she had to do was make it to her room. She had this.

Except of course that he was still right next to her. "What are you doing now? My room is only a few doors down from here. I'm sure I can make it." She walked ahead, stopping in front of 315.

"My mother would be very upset if I didn't walk you to your door. Besides, we're neighbors."

"What?" she shrieked. "Neighbors? You can't be serious."

"Oh, but I can." He flashed a key card identical to hers. A smug look settled across his face. "Three fifteen? I'm in three seventeen. Neighbors."

When would this nightmare end? It took her two tries, but Katie finally managed to open her door. She turned to Flynn. "Well, it's been, uh, interesting. Good night, Flynn."

She had almost escaped when Flynn grabbed her gently by the wrist. He reeled her in so that they stood mere inches apart. Flynn looked into her eyes. She moistened her lips. "You're not in this alone. I think about you too. All the time. In my bed. Under me. On top of me." His eyes smoldered with heat. She felt it to her toes. He released her wrist. "Good night." Flynn turned and walked into his own room, shutting the door behind him.

His words instantly sobered her. Katie went into her room. She threw herself across the king-sized bed. Rolling onto her back, she stared at the ceiling. He thought about her me? She pressed her thighs together against the heat and dampness his words had created. She fanned herself with her hand.

How could he say something like that and walk away? Since the first day they'd met, Katie had been at war with herself. He was drop dead gorgeous, with his thick, jet-black hair and a body to die for. Her fellow employees tripped over themselves when Flynn was on the critical care unit.

Not Katie. Although she did enjoy their inevitable sparring, she avoided Flynn like the plague. She might want to do all kinds of things with him. To him. But she wasn't going down that path again. She'd learned her lesson. No more doctors for her, especially not one on her own unit.

Disgusted with herself and the way her thoughts were going, Katie got up from the bed. The room still swayed a bit, but she felt better. She stripped on the way to the bathroom. She needed sleep. Everything would be better in the morning. Katie washed off her make-up and brushed her teeth. Just before crawling under the covers, Katie lowered the A/C to a chilly sixty-five. Her exhaustion finally caught up with her, and she was asleep in minutes.

*****

Next door, Flynn could hear Katie's movements through the wall. He grabbed a beer from the mini bar, not bothering to look at the price or the brand. He needed something to take his mind off the memory of her in his arms. The thin material of her dress had done nothing to mask the feel of her heated flesh against his. Flynn groaned. Knocking back half of the beer in a few gulps, Flynn set the bottle on a dresser and headed for the bathroom. He stripped off his suit and tie as he went. A cold shower was in order.

He thought about Katie as he stood under the strong spray. They had been dancing around each other ever since the day they'd met. He could picture the first time he'd seen her. She was performing chest compressions during a cardiac arrest. Her face was bright red and damp with sweat from her struggle to save the doomed patient. Wisps of her hair stuck to the sides of her face. And yet, he found her beautiful. The gentleman had died, despite their best effort. He could read the disappointment in her slumped shoulders as he pronounced time of death. She had taken the loss personally. He had admired her determination; never giving up until he called it.

It had been his first day at Windsor Memorial. He and Sebastian had just moved into their brand-new office in the medical office building. Flynn had stepped onto the critical care unit as the rapid response was being called.

He introduced himself to her later. Katie had not been impressed. She didn't even seem to remember him from the code. She shook his hand, welcomed him, and walked away. Since then, verbal jousts about patients and treatments made up their relationship. She was forever challenging him. Flynn enjoyed their battles. She was as impassioned as he about their patients. You didn't come across that every day. The fact that she was smoking hot and curvy in all the right places didn't hurt. But it did muddy the waters. Being this attracted to a coworker was the last thing he needed right now.

Turning off the water, Flynn toweled off and threw on a pair of boxers. He turned off the lights, cranked the air conditioning and set the alarm on his phone. Pulling back the covers, he slid into bed. It had been a long and demanding week. The wedding itself wasn't until late afternoon tomorrow. He wasn't on call and had no responsibilities for the next two days. He was looking forward to some uninterrupted sleep.

Chapter Three

Katie squeezed her eyes shut and pulled a pillow over her head. Why was there a jackhammer in her room? Her poor head pounded, threatening to split open. No jackhammer, she realized. Just her stupid alarm. She reached blindly towards the nightstand for her phone. Must stop its incessant ringing. Not having any luck, Katie gave up and came out from under the shelter of the blanket. Sunlight pouring through the window pierced her skull. She cursed herself for not remembering to close the curtains last night. Katie squinted at her phone and managed to silence the deafening alarm. Never again, she swore to herself. No more alcohol. It was a shame really, as she loved the occasional glass of wine.

Katie got all the way out of bed and headed for the bathroom. She had exactly fifteen minutes to be downstairs for breakfast. Then the events of the day would start. First there was make-up and hair, followed by getting dressed and photographs before the wedding. Katie grimaced as she glanced in the mirror. She didn't envy the make-up artist. She'd have to tip well.

She brushed her teeth and took the fastest shower ever before throwing on sweats and a button-down shirt. Elizabeth had reminded her to wear something that could be easily removed after having her hair done. She slid her feet into flip flops. She didn't give them up until the temperature dropped below fifty. A quick glance at her phone showed a text from Flynn. *Hope you're all right this morning. Hair of the dog?*

Acid swished in her stomach. Last night! She cringed as it all came back to her. She only had a few glasses of wine but on an empty stomach and no sleep. Then there was the ridiculous comment about Flynn. Even though it was true, she didn't need him hearing it. Katie would have slapped herself in the head, except there was already a marching band playing in it.

Nothing to be done about that. Just ignore him. She would be busy with a thousand wedding details. How hard could it be? She found out as soon as she walked out of her room. He stood there, leaning against the wall between their two rooms, arms folded across his chest. As if he had nowhere else to be.

"What are you doing here?" Great. Knowing she sounded shrill, she tried again. "What I meant was, sorry I didn't see you standing there. But what are you doing on my doorstep?"

Flynn had the gall to look perfectly put together this morning. Happy even. "I was on my way to breakfast and stopped by to make sure you were okay, Katie. You were rather tipsy when I dropped you off last night." He looked her up and down as if assessing a patient.

Katie tried to not burn with embarrassment. Although freshly showered, her wet hair was tossed in a bun. She was wearing her oldest sweats, a ratty pair left over from nursing school that threatened to slide off her hips at any moment. She wasn't wearing any make-up, and she had bags under her eyes. Great.

She returned the favor and looked Flynn up and down. Naturally, he looked his usual model self, with thick, damp hair that practically begged her fingers to run through. His khakis and polo shirt were casual but neat. No signs of a raging hangover. She hated him.

"I'm fine, as you can see." She headed down the hall towards the bank of elevators, hoping against hope he wouldn't follow. Of course, he did. Katie sighed aloud as Flynn fell into step beside her.

"Heading for breakfast? Me too." Flynn smiled down at her, and Katie forgot to breathe for a moment. Did all gorgeous men know how to smile in that way? The way that made her bones turn to mush. Was there a manual?

"Oh goodie," she muttered.

"Did you sleep well?" Flynn asked, ignoring her snide comment.

Katie inhaled deeply and counted to ten. She did that a lot around him. But she also knew she was being a bitch. It wasn't Flynn's fault he looked the way he did. She attempted a smile in return. "Yes, thanks, I did. You?" There. She had been civil to him. Would wonders never cease?

She pushed the button for the elevator, and the doors slid open immediately. Flynn, ever the gentleman, stepped aside for her to enter first. She murmured thanks and moved inside the car. Her body language didn't encourage conversation. Of course, Flynn didn't get the hint.

"I imagine you ladies have a full day before the wedding ceremony. All kinds of girlie things that I don't even care to imagine."

So much for ignoring her. "You'd be right, Flynn. I have hours of hair styling and make-up ahead of me. But no one is laying even so much as a finger on me until I've had about a gallon of coffee."

Flynn threw back his head and laughed. "Now there's my Katie. Attitude and all."

Katie turned her head towards him, wincing as she did. "Your Katie? Since when am I 'your Katie'?" Why was this elevator so slow? She had to get away from him. Now.

"Well, after what you said last night, I thought we had an arrangement." He topped that ridiculous statement with a wink.

The elevator reached the bottom floor, and Katie exited at a rapid pace. "I have no idea what I may have said to you last night, Flynn, but as you like to point out, I was a bit intoxicated. Too much wine, not enough sleep or food." She crossed her fingers behind her back at the blatant lie. She remembered every bit of it unfortunately.

"Something about finding me sexy. Ring a bell?"

Katie looked around to see if anyone was nearby to overhear their conversation. Luckily, the lobby was empty. She pulled Flynn down a side hallway. Her face flushed as she whirled on him. "Did you have to say that out loud? For everyone to hear? My whole family is here, Flynn!"

"I was only repeating what you said last night, Katie. You didn't seem to mind people overhearing you then."

"I was drunk, Flynn. My judgment was not at its best."

"So, you weren't responsible for what you said, Katie? Does that mean you didn't mean it?"

Katie caught her lower lip between her teeth and thought about how best to answer. She hated lying. Even the smallest of lies. And he knew that about her, damn him. She turned to face him and took a deep breath. "Fine," she spat at Flynn. "Yes, I find you very sexy. But then who doesn't? I'm not planning on acting on it."

Flynn closed the distance between them and leaned into her. The heat of his body burned hers. It was suddenly difficult to breathe. "What if I told you that I find you incredibly sexy too? Would that make a difference?"

Katie closed her eyes and tried for a snappy come back. Nothing. This was why she always avoided being close to him. It messed with her mind. Made it hard to think clearly. "No," she whispered in response. Even to her own ears it sounded weak.

"What if I said pretty please?" Flynn advanced, trapping Katie against the wall. He placed a large hand on either side of her head and covered her body with his own.

Katie forced herself to open her eyes and look at Flynn. She was so close to him, that she could see the small scar that lay to the right of one eyebrow. She had never noticed it before. Now she wanted to trace it with her finger. Or maybe her tongue. She struggled for rational thought instead.

"Not even with a cherry on top, Flynn. You're not my type." For an honest person, Katie was lying a lot she thought with disgust. To herself now. Of course, he was her type. He was over six feet of toned muscle. He was every woman's type.

Flynn raised the eyebrow that had been the subject of her scrutiny. "Are you sure, Katie?"

She nodded her head, not sure that she could form words at this point. He smelled like sex. Some masculine, spicy scent that tickled her nostrils and made her lower regions sit up and take notice.

"Let's see if that's true." That was all the warning Katie was given before Flynn leaned in and covered her mouth with his. It was probably a good thing she had the wall behind her. Otherwise she'd be in a boneless heap on the floor.

That was her last conscious thought as Flynn turned up the heat. He moved in until there wasn't any space between them anymore. His large, firm body made her feel small and feminine in comparison. Her mouth opened on a sigh, and Flynn plundered it with his tongue. Of their own volition, Katie's hands flattened on his chest. She marveled at the taut muscles there.

Flynn made a muffled sound, almost a growl, into her mouth. The sound alone made her damp. Without thinking, Katie moved her hips against him in a silent plea. Too many clothes, she thought. She tugged at his polo shirt, trying to untuck it. She needed to feel his skin.

Suddenly, Flynn's hands were on her arms, and he was taking a big step backwards. She felt lost and more than a little chilled. "I should have never started that," he muttered.

His words were a bucket of icy water over her heated flesh. Reality dawned, quickly and painfully. She moved a few feet to the side to put more space between them. What had she been thinking? Anyone could have come along at any time. And here she was, pressed up against Flynn, stripping him in the hallway. Her whole family was somewhere in the building for goodness sake.

Katie looked at Flynn one last time before turning on her heel to escape. But he was quicker than she was and caught her wrist. "Do I need to apologize?"

"No. But don't do it again," she mumbled more to herself than Flynn. She needed to get away from him so she could think.

"I am sorry, Katie. Sorry this isn't the right time for us."

"There's no us, Flynn. This can't happen." She gestured wildly between the two of them.

He nodded but didn't look happy about the truth. "You're right. We both have too much at stake."

She turned and walked away, head held high and spine rigid. She turned the corner and ducked into a rest room. Standing with her back to the cool, tile wall, Katie held her hands out in front of her. She watched their trembling with an almost morbid curiosity. She pressed her lips together, recapturing the taste of him. For months, she had been doing her best to avoid Flynn. This was exactly why. The attraction that had bubbled under the surface was real and had just exploded in her face.

Wishing it was just because of a dry spell, Katie tried to deny her attraction to him. But she knew better than that. Flynn got under her skin in a way that no man had before. But that wasn't a good enough reason to abandon her rules. He was wrong for her no matter how delicious he was. It wasn't worth getting her heart crushed again. She had plans. And they didn't include Flynn Reynolds.

Katie straightened away from the wall and shook off these gloomy thoughts. She exited the restroom and headed for the restaurant. She was already late and didn't want to keep the rest of the bridal party waiting. They had a lot to do in the next few hours. Being that busy might help to keep her mind off the yummy Dr. Reynolds. But, somehow, she wasn't so convinced of that.

*****

Flynn stayed where he was as she walked away. He needed a chance to cool down. His unexpected tangle with Katie in the hallway left him more than a little aroused. It wouldn't do to walk into breakfast, where her family gathered, sporting an erection. He tried to think of something that wasn't in any way related to Katie. Puppies. His mother. Anything. But he couldn't lose the memory of her lush, little body pressed against his. Or the hot sounds that came from deep in her throat as he kissed her.

Flynn paced up and down the short hallway, trying to get his thoughts under control. Not to mention his body. After another few minutes, he headed for the lobby. Outside the restaurant, he ran into Elizabeth. Scooping her up, he twirled the laughing bride-to-be around a few times before setting her back on her feet. "So, are you ready?"

Her bright blue eyes sparkled with joy. "More than ready, Flynn."

"There's still time to run away with me, you know. My car's right outside."

She threw back her head and laughed. "Very funny, Flynn. And you wonder why everyone thinks you're a flirt. You may have misunderstood your role as groomsman. Besides, it's taken me this long to get Sam to even like you. Don't ruin all my hard work now."

"Just kidding, my friend. I've seen the way Sam looks at you. And you at him. No one else will even be in the room when you say your vows."

Her eyes grew wet and Elizabeth swiped at them. "Don't remind me, Flynn. I don't know how I'm ever going to get through them without bawling."

"Nothing wrong with that, Elizabeth. You and Sam love each other, and this is a wonderful thing. I say make them all cry with you. Don't forget the water-proof mascara." He leaned in and hugged his dear friend. He had flirted with her last summer, when Elizabeth had first returned home. But he knew after kissing her once that they lacked any real chemistry. He was as fond of her as he was his own sisters. Katie Fitzgerald was another story altogether.

"Speaking of Sam, he and the other guys are waiting for you in the lobby. Y'all are going out for breakfast so that he and I don't accidentally see each other before the ceremony. Tradition and all that."

"Well, then, off to the lobby I go." He leaned in and kissed her cheek. "I can't wait to see Sam's face when he sees his beautiful bride for the first time."

Flynn walked away, smiling to himself. Elizabeth was glowing with happiness and she deserved every bit of it. And he liked Sam, even if the other man had taken awhile to warm to him. Sam had considered Flynn a rival for Elizabeth's affections. Flynn had known the truth; there wasn't any chemistry between them. But that didn't stop him from having a bit of fun at Sam's expense.

Now they were friends, and Flynn even joined their bi-weekly poker night when he wasn't on call. One or more of Katie's brothers were usually there. He liked and respected each of them. But he wondered what kind of slow death they might think up for him if they knew the thoughts he had about their sister. The ones where she was naked. In his bed. Or shower. He wasn't picky. No, they wouldn't be quite as friendly to him then. She was off limits in more ways than one.

*****

Katie took one last look in the mirror to ensure everything was perfect. She grinned at the unfamiliar creature who peered back. Far from the traditional bridesmaid gown, the dress she wore was a column of golden silk that clung to every curve. Neither a puffy sleeve nor hideous bow covering her butt in sight. Elizabeth had picked the color to reflect the wonders of autumn in her beloved Blue Ridge Mountains. The design of the dress she had left to each woman in her wedding party. She was wonderful that way, Katie mused. The bride had wanted each of them to pick something that complimented their own shape and style.

Katie had chosen a very simple sleeveless dress with a high neckline that was subtle from the front. But the back plunged, leaving most of her skin exposed. The dress flowed down her body to her ankles with a high slit up the left leg. She wore killer heels. Being vertically challenged, Katie loved the *idea* of heels. The reality not so much. She had never mastered the art of walking in them.

She wore a pair of dangling, amber earrings that were a gift from Elizabeth. Her only other jewelry was a diamond tennis bracelet that her parents had given her when she graduated from nursing school. Her hair was swept up with soft flame-colored tendrils escaping on each side. Her make-up was flawless. The team was from a local salon and had come to the hotel to help the women get ready. Katie had tipped generously, and peering into the mirror, she knew it had been worth every cent. By some miracle, or sorcery on the beautician's part, the bags under her eyes were gone.

She touched a hand to her abdomen, trying to calm the growing butterflies within. Her thoughts turned, once again, to that kiss she had shared with Flynn this morning. Although *kiss* didn't even begin to cover it. It had been all consuming, with every cell in her body crying out for more. That was exactly why she had been avoiding him for months. She wasn't stupid. Just standing near him at work set her senses aflame. But none of that mattered, because Flynn was exactly the wrong person for her. Despite that, she couldn't help smiling as she glanced into the mirror one final time. His mouth was going to drop open when he saw her tonight.

Katie turned as Elizabeth came to stand behind her. Tears sprang to her eyes. "You're so very beautiful, my friend," she whispered in a choked voice. Katie reached up and made a small adjustment to Elizabeth's veil. "There. Now, you're perfect."

Elizabeth's smile was watery. "Thank you, Katie. For everything. It means so much to me that you're here with me today."

"We promised no crying before the ceremony. I don't want ruin my perfect make-up." Katie sniffed back the tears that were threatening. "I'm so happy for you, Elizabeth. And I know that Connor is too." She *was* happy for the couple. They deserved this. But a shaft of pain pierced her heart every time she thought of her brother. Connor had died so young.

"Connor is always with me, Katie. In here." Elizabeth touched her chest. "He'll always be a part of my history. But Sam is my future."

"And I couldn't be happier. My whole family is thrilled that you're marrying Sam." A lone tear escaped down her cheek. She swiped it away with her finger. "And that's enough of that. No point in ruining all the effort they put into making us look so good."

"You're right. We do look amazing. I only wish Charlie could be here." Elizabeth sighed and turned back to the mirror to take one final look.

Katie wished that Elizabeth's friend from residency had been able to make it for the wedding. Dr. Charlotte Avery, or Charlie as she preferred, was an ER physician like Elizabeth. She lived in Chicago but was currently working as a medical missionary in some war-torn part of Africa. Katie squeezed her friend's shoulder in support.

Elizabeth gave her a shaky smile in the mirror. "I knew she wouldn't be able to make it when Sam and I decided to get married sooner rather than later." Her smile grew brighter. "But after everything Sam and I have been through, and almost missing out on each other, we didn't want to wait."

A knock on the door interrupted their conversation. and Katie answered it. Her mother and father were there, along with the rest of the bridesmaids. They all piled into the room in a chorus of oohs and ahs. She turned to see Elizabeth standing in the center of the group.

The bride was a sight to behold. Because they had planned their wedding in only two months, Elizabeth and Sam had scrambled to get everything ready. Lady luck had been kind to the couple. A last-minute opening at the hotel had given them the venue. The venue came with catering. Katie's sister, Riley, had a friend who was opening a flower shop and had time to make the flowers.

The dresses were the biggest challenge. With so little time, Katie wasn't sure what they would be wearing. But fortune had shined upon them once again. The shop's seamstress had been in tears at the story of Sam and Elizabeth and vowed to make it happen.

Because she had been married previously, Elizabeth had chosen something other than the traditional white dress. The champagne colored gown was made of silk and lace and floated around Elizabeth as she moved. It was fitted without being constraining and ended at her ankles. The bodice, with a sweetheart neckline and tiny, capped sleeves, was covered in lace for an antique feel. A similarly colored ribbon encircled Elizabeth's waist and flowed down the back. She wore amber at her throat and ears; a gift from her soon-to-be husband. Matching low-heeled sandals completed the look.

Maggie took both of Elizabeth's hands in her own. "My girl, I believe it's time."

"I'm more than ready. Besides, if we stay here any longer, one of us will start crying. Can't have that."

The bridal party grabbed their bouquets and headed downstairs. The photographer was waiting for them on the terrace. Behind them stretched the magnificent Blue Ridge Mountains in all their autumnal glory. A thousand shades of reds and yellows and oranges blazed in the late-day sun. The sheer beauty stole Katie's breath. Mother Nature had blessed them with perfect weather: warm and sunny but not humid. Nothing could go wrong today for Elizabeth and Sam.

Katie knew the moment Flynn stepped onto the terrace. He was behind her, but the small, delicate hairs at the nape of her neck stood at attention. She always knew when he was near. She chose not to think what that might mean.

Offense was the best defense, so she turned to Flynn with a blinding smile on her face. And stopped short at the sight of him in formal wear. She thought he was hot in navy scrubs, but this was ridiculous. How could he still be single? She squared her shoulders. So, what if she was faking it? Katie already had a hard-enough time not melting around Flynn. The debacle in the hotel corridor this morning had turned the tension between them nuclear.

Flynn let out a long, low whistle of approval at the site of her. "Wow, Katie. You look amazing."

"Not so bad yourself, Flynn. 'You clean up well,' as my mother would say. But you're supposed to be paying attention to the bride, Flynn. Not the bridesmaids." Her voice was harsh, but better than the low, sexy one she wanted to use on him.

"Indeed. And I will. But still, wow." He traced his finger along the line of her jaw. "Needed to get that out of my system before the ceremony." With one last, heated glance, Flynn turned away.

And Katie remembered to breathe. It was going to be a long day.

*****

Flynn ran a finger around the inside of his collar. Even though the tuxedo was custom tailored, it was killing him. Where was the chilly mountain air? But the heat he felt had nothing to do with the actual temperature and everything to do with the site of Katie in that gown. The silky material lovingly hugged her curves. He imagined how great it would look in a puddle on the floor of his hotel room. And got hard.

He loved her curves. Flynn had always preferred women with real shapes. The fashion industry could keep their "heroin chic". Give him a real woman any day. More than once, he had come upon Katie eating a salad at work. He was all for healthy eating. He was a cardiologist after all. But Flynn worried she was watching calories as well as being healthy. He longed to tell her there was no need. She was perfect. But Flynn had sisters. And a desire to live to a ripe, old age. He knew better than to ever discuss a woman's weight with her.

Flynn approached the edge of the patio, watching as Elizabeth was photographed with the stunning backdrop. He waited until the photographer finished before approaching her. Flynn raised her short veil and kissed her cheek. "You're stunning today, Elizabeth. I'm so proud of you."

Elizabeth chuckled in return. "Thank you, Flynn. You're rather smashing yourself." She cocked her head in confusion. "But why proud?"

Flynn smiled and took her hand in his. "Because you were brave enough to love again." He winked and left the terrace in search of his fellow groomsmen.

He found the guys on the opposite terrace. The photographer followed him through the door. "Okay, guys, if everyone could line up for some shots." He motioned the men towards the railing, so they too could have the stunning vista in the background.

When the photographer finished, Flynn took a moment to speak with Sam, clapping a hand to his back. As he turned, Flynn smiled. "Hey man. I wanted to tell you how happy I am that everything worked out for you guys."

Sam faced Flynn and grinned. "I guess the best man won, eh?"

"Nah, Sam. I was never in the running. Be good to each other."

Sam's face turned serious. "We will."

Flynn nodded and joined the others at the door.

Chapter Four

The opening strains of Pachelbel's "Canon" marked the beginning of the procession. The butterflies in Katie's stomach fluttered their wings. Each groomsman escorted his assigned bridesmaid down the aisle. When the party had assembled at the front, Quinn tucked her hand in his arm and followed. Katie smiled and looked around, enjoying the expressions of her family and friends. Until her eyes caught Flynn's. She forgot that the new shoes were pinching her feet. Flynn filled her mind, standing at the front in his formal wear, as if he were only waiting for her. The butterflies took flight, sending a ripple of longing throughout her.

Quinn and Katie parted ways as they reached the officiate. The guests all rose when Elizabeth appeared on Joseph's arm. The gathered crowd sighed and exclaimed at the bride's dress. When they reached the front, Joseph lifted her veil and kissed Elizabeth's cheek. She turned and handed her bouquet to Katie. The radiant smile on her friend's face took Katie's breath away. She ignored the small stab of jealousy. Elizabeth deserved this more than anyone Katie knew.

The rest of the ceremony passed in equal parts tears and laughter. Sam thoroughly kissed his bride. The wedding party gathered at the railing for more pictures. Katie watched as the guests headed inside for cocktails. She envied them that. As if reading her mind, a black-jacketed waiter approached with a tray of champagne glasses. Katie sighed in relief. If she was going to survive this night with Flynn, several drinks were called for. She just needed to make sure she ate to avoid last night's embarrassment.

The photographer shot picture after picture. Just when Katie was sure she couldn't stand for one more second in her new heels, he wrapped it up. A cheer went up from the wedding party, and they once again got back in formation to enter the reception. Soon, they would be able to sit and eat, and that couldn't happen fast enough.

The guests laughed as the wedding party entered to Pharell Williams' "Happy." Katie thought the choice was perfect. After all they had endured to get here, Elizabeth and Sam had every right to be happy on this day. She joined in and grabbed Quinn's arm as they made their way in. A few moments later, the roar of the crowd announced the arrival of the bride and groom.

Katie made her way to their table and dropped into her chair. She kicked off the offending shoes. She closed her eyes, leaned back, and sighed as she wriggled her toes.

"You look comfortable, Katie," came a deep voice immediately to her right.

She didn't bother opening her eyes. "You have no idea. Try walking in these heels, and you'd be sighing too."

Flynn pushed the table cloth aside to inspect her shoes. "I see what you mean. Sexy though. Might be worth a little pain."

"Says the man who's never tortured his feet wearing heels."

"You're right about that. I'd be happy to rub your feet for you."

Electricity zinged along her nerve endings at the thought of his hands on her body. Anywhere. Katie forced the thought from her head. Without looking at him she replied coolly. "No thank you."

Instead of being put off, as she had intended, Flynn threw back his head and laughed. This brought her gaze around to him. "I see 'Proper Katie' is here," he replied.

"What exactly is that supposed to mean?"

Flynn shrugged his broad shoulders. "You're being very proper tonight. The way you are at work." His eyes were hot as he gazed at her. He leaned in and lowered his voice. "You were different in the hallway this morning. I think that Katie is closer to your true self. Just a hunch." Much to her chagrin, Flynn raised his water goblet and took a large sip. He appeared calm. She on the other hand was having murderous thoughts. Again.

"What's wrong Katie?" Quinn asked her from her other side. He didn't look the least bit concerned with her health. In fact, the beast was smirking. "You look a bit, um, pissed."

"I'm perfectly fine, Quinn." Katie tried to take a few deep breaths without drawing attention to herself.

Quinn finished chewing his bite of salad before replying. "Sure, you are, Katie. I'm just glad the fire spitting from your eyes isn't directed at me."

She didn't spare him a glance. "Keep it up, and it will be."

Much to her horror, Quinn leaned behind her and addressed Flynn. "Dude! Whatever you did, apologize. And never do it again. Katie makes a terrible enemy."

Flynn didn't look the least intimidated. He raked his eyes up and down her. "I think I can take her."

Katie, who had chosen that moment to take a sip of her wine, sputtered as she swallowed quickly to avoid spewing it across the table. Before she could speak, Quinn chuckled. "You have no idea what she's capable of. Small but mighty is our Katie. The worst part is, you'll never see it coming. Good luck, man."

She set down her wineglass harder than necessary. "I. Am. Right. Here." Both men turned to her, shrugged, and continued with their starter course.

Katie dug deep down for a shred of patience. Sadly, that wasn't her strong suit on the best of days. This moment was far from her best. But this was Sam's and Elizabeth's wedding, and she wasn't going to waste it stewing over *that* man. Katie took a bite of her salad and tried to not grind her teeth.

"She's showing amazing restraint. Must be the setting. Otherwise you'd be a dead man by now." Quinn grinned in Flynn's direction.

"Probably. But it's entertaining. I can't help myself."

"I still think you have a death wish. It's never good to poke the bear." With that sage advice, Quinn returned to finishing his salad.

Katie kept her resolve, refusing to rise to the bait. She too finished her salad and laid the fork across her plate. A waiter came to remove it, and Katie took another small sip of wine.

"Pacing yourself I see. Probably wise after last night."

"Nice to know you're so concerned about my health, Dr. Reynolds," she bit out sarcastically.

Flynn turned to Quinn. "She only calls me that when she's really pissed. I may have gone too far this time." His joking tone belied his words.

"You think, Flynn? What is it with you anyway? Am I a game to you?"

Flynn lifted the napkin off his lap and wiped his mouth before replacing it. He turned towards Katie. His eyes were deadly serious. "You were never a game, Katie."

The pulse in her neck beat frantically like the wings of a hummingbird. She could handle a joking Flynn. But a serious Flynn was another story. His blue eyes had darkened to navy, with desire if she wasn't mistaken. He wasn't playing around anymore. Her breath caught in her throat, making speech difficult. Without another word, she rose and walked to the ladies' room for a reprieve. Even across the crowded room, Katie could feel his eyes upon her. It might be cowardly to run, but she needed a break from him. Needed time to pull herself together.

*****

Flynn watched her retreating back until Katie was out of sight. That's when he noticed Quinn watching him. Staring really. "You really do have a death wish. Unless there's something else to it."

Flynn was becoming friends with Katie's brothers, and their friends by extension. He genuinely liked them. They were good men. But he had no doubt they would view him differently if they could read his thoughts about their sister. He didn't want to lie to Quinn, even by omission, but there was nothing between Katie and him. Couldn't be. No need to muddy the waters.

Flynn cracked a smile. "I have sisters of my own. I know how far I can push Katie."

Quinn's shoulders relaxed. "It is nice to see her getting back to herself again. The past few years haven't been easy for her. Just keep in mind that she's a tough nut to crack. For all her outward bristles, Katie has a heart of gold. And that heart's been broken." At Flynn's raised eyebrow, Quinn shrugged. "Not my story to tell. And I'll deny I ever mentioned it."

"Fair enough." Flynn reached for his Scotch and took a sip. The amber liquid scorched his throat before starting a warm glow low in his belly. Not all that different from the feeling he got around Katie. He sighed with something near regret.

He had been enjoying their sparring for months now but was growing frustrated. The more time he spent with her, the more time he wanted to spend time with her. But work was his priority. It had to be. He and Sebastian had risked a lot coming to Windsor Falls to open a practice of their own. Money. Time. Professional pride. Their patient list was growing, but they had a long way to go. He needed to project a professional demeanor that would build people's confidence in him. What he didn't need to do was flirt with a beautiful nurse at work. His behavior must remain beyond reproach.

He sensed her before he saw Katie return to the table. Her cheeks had returned to their normal color; hopefully a sign that she was feeling calmer. One way to find out. Flynn stood and held her chair as she approached, waiting until she sat to retake his. "Quinn and I were about to arm wrestle for your dinner." He pointed to the fish dinner that had been served just moments prior to her return.

Katie's back was very straight as she replaced her napkin in her lap. Picking up her fork and knife, she waved the latter towards him. "Growing up in a family of six kids teaches one a thing or two. I wouldn't try it if I were you." She cut and ate the first bite.

"Noted," murmured an amused Flynn. The rest of the meal passed as Flynn made conversation with Riley. Although Katie ignored him throughout it, he kept track of her every movement. When the last plates were cleared and the music grew louder, Flynn asked Riley to dance. The younger woman smiled and held out her hand to him.

As soon as they were far enough away from Katie, Riley grinned at Flynn. "Why are you dancing with me and not Katie?"

"What makes you think I wouldn't rather be out here with you?"

She gave him a look that women have been giving men since the beginning of time. The one that says they might not be all that smart. Words weren't necessary.

Flynn laughed. "You remind me of your sister."

"I'll take that as a compliment. You're clearly not stupid, Flynn. And neither am I."

"I never thought you were."

"Good. So, I thought I'd give you some advice."

"I'm all ears."

"Anyone with eyes in their head can see that something is going on between you two. I don't know what exactly. But know this. Katie loves with her whole heart. And every fiber of her being." Riley's eyes darkened with shadows. "Or at least she did. Until that jackass came along. She's sworn off men since. If you have interest in her, you have your work cut out for you."

Flynn nodded, understanding Katie's "back off" vibe a little better. "Your sister and I are co-workers. That's all." He ignored her skeptical look. "But let me guess. He was a doctor."

"Got it in one." Riley sighed heavily, her eyes still troubled. "I won't say anymore, but I will tell you this. You're good for her."

The song changed, but Flynn didn't release his partner. Cocking his head, he leaned in a bit closer to Riley and lowered his voice. "In what way?"

"Katie was sort of a shell of herself for a while. We worried about her." Riley's brow furrowed, backing up her words. "But for the past few months, she's been more like her old self. Livelier. Fun again."

"A few months, huh?" Flynn was secretly pleased. He liked to think he had something to do with that.

"Let me be clear, Flynn. You've been good for her. But if you're serious about pursuing something with her, then you need to be all in." Riley grabbed Flynn's lapels and drew him in closer. "I may not be one of the boys, but I can still hurt you. And with all those construction sites I'm on, they'd never find the body." Riley stretched up on her toes and pecked Flynn's cheek before walking off the dance floor.

Flynn laughed and made his way back to the table. He really liked the Fitzgeralds. They were a loud and sometimes rowdy bunch, but they had each other's backs. He could appreciate that. Hurting Katie was never part of the plan.

*****

Katie watched from the side as Flynn danced with her sister. Acid churned in her stomach. The two certainly seemed to be having a fabulous time as they twirled around the floor. Each time one of them laughed, she clenched her fists. A few hours ago, he was kissing the stuffing out of *her*. She was right to never trust Flynn Reynolds. He flirted as easily as he breathed and with the same lack of conscious thought.

Which was exactly why she said yes to Quinn when he asked her to dance. She had known Quinn, through Sam, for years. The fact that he was more than easy on the eyes didn't hurt. His legendary avoidance of long term relationships sealed the deal. He would do. She placed her hand in his and allowed him to pull her up from her seat. They passed Flynn on the way to the dance floor, and Katie couldn't help smiling at Quinn as they did. She added a flirtatious laugh for good measure. There. Let him stew on that. Two could play that game.

Quinn gathered her in his strong arms, and they swayed in time to an old love ballad. "Should I even ask what you're up to?"

Katie eyes widened. "Quinn, I have no idea what you mean."

He shook his head. "We've known each other for years, Katie Fitzgerald, and you've never looked at me like that before. So, I'll ask you again. What are you up to?"

Busted. "Okay, fine, but you're sworn to secrecy." She waited until he crossed his heart. "It's Flynn. Some days I could just kick him." She blew out an angry breath.

"What's wrong with Flynn? He plays poker with us sometimes. Other than being a bit of a card shark, he seems like an all right guy." Quinn stopped dancing and stared at her. He shook his head knowingly. "Oh. You like him. It all makes sense now."

Her green eyes snapped. "I do not like him. He makes me crazy. Did you see him out here with Riley for God's sake? She's way too young for him."

"Riley is thirty, as you are aware. And she is also more than capable of taking care of herself."

Katie resisted stomping her foot. "Of course, you would side with him. That's what guys do."

Quinn shook his head but didn't stop the smile from spreading across his face. "I'm not siding with anyone. Want me to rough him up a bit for you? Just say the word."

Despite herself, Katie burst out laughing at the sheer ridiculousness of Quinn's question. "No. As tempting as that is, I can handle Flynn Reynolds."

"You're trying to make him jealous. Then we should have sex. That might work." He wagged his eyebrows suggestively at her.

"Wow, Quinn, way to take one for the team. Nice to know you have my back, but no thank you."

"May I cut in?"

Quinn looked amused as he stepped aside. Flynn gathered a shocked Katie into his arms.

"How much did you hear?" she managed to eke out. Would there ever be a day when she wouldn't make an idiot of herself in front of this man?

Flynn swept her to a less crowded area of the dance floor. "I came in at the part where you were turning down Quinn for sex."

"Maybe, you shouldn't be eavesdropping in the first place."

"Maybe, you should be more careful where you discuss sex if you don't want people overhearing," he countered.

Katie looked up into his smug face. Too bad he was also hot as sin. "Whatever," she muttered, knowing she sounded twelve at best.

"Nice comeback. So why was Quinn offering to have sex with you in the middle of the wedding reception?"

Katie kept her eyes averted and mumbled into his chest. "It's a long story."

"I have nothing but time."

"It's a long story that's none of your business," she threw out. What was it about this man? When she was around him, she was either dumb with lust or a shrew. Sometimes both.

"Quinn's not your type, Katie."

She arched an eyebrow. Her eyes glittered dangerously. "And who is my type, Flynn?" Her mild tone should have been a warning to him.

But it wasn't. "Why I am of course." He drew her flush against his body to drive home his point.

Of all the arrogance, she fumed. Katie would have cut him off at the knees, but she was having a tough time putting two words together. Who could think with his glorious body against hers? His arms wound around her back, securing her to him as his hands splayed at the top of her butt. His intoxicating scent enveloped her. Katie laid her cheek against his chest. She heard a soft moan and wasn't sure if it came from her or him.

They stayed wrapped around each other, swaying in time to the music, through the next song. In some distant part of her brain, Katie knew this was a bad idea. Her lower parts had a different take on it altogether. They fit together perfectly.

Katie thought about how incredible it would be if they were naked. And that was a perfect example of why dancing with him was a bad idea. Katie pulled back and looked in his eyes. They were blazing hot. "This thing is never happening, Flynn." She tried to turn away but remained trapped in his strong arms.

"What thing, Katie? I thought we were just dancing?"

"You know exactly what I mean, Flynn Reynolds. This crazy attraction between us doesn't mean anything. It can't."

"I know," he agreed with more than a hint of regret in his voice.

"Then why are we having this conversation?"

Flynn stared into her eyes. His deep voice rumbled in his chest. "Because I can't help myself when I'm near you."

The music and crowds disappeared. Katie couldn't take a full breath. "Please let go of me," she whispered.

Flynn immediately dropped his arms from around her. "Of course."

Katie felt an immediate chill at the lack of his touch. She missed the feel of his body pressed to hers. She shook her head to clear it from the spell she was under. "We both know we're wrong for each other, Flynn. We must work together, and I need the health fair to be a success. It means everything to me right now. Please don't make this hard for me."

Flynn nodded. "I would never do anything to jeopardize that for you."

Katie stared into the depth of his navy-blue eyes. Sincerity shone from them. She could easily lose herself in them, so she took a shaky step backwards. "I'm sorry." She turned and rushed off the dance floor without looking back.

Katie ducked into the nearest restroom and locked herself in a stall. A few tears slid down her face, which only made her angrier. She wiped them away and refused to let the rest fall. She was never going to cry over another man. At least that's what she had promised herself after David left.

She cringed when she heard the outer door open, followed by a soft knock on her stall. "Katie, is that you?" came Elizabeth's voice.

Maybe if she didn't answer…

"I can see your shoes."

Katie grimaced. So much for hiding. "If I said 'no' would you believe me?"

"Only if that's what you want."

What she wanted was to not like Flynn. To be completely indifferent to him. And his incredible body. She rolled her eyes at her own stupidity. Sighing, Katie unlocked the stall door.

Elizabeth peered at her face. "No tears. That's a good sign. What's wrong?"

"Nothing earth shattering. Just being a stupid female and falling for the wrong guy." She moved to the sink to wash her hands, for something to do more than anything.

"Why is Flynn the wrong guy?"

A startled Katie met Elizabeth's gaze in the mirror. "How did you know I was referring to Flynn?"

"Because I'm neither blind nor stupid." Elizabeth chuckled to take the sting out of her words. "There's also the amount of electricity snapping whenever you're within ten feet of each other. You could give the utility company a run for its money."

Katie turned to face her friend. "Really? I thought only I could sense that."

Elizabeth merely raised an eyebrow. She placed a hand on Katie's arm. "What's the problem? Flynn's a great guy. I would have considered dating him."

"I won't tell your brand-new husband you said that."

Elizabeth laughed. "I meant when I first came home. Before I fell in love with Sam."

"So, what stopped you?" She couldn't help it, Katie was dying to know.

"Well, there was a complete lack of chemistry. Besides, it was pretty evident how you felt about him."

A warm glow spread throughout Katie's chest. A genuine smile touched her eyes for the first time that night. She hugged her fiercely. "I'm so glad you're back, Elizabeth." Katie bit back the sob that was forming. She had missed her friend so much when she was in California. Desperate to lighten the moment, Katie released Elizabeth. "It's not just that. Guess who's the new chair of the Heart Health Day?"

Elizabeth clapped her hands and shrieked. "Oh, my goodness, Katie. Congratulations! That's wonderful!! Tell me everything."

"All you need to know is that Flynn is my co-chair. Because the universe hates me. So now, more than ever, that man is hands off."

Elizabeth bit her lip. "Are you sure? I know workplace relationships can be tricky, but they don't have to be. You're both adults."

Katie shook her head, refusing to even allow that thought to take root. "There's more. I'm applying to graduate school. To become a nurse practitioner. And pulling this off is the edge I need."

Elizabeth met Katie's eyes in the mirror as she reapplied her lipstick. "Wow, Katie, anything else I don't know?"

"No, that's it."

"That's fabulous news, Katie. You're going to be a fabulous NP." She hugged her hard. "I'd love to write a letter of recommendation for you."

"Thanks, Elizabeth. That means a lot to me. I'll take you up on that. Now shouldn't we be out there? At your reception?"

Elizabeth sighed. "Fine. You're off the hook for now." Elizabeth paused and tucked a stray hair behind Katie's ear. "Flynn is a good guy, Katie. I know it's complicated, but you should at least think about giving him a chance." She smiled warmly at Katie and left the restroom.

Elizabeth's parting words echoed in Katie's head. Flynn might be a good guy as Elizabeth stated. But he wasn't the guy for her. The problem was she wasn't sure who was. She frowned in the mirror. Faint lines radiated from her eyes and mouth. She wasn't getting any younger. That was for sure. Thirty-three, she thought with disgust. Her mother had already had her children by this age, and here she was still single. She thought for sure that she and David would have… No, she wasn't going down that road again. She didn't even miss him anymore. Just the *idea* of him. She wanted to get married and have at least two kids, but she no longer knew if that was in the cards for her.

That's why the idea of graduate school had become so important to her. Katie loved being a nurse, and becoming an NP was perfect. She would be able to do so much more for her patients. And now was the time.

Katie shrugged off her gloomy thoughts. This was a night for fun and celebration. And dancing was an excellent way to get in some cardio. She exited the bathroom and made her way to her seat. Placing her purse on the table, Katie spotted her whole family on the dance floor. A smile lit up her face. No matter what happened, she would always have them. She kicked off her painful shoes and rushed out to join them.

Chapter Five

Katie finished taking report from the outgoing day shift nurses and settled into her area at the desk. The unit was full, and the moon was not. They had a chance at a decent night. All she had to do was keep everyone alive all night. She signed into the computer and pulled up the patient list. This was her first shift back after the wedding. Katie muffled a huge yawn. Four days off in a row was wonderful. The first night back, not so much. She had never gotten great at sleeping during the day, despite working night shift for over ten years. Especially when she had slept the whole night before.

"Looks like a quiet night for sure," came a way too bubbly voice from behind Katie.

She resisted, barely, ripping off the head of their newest nurse. Instead, Katie swiveled in her chair. "Annie, how many times do I have to tell you?"

The smile on Annie's face froze. "Oops. I said it again, didn't I?" Her cheeks flushed prettily. She averted her crystal blue eyes.

That was another reason to hate her. Katie was a natural red head. When she blushed, it wasn't pretty like Annie's. No, her face became blotchy and blended in with her bright hair. Not to mention the fact that Annie was a size zero. She took a deep, calming breath, in through her nose and out through her mouth. Despite her obvious flaws, Annie was very bright and a fantastic addition to the night shift.

"I'm sorry, Annie. I'm tired. No reason to snap off your head. I know it's superstitious, and I'm not usually. But just don't say the q word. Okay?"

"Sure, Katie. I promise. You won't hear me say quiet again ever." Her hand flew to her mouth.

Too late. An alarm pierced the stillness of the unit. Katie didn't even have time to shake her head before Pam, one of her most seasoned nurses, stuck her head out of room four.

"Page trauma! His abdomen is rigid and distended, and his pressure's falling fast." She ducked back in her room, confident that someone would respond.

Katie turned to Annie. "Page Trauma please. I'll go help her." She ran to room four. Although he was not her patient Katie was up to speed on all twenty people currently filling their beds. That was part of being in charge. They were fully staffed tonight, meaning Katie had the 'luxury' of only taking one patient of her own. This freed her up to help in situations such as these.

Room four was a young man in his twenties who had been admitted on day shift. Robbie Phillips had made the mistake of not looking both ways before darting out between two parked cars on his skateboard. In a pedestrian versus car scenario, the car generally won. The only saving grace was that he had been smart enough to wear a helmet. Unfortunately, that didn't protect his abdomen. He had been admitted with a splenic laceration that the surgeons were keeping an eye on. The hope was that it would heal on its own. That didn't seem likely now.

Entering the room, she took a moment to survey the patient. It wasn't pretty. Katie ran her hands over the patient's abdomen. Pam had been right. His upper left quadrant was hard as a board. Although not fully conscious, he groaned and tried to cover his belly with his hands when she palpated it. The rest of the picture was equally alarming. His skin was slick with sweat and cool to the touch. While his blood pressure was plummeting, his pulse was over one fifty.

"Robbie, wake up. I need you to open your eyes for me." After a moment or two, Robbie opened his eyes to slits. Although he was still following commands, he was sluggish. Another thing not in his favor.

"Hey, ladies, what's going on?" Dr. Slater, a second-year trauma resident, appeared in the doorway.

His casual attitude set Katie's teeth on edge. He was her least favorite surgical resident; way too cocky for his own good, not to mention his patient's. Dr. Slater also thought he was God's gift to nurses everywhere.

Pam spoke through gritted teeth. "What's going on is that Robbie here is not doing so well. You need to get your attending in here now."

"I'll be the judge of that," he exclaimed. Katie watched with growing alarm as Dr. Slater assessed the patient. His casual attitude and lack of haste were disconcerting. Surely, he could see just by looking that Robbie was going downhill. Fast.

"Would you like me to call the on-call surgeon for you?" Katie asked with contempt.

Dr. Slater straightened up and turned to Katie. "I've got this. Let's up his fluid a bit to support his pressure. Call me in an hour with his latest vitals."

Pam stepped in front of him as Dr. Slater attempted to leave the patient's room. "With all due respect, he's past 'upping his fluids.' His abdomen is rigid and he's barely maintaining his pressure.

The resident unfortunately wasn't the type to remember that he was still learning. "Thank you for your concern, *nurse*. I'll check back in an hour." He strode out of the room checking his phone as he went.

Katie and Pam exchanged a look. Words weren't necessary. They both knew what an incompetent ass the resident was. Pam adjusted his IV rate as ordered. She looked at Katie over her shoulder. "Which one of us is going over his head?"

Katie heaved a sigh. "I'm the charge nurse. I'll do it." She went to the desk and called the on-call trauma attending. She outlined what had happened and the patient's condition. Katie repeated the verbal orders and entered them into the computer. She hung up the phone as Pam approached the desk.

"Dr. Kilpatrick is on her way up from the ED. Unhappy doesn't even begin to cover it." She grinned at the same time as Pam. "Dr. Slater has a lot to learn."

"Annie, I'm going to need you to keep an eye on my patient for a bit. She's in one and stable. Four is on his way to the O.R. I'll be in there with Pam getting things ready. Please send Dr. Kilpatrick that way when she gets here."

Annie waved a hand in acknowledgement. Katie spun on her heel and jogged back to room four. Robbie wasn't looking any better. If anything, he had lost some color. The fluids weren't enough, as Katie had already known. She gnashed her teeth before letting out a huff of breath. No use losing it over a resident who thought he was God.

Katie and Pam worked in silence, prepping their patient for his trip to the operating room. Neither one had a doubt about his condition. Although she was sorry for his plight, this was exactly the reason Katie loved being an ICU nurse. If they had just accepted Dr. Slater's orders, and not used their own critical thinking, this patient would be "circling the drain" in the next half hour.

"What the hell happened in here?" Katie looked up to see Dr. Kilpatrick rush into the room. "And where is my resident?"

Katie chose her words carefully. It would be easy to throw Dr. Slater under the bus. And heaven knows he deserved it. But they had all been there, she mused. Too new to know how dangerous they were. "He's been and left already. Robbie here is not cooperating. Despite his fluid bolus, his pressure is eighty over sixty with a pulse pushing one sixty. He's diaphoretic, mostly unresponsive and his abdomen is rigid and hard."

"Damn it, I was afraid of this. I had hoped with his age and otherwise good health, he would be able to recover without surgery. That's not happening. Let me take a quick look. Katie, can you throw him on six liters via nasal cannula for me?"

Katie applied the oxygen tubing as Dr. Kilpatrick grabbed the portable ultrasound. After squirting some gel on the patient's abdomen, she moved the probe around to get a glimpse of his spleen. A string of inventive curses colored the air. Katie turned to hide a smile. She loved working with this trauma surgeon. Not only did she treat nurses with dignity and respect, but she cursed like a sailor.

"Good catch, ladies. Robby bought himself a ticket to the O.R. We'll talk about Dr. Slater another time."

The doctor in question ran into the room, huffing and puffing. "I'm right here, Dr. Kilpatrick." He turned and glared at Katie and Pam who weren't in the least bit intimidated. "What's up with the patient?"

Dr. Kilpatrick turned to stare at her resident. "'What's up' is that this young man is bleeding out. A fact that you apparently missed earlier. Thankfully, his nurses did not and called me. You can thank them for saving your ass. Later. Right now, we have to go." She turned and hurried from the room.

Dr. Slater followed on her heels but turned to hiss at the two nurses. "What did you tell her?"

Katie and Pam ignored him, busy readying the patient for his short trip downstairs. She switched him to the portable cardiac monitor and placed it on the bed, doing the same for his oxygen. Pam tucked his various wires and apparatus into the bed and released the brakes. They rolled him through the department and out to the elevators. Only then did Katie give way to her temper.

"Of all the arrogant little pricks," she fumed to Pam. "What did we tell Dr. Kilpatrick? That's what he's worried about? Try worrying about almost killing this patient. Not to mention thanking us for saving his ass and the patient as well."

Pam chuckled and shook her head as the elevator doors opened. "Now, Katie, you know better than that. The devil will be playing ice hockey in Hell before that man apologizes. Or thanks us."

"My momma didn't raise any fools. I know he won't. But he bloody well should."

"Not a chance," Pam murmured. "That one is way too big for his britches. Dr. K needs to bring him down a peg or two."

"I know he's young and green, but he's going to kill someone one of these days with his arrogance."

They wheeled the bed off the elevator and headed for the operating theater. Once inside, Pam gave report to the nurses before transferring Robbie to the table. When they finished, Katie and Pam took the empty bed back to their unit.

Annie was at the desk. Katie waved as they walked by. "Anything going on?"

Annie looked up from her monitor. "Everyone's fine, Katie. How'd it go with wonder doc?"

"As well as you can imagine," she threw over her shoulder as she and Pam entered room four. After tidying up, Katie went back to the desk.

"I keep telling myself that he's still learning." Her clenched teeth and stiff shoulders told another story.

Annie shook her head. "Not sure what's worse. His arrogance or the constant hitting on me."

Katie whipped her head around to face Annie. "You know that's not tolerated, right? If he's harassing you, talk to human resources."

The young woman dropped her eyes. "I know. I was trying to give him the benefit of the doubt. I don't want to get him into any more trouble than he already has."

Katie placed a hand on the younger nurse's shoulder. "I get that, Annie, I do. But if saying 'no' isn't enough, you have to report his behavior."

"I will. Thanks for caring, Katie."

"No worries! That's why I make the big bucks." She grinned. They both knew the extra dollar per hour wasn't worth it, but Katie enjoyed looking out for her fellow nurses.

The evening passed quickly, and Katie was happy that the rest of their patients remained stable. The night had started off with enough drama. When she had finished charting her assessments, she got up to get some caffeine. Stopping to stretch, she didn't see Dr. Slater approaching.

"What the hell did you say to her? Do you know how much trouble I'm in now?" Before Katie could respond, Dr. Slater closed the space between them, looming over her. His angry expression and clenched fists didn't have their intended effect. Katie was pissed, not afraid. But she never got a chance to tell him.

"Is there a problem here?" Flynn's words might have been mild, but his tone and body language were far from it.

The change in the resident's countenance would have been funny if the situation weren't so serious. "Dr. Slater and I were discussing his patient. Weren't we, Dr. Slater?" Both men turned to look at Katie. Neither looked happy. She sighed. As if this situation wasn't stupid enough already.

After a long moment, Dr. Slater addressed Flynn. "This nurse and I were discussing my patient." A smile appeared on his face. "I was about to remind her that there's a chain of command to follow. I don't appreciate her going above my head to Dr. Kilpatrick." His smile broadened. He seemed to think that Flynn would back him up. Katie's blood began to boil.

"I only went over your head because you missed the fact that the patient was critical and needed to go to surgery. 'Pushing fluids' bought us a few minutes. If you'd take your head out of your ass long enough, you would have known that."

Dr. Slater's face darkened immediately. "Who do you think you're talking to?"

"The doctor who's license I just saved." Katie could feel her blood pressure rising. Arrogant jerk.

Dr. Slater made his fatal mistake when he took a threatening step towards her. The rest happened in a blur. Before she could understand, Flynn had grabbed the younger man by the arm and escorted him off the unit.

Annie looked up from her computer, grinning. "Go, Dr. Reynolds."

Katie's mood darkened even further at her words. She whirled on the unsuspecting nurse. "The last think I needed was Dr. Reynolds butting in."

Annie's smile faltered. "Oh. I thought it was great the way he stepped in. Not all doctors have our backs like that. Sorry."

Katie blew out a quick breath. "No, I'm sorry, Annie. I shouldn't have snapped at you. But I was fine and didn't need any help. What I need is coffee." She headed to the employee lounge.

Of course, there weren't any clean mugs. Katie opened her locker and pulled out her covered travel mug. Choosing a flavor, she placed the Keurig cup and a paper cup into the machine and waited for the magic. Last May, for Nursing Week, her manager had given the coffee maker to her staff. The nurses and techs all chipped in to keep them in assorted flavors of coffee.

When the coffee was ready, Katie transferred the hot beverage into her travel mug. As the steam swirled, Katie drew in a deep scent of the delicious aroma. Pumpkin spice filled the air. She loved this time of the year. Sweater weather, as her mom always called it. The air had a nip in it. The leaves were brilliant, turning the Blue Ridge Mountains into nature's canvas.

Even her hometown went a bit crazy with it. Windsor Falls was a competitive place. About everything. All throughout the year, there were contests galore. Best roses. Largest tomato. All kinds of ridiculous things. But fall was ripe with it. First there was the pumpkin carving contest next week-end. Next up was the scarecrow decorating contest in the beginning of November. And of course, the best of all was the Christmas decoration contest in December.

Katie smiled into her cup at that last one, feeling her bad mood evaporate. A few years back, some goofball tried to squash the Christmas decorating contest. A sad attempt at being politically correct. The Save the Christmas Decorating Contest Campaign resulted; a joint effort between the Muslim and Jewish population of Windsor Falls. The contest remained.

Katie sat and drank her coffee, resting her tired feet on a low coffee table. She sighed and stretched, enjoying the moment of peace. She had closed her eyes for a second when the door opened. The tiny hairs at the nape of her neck stood up. No use opening her eyes. There was only one person who could crush her serenity merely by entering the room.

"There you are, Katie. Are you okay?"

Katie bit her lower lip to contain her frustration. "Why wouldn't I be okay, Dr. Reynolds?" She jumped to her feet and paced to the other side of the room.

"How long has Dr. Slater been a problem for you?" Flynn's face was carved of granite. His usual humor was nowhere in sight. "Why didn't you ever tell me?"

Katie's green eyes flashed. "I'm not even sure where to start with how ridiculous those questions are. I was handling things fine before you stuck your nose into the middle of it. Dr. Slater is a way too confident resident who is a pain in my ass. Not the first and not the last. This is a teaching hospital, so there you have it. But I have to work with him. All you did was make things worse."

Flynn's blue eyes darkened, the pupil disappearing. "That was 'handling it'? I walked onto the unit to find him threatening you. And I was supposed to keep my nose out of it? Never gonna happen."

She clenched her hands and counted to ten. "He was not threatening me. He was angry that I went over his head to his attending. He screwed up, and he knew it. My patient was circling the drain. I'd do it again."

"Well he looked more than a bit threatening to me. What was I supposed to do, Katie? Let him hit you?"

Katie threw her hands in the air. "Oh, for the love of all things holy, Flynn. He wasn't going to attack me. Dr. Slater screwed up, and he knows it. I hurt his pride. I never felt unsafe for even a second. And I *was* handling it."

It was Flynn's turn to pace. He raked a hand through his thick, dark hair. "Yes, Katie, I got that message. So, next time I see you in danger I should walk by? Is that what you're telling me?" He stopped and faced her, his breathing rapid and rough. "Well you can forget it. I have too many sisters for that. Protectiveness is bred into me."

The mention of his sisters sent Katie over the edge. He thought of her as a sister? She wasn't interested in him like *that*. But still. A sister? What woman wanted to be thought of like a sister? Katie's conflicted view of this didn't help and added to the strident tone of her voice. "You don't get it, Flynn. I'm not some little girl who needs your protection. I was handling it. And I'm not your sister."

Flynn's eyes narrowed again. But for a different reason. He stepped in until there were mere inches between them. "No, Katie, you are not." Before she could read his intention, Flynn hauled her against him and kissed her. All thoughts of why she was mad at him fled. Her mind emptied as her senses filled with the delicious sensations of Flynn's hard body against hers. She moaned deep in her throat, and Flynn took advantage, sliding his hot tongue against hers. Her eyes drifted closed on a cloud of pure lust.

Somewhere deep in her brain, Katie knew this was a bad idea. But her hands had a mind of their own. The thin cotton of Flynn's scrubs did little to contain the heat of his skin. She slid her palms across his chest, reveling in the hard plains. Katie snuggled in closer to better reach him and pressed up against his erection. And that was the wake-up call she needed. She dropped her hands as though burned and jumped back.

Because he apparently lacked in survival skills, Flynn grinned at her. "Nope. Never kissed any of my sisters like that."

Katie cursed under her breath and spun away from him. She needed to be in the safety of the unit, with patients and co-workers surrounding her. There'd be no possibility of kissing Flynn again.

She stopped at the sound of his voice right behind her. "I know we both have our reasons, Katherine. But there's something between us. Something that doesn't come along every day."

His warm breath stirred the tiny hairs at the base of her neck. And her heart rate. Katie didn't turn to face him. "You're right, Flynn. There is something between us. Chemistry. That's all it is, and I have no intention of doing anything about it." She walked out of the room, closing the door behind her.

*****

Flynn turned and made himself a cup of decaf. He needed to get some sleep tonight. As the machine went through its paces, Flynn leaned against the counter. He couldn't stop the grin from spreading across his face. There was something between them. Something more than chemistry. Katie's being so quick to dismiss it only made him grin broader. She could deny it all she wanted, but that didn't make it any less true.

Flynn stirred some low-fat milk into his coffee and grabbed a yogurt from the fridge. It had been a busy day, and he missed the cafeteria. Again. This would have to suffice. He sat down at the break table and thought about Katie. As usual. Even in her less than flattering scrubs, Flynn couldn't miss her heart stopping figure. She had curves in all the right places. But it went so far beyond the physical. Her razor-sharp tongue kept him on his toes. He enjoyed sparring with her. And that was the problem. He had to stop thinking about her. Stay away from her, except for work. His brain knew that. If only his body would get the message.

Chapter Six

Katie loved being a critical care nurse, but she was always happy to see day shift arrive. Although the night had been a calm one, she was exhausted. Especially after having a few days off. She was back the next two nights and wanted nothing more than sleep. Katie preferred to do her three days in a row, which then gave her a chunk of time off. But those three days on were lost ones. She was either at work or sleeping. Having a social life was never easy.

Grabbing her purse and keys, Katie clocked out and headed for the stairs. She wasn't surprised to see Flynn exiting room ten. He and his partner, Sebastian, were deep in conversation. Now there was a handsome pair, she thought. With their heads together, the two could easily be a GQ cover. As fair as Flynn was dark, Sebastian was a similar height and build. Both men dripped sex appeal, but Sebastian had never caused her ovaries to tighten at the sight of him. Not that it mattered, as she still wasn't getting involved with another doctor.

"Goodnight, gentlemen," she called as she passed them in the hallway. Both looked up as she walked by. Sebastian waved in greeting. Flynn fixed her with his trademark smoldering glance. The one that made her toes curl and panties want to fly off. For self-preservation, Katie kept going. Right down several flights of stairs and out of the building. She wasn't running from Flynn exactly. More like preserving her sanity.

By the time she arrived home, Katie felt the long night in every sore muscle. She pulled into her attached garage and parked. This was one of the selling points when she bought her home two years ago. Katie didn't like to carry the germs of her work into her home. She had a laundry basket and a small cabinet with clean changes of clothing. Katie pulled off her soiled scrubs and pulled on cotton shorts and a tank top. Pulling off the ponytail holder, Katie shook out her long red tresses. It was necessary to wear her hair up at work, but it always felt good to let it down.

Katie continued through to the kitchen. She had put a lot of effort into decorating her townhome. Making it her own. It was a comfortable haven from the demands of her professional life. She grabbed a quick, healthy breakfast before heading into her master bedroom. Stopping in the bathroom only long enough to wash her face and brush her teeth, Katie flopped into bed. She sank into the pillow-topped mattress and pulled the thousand thread count sheets up to her chin. The cotton, soft and cool against her skin, was a balm that lulled her into sleep. Usually.

Not this morning. Can't blame the room darkening curtains, Katie thought with disgust. No, she knew exactly what to blame. Or rather whom. Flynn. Memories of his hard body beneath her hands. His lips on hers. She flipped over, turning the pillow to find the cooler side. But it wasn't cool enough. Her face, her whole body, felt hot. She needed to get back out there, she thought in desperation. Once she met someone else, thoughts of Flynn, and his sexy, hard body, would be a distant memory. At least she hoped so.

*****

The doorbell rang as Flynn hung up with the local pizza place. It was his turn to host poker night, and those guys could eat. Jogging to the door, Flynn took a last look around. It wasn't going to be featured on HGTV anytime soon, but his friends wouldn't care. They just wanted to play poker and blow off some steam.

The bell rang again as Flynn reached for the door knob. "Hold your horses," Flynn yelled as he pulled open the door. The three Fitzgerald brothers, Donovan, Aidan, and Brendan stood there. Each was carrying some sort of contribution to tonight's game. Flynn grabbed the beer from Donovan to put in the refrigerator.

"Come on in. I hope you brought your money. I'm feeling lucky tonight."

"That's the only 'lucky' he's getting lately. And I wouldn't count on that if I were you," joked Brendan. His two brothers laughed in unison at the slam.

"Ha-Ha very funny, Fitzgerald. You're jealous because I'm better looking than you are."

"Yeah," agreed Brendan. "That's it exactly."

A round of laughs almost drowned out the doorbell. Flynn answered it again. Quinn and his friend A.J. from the town's fire department stood on the porch. "Right on time, gentlemen. Come on in."

"What have we missed?" asked Quinn as they joined the others in the kitchen.

"Not much," quipped Flynn in response. "Brendan was just commenting on my lack of a dating life."

"And by that, I meant he's not getting any." Another round of jokes, one cruder than the last followed. The six men each grabbed a seat around Flynn's table as Donovan began to shuffle. Quinn grabbed some beers from the fridge, and the game began.

A few hands later, Flynn looked around his table. He liked the friends he had made in Windsor Falls. Flynn took a risk moving from Atlanta to this small town in the Blue Ridge Mountains. But he had taken the chance and was very pleased with how things were going. The practice that he and Sebastian had started was small still, but they were working on that. That was why he had volunteered to help with the Healthy Hearts community event. They were sure to drum up some business. Of course, it had been longer than he cared to remember since he had sex. Well, two out of three wasn't bad he mused.

A well-aimed potato chip broke his reverie. He blinked to focus and grinned at Quinn. "Lose something?"

Quinn laughed. "Nope. It's your turn." He gestured to the table.

"Oh. Lost in thought for a moment I guess." Flynn perused his cards. "I'm out," he declared as he threw down his cards in disgust. Several others followed suit, until only A.J. and Donovan were left to battle out the hand.

Flynn got up and walked into the kitchen for another beer. Aidan and Quinn joined him, each grabbing a Corona from the fridge. "Hey, where's Jack tonight?"

Quinn grimaced. "He has a date. Imagine that."

"Lucky man," quipped Aidan. "I almost remember what that is."

"Well Jack won't be forgetting any time soon. He's got a new woman every week."

"Wow. I had no idea. Lucky guy."

"I don't know," remarked Flynn. "That was fine in my twenties. But I'm too old for that now."

"Yeah, you're a regular Methuselah," joked Aidan.

Flynn laughed. "I'm not saying that, Aidan. But I've done that already. Been the party guy, etc. Now that I'm here and settling in, I want more."

"You have to actually go on a date for that to happen, Flynn."

Flynn smiled at Aidan. "I know. I will. Right now, Sebastian and I are pretty much swamped with building the practice. What's your excuse?"

Aidan shrugged, and they headed back to the table as Donovan was scooping up his winnings. He looked up and smirked at them. "We could hear you guys in there. You're all pathetic. Find a good woman. Grab her. Don't let go. Then make her so happy she doesn't want to anyway." He took a long pull from his beer. "It's that simple."

His suggestion was met with total silence. And some skeptical expressions. "Do I need to remind y'all that I'm the only happily married one of the group?"

Flynn shook his head. "No need to rub it in. When Elizabeth and Sam get back from Hawaii, you and he can share stories of domestic bliss." This brought a lot of comments from the other guys. After a few moments of good natured ribbing, the noise level dropped to a dull roar, and their poker game resumed.

Flynn was finally dealt some decent cards when the doorbell rang. "That'll be the pizza. No one move until I get back." He paid the delivery boy and carried in the pizzas. Everyone put down their cards and descended on him like a pack of starving wolves.

"Wow! When was the last time you guys ate?" The only sound was them chewing. And a few moans of appreciation. Flynn grabbed a paper plate and a few slices before it was all inhaled. Within minutes only a single slice of pepperoni remained.

Donovan took a long sip of his beer and then wiped his mouth before speaking. "Some of us work hard for a living. Now, let's get back to me taking all your money." Quinn gathered up the trash as the others picked up their hands. There was a heated debate about who was going to break Donovan's lucky streak tonight.

As much fun as he was having, Flynn was having difficulty keeping his head in the game. He hadn't gotten much sleep last night and then put in a long day at the practice. A certain red-headed nurse had something to do with that. Once again, his thoughts drifted to Katie. And the sounds she made deep in her throat when he kissed her. Not to mention the feel of her hands on his chest. He shifted in the chair, his pants a bit tighter in the crotch. He thought about cranial nerves instead. Their names, locations, and what they controlled. Anything to take his mind off Katie, and what he wanted to do to her. Especially while playing poker with her brothers. Her three very large brothers.

He looked up, realizing too late that five pairs of eyes were watching him. "Sorry, long night at the hospital followed by an equally long day at the office." He crossed his fingers mentally.

Aidan raised one eyebrow and grinned. "Long night at the hospital, huh? Is that what you're calling it now?" An assortment of whistles and crude comments followed.

Flynn took a deep breath. "That's what I'm calling it, because that's what it was. I was there late admitting a patient, so I slept in a call room. Then I had early rounds before heading into the practice."

Donovan took his turn. "Katie worked last night; she can give us the dirt."

Flynn's gut tightened at the thought of her brothers finding out how he felt about her. They were protective of their sisters. Not that there was anything to know. Except the fact that he wanted her under him. Naked. Better not to think about that right now. Or ever. Better to throw them off the scent. "I saw Katie. In fact, we had another of our legendary battles." Now he had their full attention.

All three of her brothers laughed. Brendan leaned towards Flynn. "Do tell. Few mortals come away from a battle with Katie with all their limbs still attached."

"In my defense, I was actually trying to protect her. She didn't see it that way." He told them about the resident that was giving Katie a tough time. They morphed into big brother mode. Even Aidan, who was technically her little brother.

"Who is this jackass that gave Katie a problem?" Donovan uttered the words through clenched teeth. His manner was deceptively calm.

"I handled it. I have sisters, so I get it. We had a little chat. Let him know that his manners were off a bit." Flynn grinned, showing a lot of teeth. "I don't think he'll make that mistake again. The bigger problem is that this was not the first time. Katie has been handling this on her own. She was not appreciative of my stepping in. Too bad." Flynn picked up his cards and made a show of looking at them. "Shall we get back to the game, guys?"

The others followed suit, examining the hand they had been dealt. Brendan nodded at Flynn. "Thanks for being there for Katie. Even though she didn't appreciate it. We do. Nice to know someone has her back at work."

Flynn felt badly about deceiving them. But since nothing could ever come of a relationship between them, what was the point? He was thankful when they called it a night early. Everyone had work in the morning, and he was exhausted.

*****

Thursday morning dawned dreary and wet. Chilly too. Perfect sleeping weather, Katie thought as she finished up her third shift in a row. The first two nights had gone relatively smoothly. Not so much last night. It seemed like everyone was trying to die on them last night. One did. A ninety-year-old man who had been admitted on her shift Tuesday. Brought in with a massive stroke, he had never regained consciousness. His family had camped out around the clock, hoping for a miracle. But Katie knew they were few and far between when the patient was that old and the prognosis that bleak. She was amazed he had held on so long.

Although she took every patient death as a personal loss, this one was particularly hard. Katie had watched Ruth, his wife of seventy years, kiss him one last time. It was almost more than she could bear. But that was part of her job. To support families in their time of need. So, she had stayed with Ruth until the very end. Now she was off for several days, and all she wanted was her bed. As much as Katie hated to "waste" her days off sleeping, the three in a row had taken their toll. She needed a solid ten hours of sleep.

She stood under the overhang at the employee entrance, cursing the fact that her umbrella was in her car. She kept one in her locker for situations just like this. It wasn't there when she looked for it. She must have forgotten to bring it back last time. Katie had decided to make a run for it when a sleek, black Mercedes pulled to a stop in front of her. The passenger window lowered.

"Get in," yelled Flynn.

Katie didn't hesitate. She hated getting wet more than most other things. Except snakes. "Thanks," she muttered as she slid into the front seat of his car.

"You're welcome, Katie," murmured Flynn. "Not a morning person, eh?"

"Maybe because this is my night, not morning." Katie refused to look at Flynn. That would be a huge mistake. It was bad enough that he smelled like sin. She smelled like a twelve-hour shift in the critical care unit.

"How about some breakfast at Bob's? I have a little time before I have to get to the office."

Katie rubbed a weary hand over her face. "Thanks, but no. All I want is my bed." She caught his cocky grin out of the corner of her eye. "Alone," she added for clarification.

Flynn braked at a stop sign. Turning to Katie, he held up his hands. "I wasn't offering. But nice confidence you have going for you."

She couldn't help it. Katie burst out laughing. "Flynn Reynolds, you are something. And that was what I needed after the night we had." She pointed across the wet parking lot. "I'm in the far corner, under that light post."

Sorrow with a little resignation dripped from her voice. He drove across the lot and pulled in next to her SUV. Before she could bolt, he laid a hand on her arm. Flynn lifted her face with a gentle finger under her chin. "Want to talk about it?"

Katie was silent for a long moment. Then, in a quiet, subdued voice she told him about her patient.

Flynn stroked her arm in sympathy. "That's the hardest part of this job. It sucks. No way around that."

She laughed bitterly and shook her head. "Want to hear the worst part?"

"Losing your patient wasn't it?"

Katie shrugged off his hand and turned towards the window. She couldn't believe she was going to tell him this. But sometimes you had to let things out. "I felt sorry for myself. Don't get me wrong. My heart breaks for them. But I can't help feeling more than a bit jealous of what they had. Seventy years together."

"That is something to be envious of, Katie. Nothing wrong with that. Most people want that, deep down inside."

Tears welled in her eyes. Katie reached for the door handle. "I have to go," she said as she tried to open the door. Scrapping with Flynn at work she could handle. No problem. This softer, gentle side of him not so much. Her resolve to keep her distance weakened in moments like this.

"Please unlock the door."

Flynn did so immediately. "I'm sorry you had such a rough shift, Katie. How about having dinner with me tonight? Anywhere you want."

She shook her head. "You know I can't do that, Flynn. We work together. That's all we are." She was out of his car before Flynn could respond.

Katie noticed that he waited until she was safely in her own car before driving away. If nothing else, Flynn Reynolds was a gentleman. Unfortunately, he was also trouble. She wasn't going there. She had learned the hard way to not date doctors, especially ones she worked with. Better to keep her eye on the prize.

She was thankful for the short drive home. Her eyelids were at half-mast by the time she pulled into her garage. Katie kicked off her sneakers and pulled off her scrubs inside the garage. She grabbed her dirty scrubs from her earlier shifts and then walked into her house and headed straight into the laundry room.

After starting the laundry cycle, Katie briefly debated breakfast. She was hungry but more tired. As it usually did, fatigue won. Taking a brief but hot shower first, Katie was almost asleep when her head hit the pillow. Like most night shifters, her bedroom was her cocoon. The room-darkening shades and curtains kept out the morning sunshine. Not that there was any today. She kept her bedroom cool as well, to help promote sleep. The last thing Katie did was plug in her phone and make sure the ringer was off. Being awoken by a sales call, or even her mother, was unacceptable.

On Friday evening, Katie sat in her car outside The Watering Hole, a local bar. Referred to as 'The Hole" by local patrons, the bar was more pleasing than its name. Katie looked up at the sign. Nothing had changed. The owner, a genial man in his late sixties, had died a few weeks back. She hadn't been in since then.

Getting out of her car, Katie resisted the urge to check herself in the mirror one last time. Her palms were moist, and she wiped them on the sides of her jeans. She had gone for nice casual for this date, choosing her favorite jeans, sweater, and low-heeled boots. This was her first time out there since David. She wanted to make a good impression without looking like she tried too hard. She really wanted to be on her couch watching a chick flick. Eating chocolate. But here she was.

Katie pulled open the front door and stepped inside. She waited until her eyes adjusted to the dim interior. Bill, her date, was about her age, five eight with blonde hair. Katie grimaced as she glanced around the room. That very generic description could have fit half the guys in here tonight. She shifted from one foot to the other, still hoping someone would approach her. When they didn't, she moved to the bar. Taking one of the stools, she signaled for the bartender. She had known Scott since grade school. He was a nice guy and Katie's not-so-secret crush from long ago who had never noticed her. Story of her life.

Scott approached her now. "Hey, Katie! Haven't seen you in here for a while. How've you been?"

"Hey, Scott. Doing good, thanks. I haven't been here since it changed hands. How's the new owner?"

Scott smiled at her; a smile that would have melted her teenage heart. Thankfully she was past that now. "I guess you didn't hear then. It's mine now."

Katie's mouth fell open. Literally. She knew that was rude, but she just couldn't help it. Scott Anderson was a great guy. But the most motivated she had ever seen him was to get to the waves. Or the slopes. Her face burned as he laughed at her response. "I'm so sorry, Scott. I'm just shocked. I hadn't heard." Windsor Falls was not a large town. Everyone pretty much knew everything about each other. Except for her apparently.

"No worries, Katie. I can hardly blame you. Nothing I've ever done would make you think business owner."

"Oh, no Scott, it's not that. I, uh." Her face burned even brighter. "Okay, it is that. Again, I'm sorry, Scott. I shouldn't have misjudged you like that."

"Katie, it's fine. I know what people think of me, and I'm fine with that. You, of all people, have the right to be shocked." He laughed at her puzzled expression. "Who tutored me all through high school so that I could stay on one team or another? I know that wasn't easy for you. You were so smart and stuck with this dumb jock." Scott jabbed his chest with his thumb.

"I wouldn't say dumb, Scott, more like distracted." By every pretty blonde who came into the tutoring center. If it wasn't a girl, then it was practice or a game. Scott played various sports for their high school around the calendar. Baseball, soccer, basketball, you name it.

"Katie Fitzgerald, you were a saint. You are the reason I got through high school. The reason I could play all those sports that were so important to me back then. And I know it can't have been easy for you. Trying to get that stuff through my thick skull, when all I wanted to do was be outside on a field somewhere."

Katie cleared her throat. "It wasn't a big deal, Scott. Tutoring you was my job. If it wasn't me, it would have been someone else."

He shook his head. "But it wasn't anyone else, Katie. It was you. And I never thanked you. So, I'm thanking you now. You'll be happy to know that I've been taking some business classes at the community college for the past two years. Hank and I had talked about me taking over when he retired." He dipped his head for a moment. "Hank always talked about moving to the Keys when he retired. He loved to fish. I wish he had gotten that chance."

Katie knew that Scott and Hank had been close. Hank was like a second father to him. Scott's own father had been the town drunk. And a mean one at that. He had finally left for good right around the time they graduated from high school. Katie wasn't sure what had ever happened to his mother.

"I'm sorry too, Scott. I know Hank meant a lot to you."

"Thanks, Katie. He really did. Hank was the only person who believed in me. Other than you, of course."

There was a warmth and honesty to his words that touched her heart. "That's very sweet, Scott. Not true, but sweet."

His trademark smile was back. "It is, Katie. And I appreciate it." He leaned over the bar and hugged her. "Now, that's enough of that. What can I get you? It's on the house. A token of my appreciation."

"Thanks, Scott. I'm meeting someone, but I'll have a beer while I wait. Whatever you have on tap is fine."

"Okay. I'll be right back."

Katie looked up and was startled to see Flynn in the reflection of the large mirror behind the bar. He was standing right behind her. For once, her Flynn radar had failed her. She swiveled on her seat. "Hey, Flynn. I didn't know you were there."

"I guess you were too busy chatting with the bartender." His tone was stiff, unlike him.

If she didn't know better, she would have thought he was jealous. But that didn't seem likely. Flynn Reynolds was a drop-dead gorgeous cardiologist. No way would he be jealous of her talking with another guy.

"Well don't let me get in your way. I'm meeting your brothers for some pool and drinks. Have a wonderful time." He walked away before she could respond.

Katie was trying to figure out what had happened when a man walked into her line of view. If this was Bill, then five feet eight was generous. His hair was more not there than blonde as well. He had massive arms and pretty much no neck.

"Katie?"

Yep, no neck must be her date. "Bill?" Not a witty reply, but Katie was a bit flustered. She stuck out her hand to shake his, not sure if that was the right thing to do. But she wasn't going to hug a strange man in a bar.

Without shaking her hand, Bill hopped, no other description would fit, onto the closest bar stool. He looked her up and down as he did so. Katie got the vague feeling that he wasn't thrilled with what he saw. "Yeah, I'm Bill. Debbie's brother."

Scott arrived, thank all that was holy. The bartender smiled at her and handed Katie her draft beer. "What can I get you?" he asked Bill.

"Diet cola." Scott nodded and walked off.

"Debbie told me that you're a gym teacher at the high school. Do you like teaching?" Katie already knew this wasn't going to be a love match. But at least she was out there. Right? She must be getting karmic credit for trying.

"I love it! Physical fitness is my life. Speaking of which," he looked her up and down once again. "Do you belong to a gym?"

She didn't have a membership to one, preferring to run (when she could no longer avoid it) outside in the fresh air. "No, I don't, Bill. Is it that obvious?" She laughed, hoping he would take it as a joke. He didn't.

"Actually, it is. But I could help you with your problem areas." Bill waved a hand near her midsection. He could have meant abdomen, hips, thighs, or all three. She had no idea. "What are you, around a hundred fifty?"

The "date" was over. She slid off her barstool. This time she didn't put out her hand. "Well, Bill, I don't think we have anything in common. Thanks for coming." Without thinking about it, Katie turned around and headed for the pool tables in the back.

Chapter Seven

Katie stopped at the entrance to the pool room. There were three tables, all occupied. But the one she wanted was in the back corner. Five gorgeous men stood around it. The sight was something to behold, although three of them were her brothers. The other two were Quinn and the devil himself, Flynn. Brendan and Quinn were currently enjoying a friendly game, if the heckling was any indication. Something about someone's mother.

Katie strode right up to the table, beer in hand. "Hey, boys! Can I play?"

Donovan saw her first and came over, sweeping her up in a bear hug. "Hey, it's one of my two favorite sisters."

She laughed at Donovan, as she always did. "My favorite, oldest brother," she exclaimed in return. They had always enjoyed the easiest relationship of the family for whatever reason.

Katie joined the group. When she had their attention, she asked, "Do I look like I weigh one fifty?"

Silence reigned. There were perhaps even crickets in the background. Not one of them was brave enough to answer.

Aidan, with the table between them, finally responded. "Is that a trick question?"

She shook her head, glorious red hair moving as she did. "No. It's simple enough. My blind date decided that's how much I weigh and was busy recommending a fitness plan for me."

"I'm guessing there won't be a save the date card in the mail anytime soon," quipped Brendan. He turned back to the table and sank the eight ball, much to Quinn's dismay. Quinn placed a crisp twenty into Brendan's outstretched hand.

"Well, that was fun. Anyone need another?" Quinn gestured with his glass and walked out the way Katie had come in.

She stepped up to the table. "I want to play. Who's up?"

Flynn grabbed two cue sticks from the rack. "Sure, Katie. But it'll cost you." His perfect white teeth flashed.

Katie's smile was less sure. "What are we betting, Flynn?"

"Anything you're not afraid to lose."

His comment was met by a murmur from her brothers. Katie grabbed the chalk. "I'm supposed to do something with this, right?" She tried to chalk the tip of the cue stick, getting more on her hand than it.

Being a Southern gentleman, Flynn stepped forward. "Here. Let me." He took both items from her hands, leaving a trail of sparks where her skin touched his. She needed to avoid any contact with him. They were playing a dangerous game. And it wasn't pool.

Donovan rounded up the balls and placed them in the rack at the opposite end of the table. "Are you sure you want to do this, Katie? I've seen Flynn play. He's not bad."

Flynn laughed. "I was good enough to beat Brendan's sorry ass last time."

Katie gnawed on her lower lip. "Maybe this isn't a good idea."

Flynn handed her cue stick, freshly chalked, back to her. "It's okay, Katie, I'll be gentle with you."

She took the proffered stick, careful to avoid touching him this time. "Okay. I'll try." She turned to face the table. Flynn never saw the calculating gleam in her eye.

Donovan winked at her as he removed the rack from the balls. They gleamed under the light, a perfect triangle. Katie moved to the side of the table facing them. She looked at Flynn for guidance. "I just have to hit this white ball into those, right?"

Flynn hid his laughter in a cough. "Well, you have to do a bit more than that, Katie. You're going to break first. And by that, I mean use the cue to hit the white ball into the triangle. If you hit a ball into one of the pockets, either stripes or solids, then that's what you'll want to hit again. I won't even make you call which pocket it's going to land in. Understand?"

She bit the inside of her cheek. His arrogance, not to mention condescension, was showing. She took a deep breath and let it out. "Okay. Knock one in. Got it." Katie leaned over the table, accidentally on purpose giving him a nice view of her butt. She aimed her cue stick at the white ball and sent it sailing. The fourteen-ball slid right into the side pocket with a resounding thunk.

Katie jumped up and down with excitement. "I did it. I did it. I got one in. I guess that means I have to get the other striped ones now, right?"

"Yes, Katie. Knock in the rest of the striped ones and then finish with the black eight ball." He shook his head and muttered "beginner's luck" under his breath.

"Maybe. Maybe not," she replied before lining up the next shot. She pointed to the far, right corner with her cue and sank the ten ball. There was great personal satisfaction at the sight of Flynn's face. His jaw was slack. And for the first time ever, he was speechless.

Katie made short work of the remaining striped balls. She stopped to chalk her cue stick before lining up her final shot. Without even breaking a sweat, Katie sank the eight ball. "Guess you were right, Flynn. Beginner's luck." The gleam in her eye said otherwise.

There was a moment's hesitation before the Fitzgerald brothers burst out laughing. Quinn joined in as he walked back in the room. They had all been dusted by the great Katie Fitzgerald many times.

Katie walked over to where Flynn was standing. She held out her hand for payment. Without a word, he placed a twenty-dollar bill in it. Katie folded it and slid it in her back pocket.

Brendan finally stopped laughing long enough to speak. "Oh, Flynn, I'm so sorry." He tried to wipe the smile from his face without any luck. "Actually, I'm not sorry. But don't feel too badly. I've never seen her lose yet."

"It's true," bragged Katie.

He turned to face the other men, whom were trying to not laugh. "And y'all set me up?"

Quinn took a pull from his beer. "Yeah, pretty much. Consider it a rite of passage. I lost twenty myself when I first met these guys."

Flynn's blue eyes crinkled with delight. "Feeling better now, Katie?"

"Yes," she replied. "And now I'm off. Night boys."

Katie walked out to the parking lot and got into her SUV. She glanced at the time. Too early to go home. A bitch session about the evils of men with her best friend Kat De Luca would help her mood.

Katie drove down the street, admiring her hometown as she went. Lots of people her age had left after high school, eager to live in a bigger place. Not her. Sure, it was a big world, but Katie had everything she needed right here. The town square was dressed for Fall, decked out in pumpkins and the like. Windsor Falls was big on celebrating the holidays and seasons. All of them.

Pulling into the back lot behind De Luca's bakery, Katie parked next to Kat's Beetle. She was glad that her friend was home. She needed a sounding board. It was a safe bet that Kat would be here. She was in the bakery every morning by four thirty. And she was suffering a similar dating dry spell. She got out of her car and walked to the entrance to Kat's apartment over the business. She knocked once and stepped back to wait.

Kat's feet could be heard pounding down the stairs within seconds. Katie always joked that her friend had one speed only; warp speed. The door opened to reveal her friend, wearing old work-out clothes and dripping sweat.

"Did I interrupt something?" She arched one perfect eyebrow.

"Very funny." Kat inhaled deeply, wiping the sweat from her face on the sleeve of her t-shirt. "I should be so lucky. The only thing you interrupted was my cleaning frenzy. And I'm eternally grateful. Come on up." She turned and darted back up the stairs, earning a chuckle from Katie who followed at a slower pace.

At the top of the stairs, Katie moved to the small table and dropped her purse. "Please tell me you have some adult beverages. And some pastry. Oh, that's right. I need a gym, not a pastry." The last Katie muttered through gritted teeth as she flopped on the couch.

A colorful oath came from the kitchen. Kat popped her head around the wall. "Who told you that?"

Katie smiled at the righteous indignation she could feel from across the room. And that's exactly what best friends were for. "Bill. The gym teacher/blind date."

"Here, drink this and tell me everything." Kat handed her a glass of white wine. "I'll be back with reinforcements," she said before returning to the kitchen.

Katie's mouth watered at the thought of what Kat would be bringing back with her. Kat was a phenomenal baker, always experimenting with new recipes in her free time. Katie was her more than willing test audience. Sadly, the waist of her jeans could attest to that. She shrugged her shoulders and took a sip of the wine. Life was short.

Kat came back in with a plate of delicacies. "These are my fall edition of the classic petit fours. Not just for Christmas anymore, not that my Dad will listen."

Katie grabbed one and bit down, moaning in ecstasy. She didn't comment on what Kat had grumbled. The argument between Kat and her very traditional father were legendary. Even more so since Kat had joined the family business after studying her craft in Europe.

"These are amazing, Kat! Not that I need to be eating them."

"Of course, you do. That's what pastry is for. Now tell me about the schmuck. From the top. Don't leave out any of the gory details."

Katie told her about the blind date that lasted less than five minutes. Then she regaled her friend with the story of her pool triumph, leaving out the sparks between her and Flynn. That was something she didn't want to discuss with anyone. Not even her best friend.

But she should have known better. Kat was sharp as a tack.

"So, you happened to run into the handsome Dr. Reynolds? Interesting."

Katie smiled. "The interesting part was when I cleared the pool table in under two minutes."

Kat, never a fan of pool, waved that comment away. "No, the interesting part is how you try to skip right over Flynn. What are you not telling me, Katie?"

Katie picked up her wineglass, trying not to squirm. They had known each other since the sandbox days. Kat could read her like a book. Instead of answering, she took a sip of her wine. A large one.

"Katie? Come one. Tell Dr. Kat all about it. You know you'll feel better when you do." She grinned at Katie and snatched a petit four from the plate. "Mmmm, these are phenomenal. If I must say so myself." She licked a crumb off her lip. "And I must."

"Agreed. Have you shared these with your dad?"

The teasing lilt to her voice was gone. "Ha! Like he'd let me do anything but 'traditional Italian pastries.' The man is stuck in the past, Katie." A frown marred her beautiful face. "But nice try, Katie. Avoiding my question, I see. Makes me think there's something about the good doctor that you don't want me to know."

Katie sighed. "All right. You're correct." She grabbed another pastry for courage. "I like him, Kat. A lot."

"Well, duh. Katie, you're my oldest friend. You can't hide anything from me." She leaned over and hugged Katie. "So, you like him. What's the problem? You're a beautiful, funny, intelligent woman. You're single. He's not married, is he? I never see a ring. Not that that's a guarantee."

"Yes, as far as I know." Flynn might be the devil, but he was honest.

"Okay, then. What's the problem?"

Katie grimaced. "You know what the problem is, Kat. He's a doctor. With whom I work. And I'm not going there again. Ever."

"Ugh," groaned Kat. "Is this because of David?"

Katie shook her head. "No, Kat, you know it isn't. But before I ever got involved with David, I swore I'd never date a doctor. And look where that got me."

"While it's true that David was not a smart choice, that had nothing to do with his being a doctor. It had everything to do with his being an ass." She raised her wineglass. "A toast. To no more stupid men in our lives."

"Here, here," replied Katie as she clinked hers against Kat's.

"So, now that that's done, tell me again why you can't go out with Flynn. Other than he's a doctor. That's a poor excuse, Katie."

Katie took another sip for fortitude. "I'm filling out applications."

Kat let out a squeal that could be heard all throughout the Blue Ridge Mountains. She put down her wineglass and pulled Katie into a hug. "You finally did it! I'm so proud of you!" She leaned back and shook a finger at her. "Why am I just hearing this now?"

Her friend's praise warmed Katie's heart. "You know this idea has always been in the back of my mind. I was waiting for the right time. And that time is now."

Kat's beautiful face scrunched in a frown. "You mean now that you're out from under the influence of that man."

Katie had no doubt what her friend meant. She sighed and took another sip. "I know, Kat. You don't have to remind me. David was never supportive of me."

The Italian in Kat raced to the surface as her hands flew. "Not supportive is the least of it, Katie. David was all about David. Period. You were arm candy for him. He didn't care about you or what was important to you. He was threatened by you. That's why he didn't want you to go to graduate school."

"You're right. About everything."

Kat stared at her. "While I'm on a roll, can I suggest something else?"

Katie laughed. "Could I stop you?"

"Probably not." Kat pulled back her shoulders as though fortifying herself. "You didn't love David. At least not in the way you should have considering you were planning a life with him. When he left, you were disappointed that your plans got taken away, not actually heartbroken." The words came out in a rush, and now Kat seemed to hold her breath.

"Right again, Kat." Katie found saying the words cleansing. David humiliated her when he slunk back to his ex-girlfriend. But it wasn't heartbreaking. "Flynn is off limits. I will not go through that again. Having a relationship with a colleague, while the whole hospital watches. And takes bets. No thanks."

"It was awful. I remember. But you could give Flynn a chance. He's not David."

Katie held up a hand to stop Kat. "There's more. I am the new, last minute chair for the community heart health event. This will look great on my applications for NP programs. But only if it's a success. I can't take any chances. If I get involved with him, things could go wrong. Or people at the hospital might not take me as seriously." She shook her head, maybe to convince herself as well as Kat. "No, I can't risk it."

"Then what's your alternative, Katie? Bill the high school gym teacher who thinks you're fat?" She grimaced. "Which you aren't, by the way."

Katie smothered a giggle. "I'd like to think there's some middle ground between Flynn and Bill. Besides, tonight was the first time I even tried to go on a date since David. I say full credit for me. And besides, I can only go up from Bill the gym teacher."

Kat shook her head. "Not necessarily. Believe me, I know. While you've been in hibernation, I've been out there trying. Remember? First, there was the one with mommy issues. As in she was at the next table rating me. Then the guy who kept asking me my bra size. Couldn't figure out whether he wanted to try it on or was a serial killer. Then there was the guy with cats. Fifteen of them! Need I go on?"

Katie was rolling on the couch by now. She held up her hand weakly. "No." she gasped, holding her sides. "Please stop. I'm begging you."

Kat sipped her wine. "Just saying. After all that, a doctor doesn't seem so bad."

"Then why don't you go out with him?" She could have bitten her tongue the moment those words left her mouth. Katie tried to not show her dismay. Kat was beautiful. And funny and terrific. Flynn, or any man, would be mad to not want to date her.

"Hmm," murmured Kat as if considering. "Maybe I will. I see him regularly in the bakery. One morning I could ask him out."

Discomfort rushed through Katie, making her feel as though her head might explode. The idea of Kat and Flynn was… Well it was something. And not something good.

Kat burst out laughing. "Oh, Katie. If only you could see your own face. You look like you're plotting my untimely death. Don't worry. The code is still intact. I would never go out with Flynn, knowing how you feel about him."

Katie laughed at the mention of their old code. When they were teens, and boys became something other than cootie-carrying pains in the butt, the two friends had vowed to never date someone the other liked. An actual blood oath. Scott the bartender was a prime example. He had asked out Kat several times, but she had always said no, invoking the oath. Katie hadn't thought of that in years.

"I'd be happy to put in a good word with him, if you want. Not that you need one." The words practically stuck in her throat.

Kat laughed. "Like I said before, Katie, I know you. You may not want to admit it, to me or yourself, but there's something between you guys. No thanks. There's got to be a non-mommy issue, creepy cat lover out there somewhere for me."

Katie finished the last sip of her wine and got up to rinse her glass. "Well, I'm out of here. You're alarm clock will be ringing before you know it."

Kat walked her to the door. "Sad but true." She hugged Katie. "I'm proud of you. Wait until I tell my dad."

Mr. DeLuca had always been like a second father to her. "Maybe he'll bake me something special when I get accepted to NP school."

"Well, you now I will! Something rich and delicious, full of all kinds of fat and calories. And we won't even count them."

Katie laughed. "It's too bad we aren't lesbians. You'd be perfect for me." She hugged her friend goodbye and headed to her car. Kat's laughter followed her all the way there.

Chapter Eight

Saturday came way too early, even though Katie had gone to bed at a decent time. She hadn't slept well with Kat's insights rolling around in her head. Not to mention the memories of playing pool with Flynn. Shrugging off those thoughts, she got up and put on warm, comfy sweats. Bill's comments, while way off base, had a hit a bit too close to home. She was a busy woman, but going for a run was always going to be last on her to-do list.

Katie made herself a healthy breakfast and fired up her laptop. Since she had made the decision to go ahead with school, she couldn't act on it fast enough. She was interested in several programs and needed to narrow the choices. Then, she would apply. She loved the idea of Chapel Hill or Duke, but both were a hike from Windsor Falls. And even though many classes were on-line, there would still be the need for some back and forth. They were also very competitive programs. On the other hand, Western Carolina was a third of the distance and a safer bet.

She spent an hour or so perusing these and a few on-line programs. This was really a review. She had done her research. She rinsed her breakfast dishes and committed to applying to those three. Katie also chose Georgetown University as an on-line alternative. She hoped that running the community event would give her an edge on other applicants.

Having put it off as long as she could, Katie laced up her sneakers and grabbed her phone and keys. Running was never fun for her, but then neither were tight clothes. Katie strapped her phone to her upper arm and selected her work out playlist. The upbeat songs always helped her mood. And her pace. After locking her door, she stretched and took off at a slow jog. After a block or two, she picked up the pace, pushing herself a bit.

When she reached the local park, Katie was moving along at a decent clip. Mark Ronson's "Uptown Funk" blared in her ears. Although it was chilly, many people were in the park. Katie ran by several fields where small children played soccer. She could imagine the sound of them as she moved along.

She had run into a wooded area when a hand came out of nowhere and touched her arm. Screaming, Katie lost her balance and went down in an undignified heap. The hard asphalt shredded the fabric of her sweats and the skin of her knee underneath. She forgot to be afraid as anger boiled up to the surface.

Strong arms wrapped around her and lifted her to her feet. It was then she realized Flynn was her would-be rapist now rescuer. She glared at him. "What the hell is wrong with you?"

Dark sunglasses shaded his eyes. He pushed them up on his head. Regret lined his face. He plucked the earbuds from her ears. "I called your name several times, Katie." He gestured with the earbuds hanging from his fingers. "You couldn't hear me."

Her chest rose and fell from the effort of breathing. Now that she wasn't in any danger, unless you counted his nearness, everything hurt. "Ouch," she muttered as she looked down at her knee. There was a ragged tear in the sweats. Blood was trickling down her leg. She raised both hands. Yep, both had battled the pavement and lost.

Flynn grasped her hands in his, turning them over so he could inspect the damage. "I'm so sorry, Katie. I never meant to hurt you. I saw you running from across the parking lot and came over to say hello."

"Great, Flynn. Your hello cost me my favorite sweats and a fair amount of flesh. Satisfied?" She knew it was a simple accident, but she wasn't feeling generous today. She hurt too much for that.

"I am sorry. Let me clean you up a bit. Tend to your wounds." His smile was beguiling. "I am a doctor you know."

"No thank you," she said with more than a little starch. "I'm perfectly fine." Katie turned to head home. The first few steps reminded her how sore she was. It was going to take her a long time to get home at this rate.

Flynn jogged in front of her. "Please. At least let me drive you home. My car is just around the bend, near the soccer fields."

Pride was wonderful but foolish in this situation. She hurt. Everywhere. And the idea of walking home sucked. "Okay, Flynn. But only because I hurt way too much to make it home." She mumbled, "This is what I get for being healthy" under her breath.

"Do you need me to carry you to the car? I can't pull it up here."

The look she gave him gave Flynn his answer. Katie concentrated on putting one foot in front of the other. She also tried to ignore the pain that radiated up her legs. "You really are a nuisance."

The corners of his mouth twitched. "I just wanted to say hello, Katie."

"Next time, think about running ahead so I can see you. Grabbing a woman from behind is never a good idea. You're lucky I tripped. Otherwise you'd be the one wincing in pain. I have brothers. They taught me things."

Flynn made a show of covering his "family jewels." "I'm glad they did."

She limped along, trying to ignore him. But in workout clothes, ignoring Flynn wasn't easy. His shorts nicely highlighted the long, muscled length of his legs. She noted they were covered in dark hair, but not overly so.

"By the way, are you married?"

It was Flynn's turn to miss a step. But unlike her, he didn't end in a bloodied pile on the ground. "Excuse me?" The look of incredulity on his face almost made her laugh. Almost. That would hurt too much.

"Not a hard question. Are? You? Married?"

"Uh, no. I've had my tongue down your throat, Katie. That would not have happened if I was married. Not my style." His tone was not amused.

Somehow, she had managed to hurt his feelings. Great. Now she had to apologize. "I know that. I'm sorry." And she did. He might be a flirt, but he wasn't a cad.

One dark brow raised. "Why are you asking?" His voice lowered, sending waves of sensation through her belly.

"Because Kat is single." She blurted out the words as though they were one, long one.

Flynn's blue eyes bored into her green ones. "Kat is single, huh? Should I ask her out?"

Katie kept walking, thinking before answering. "Kat's a wonderful woman. Bright, funny, beautiful. And she can bake."

Flynn jogged ahead of her and blocked her path. "I do like Kat." Flynn took a step closer. Just one. But it brought him almost up against her. She could smell the light layer of sweat on him. It wasn't unpleasant. In fact, it made her think of ways they could get sweaty together. She swallowed heavily.

In a low voice that only she could hear, Flynn asked "So should I ask her out? Dinner? A movie? You haven't answered me yet."

"Why would I care?" Katie stepped around him and kept walking. She needed to get off her injured leg. And to put distance between them.

He fell into step with her. "See, you still haven't answered."

He had pushed her over the line. She whirled on him. Bright red slashed across her cheekbones. "No, Flynn, I don't want you to ask her out. But then, I don't have the right to ask that of you."

She turned away, resuming her walk towards the parking lot. She wasn't sure, but thought she heard him reply, "You're the only one who does." But that was dangerous thinking on her part. Flynn was exactly what she didn't need in her life.

He caught up to her, and they reached his car without another word. When they pulled out of the lot, he asked for directions. She gave them without looking at him, watching out the window but not seeing. How did she keep ending up in this situation with him, when she meant to avoid him at all costs?

The silence in the small car was deafening. Katie had never been happier to see her home. She would have jumped out before he even pulled to a stop, but her knee was now throbbing. "Thanks," she muttered over her shoulder before limping up the front walkway.

But Katie knew she hadn't escaped. She wasn't stupid. Sure enough, Flynn caught up to her by the time she reached the front door. He took the keys from her hand to open the door. Katie gasped at the electric tingles where their fingers touched. The sensation spread up her arm.

He opened the door, and Katie stepped inside. Flynn followed behind, turning to shut and lock the door. She heard the metallic clink as he dropped her keys in the dish on the entryway table.

"Where do you keep your first aid stuff?"

There was no point in telling him she could take care of herself. He was a man on a mission. She pointed to the short hallway. "In the guest bathroom, under the sink." She sat on the couch, toeing off her shoes as she did. Katie grimaced when she saw the ragged skin of her knee poking through the hole in her now ruined pants. She gripped the fabric and pulled, creating an even bigger one. Katie picked a small piece of gravel from her knee, wincing as she pulled it from the dried blood. As injuries went, this was minor. But it didn't feel that way right now.

She propped her injured leg on the low coffee table and leaned back, closing her eyes. Katie could hear Flynn puttering around in her bathroom. The noise drifted closer as he moved into the kitchen. The refrigerator door opened and closed. Or the freezer door. She had no idea and didn't care.

Katie didn't open her eyes when the couch dipped under Flynn's weight. "You know, I am a nurse. I'm trained to fix boo boos."

A small chuckle escaped him, lightening the tension that was there since the jogging path. "Yes, I know. But I caused this mess, so let me fix it. Please."

Katie sighed and nodded. She opened her eyes to see his dark head bent over her knee. It was almost her undoing. He had put a paper towel on the coffee table and was using tweezers to pick out more gravel.

"Luckily, this looks much worse than it is. Road rash. I'll just clean it."

His head was so close to her knee that his words sent his hot breath wafting over her skin. And shivers to all the right places. Katie gripped the couch cushions on either side of her to keep her hands from roaming though his hair. Or down over his broad shoulders.

He must have mistaken her tension for pain. Glancing up at her, kindness and regret filled his eyes. "I truly am sorry, Katie. I'm almost done here. Just need to disinfect."

"Okay." Witty repartee was beyond her now.

Flynn grabbed the disinfectant. "This might sting," he warned. She watched as he poured it on some gauze. Flynn patted the bruised areas, and Katie hissed out a breath between her teeth. Sting? Her knee felt like it was on fire.

"Sorry," he whispered before blowing cool air over her knee.

The tingles shot straight from her knee right up to the very center of her. It was more than she could take. He was too close. Too male. She shot up off the couch then put some space between them. "Okay. All good. Thanks for the ride home." She didn't want to sound ungrateful, but he had to leave. Now. Before she did something stupid. Like jump him.

Flynn stood, approached her slowly as one would a spooked horse. "You feel it also. I know you do, Katie." He stopped moving when mere inches separated them.

"I don't want to feel it, Flynn." She turned to face him, gazing into his striking, blue eyes. There were many good reasons for resisting him thus far. For the life of her, Katie couldn't remember one. And she gave in. She leaned into him, closing the gap. Reaching up on her toes, Katie placed her lips against his. "Stay with me," she murmured against them.

*****

Flynn's blood rushed from his head to parts further south at the touch of her lips on his. Her words haunted him. "Stay with me." How long had he longed to hear them? But there were reasons for not getting involved with Katie. Good reasons. Not that he could remember them right now. Even more, he knew he would always regret saying no.

With every ounce of will power he possessed, Flynn backed away from Katie. The hurt that flashed through her eyes was almost his undoing. "Don't misunderstand me, Katie. There's nothing I want more than to go up those stairs with you. Nothing."

Confusion mingled with the hurt. "Then why aren't you, Flynn?"

He took another step away from her. "We agreed that this isn't happening. Us getting involved. We both have other goals right now. Ones that conflict with this." He waved a hand between them in a desperate gesture.

A smile spread across her face. There were hidden depths of meaning in it. "Is that the only reason, Flynn?"

It was his turn to feel confused. He glanced towards the stairs. "Yes."

"Because nobody has to know. It's just us here." She placed an open hand on his chest. His breath hissed in at the contact. Flynn felt branded by her touch. "I do feel it, Flynn."

He pulled her hand off his chest and turned it over. Ever so gently, he placed a soft kiss on her scraped palm. A shudder ripped through him. "Never doubt that I feel the same attraction, Katie."

The green of her eyes darkened to jade. "Then why are we still talking?" She placed her hand in his and turned to the stairs. Flynn followed along. He might have lingering doubts, but there wasn't enough blood left in his brain to process them.

Because he needed to know for sure, Flynn turned to her and asked one more time. "Are you sure about this, Katie?" Her seductive smile gave him all the answer he needed.

Flynn took her face in his hands. Lowering his mouth to hers, Flynn tasted her lips, drinking greedily from them. When she moaned in her throat, he slid his tongue into her mouth. He plundered. She did the same. Soon, he was moaning along with her.

But tasting her wasn't enough. His hands itched to touch her. Everywhere. Flynn buried his hands in her hair, the silken strands becoming tethers. Whether she was bound to him or vice versa, he didn't know. Or care. All that mattered was the feel of her body pressed against his. Her curves were tight up against him, making him harder than he could bear. He shifted his pelvis away from her to slow things down a bit. This was a fantasy many months in the making. He didn't know why today was the day. He wasn't questioning his luck, but he damn well was going to make it last.

Katie lifted her head. Her green eyes were now clouded with passion. "What's wrong?"

He placed an affectionate kiss on the top of her head. "Nothing's wrong, Katie. Quite the opposite. But I don't want to embarrass myself by finishing before we even start."

"Oh," she said, her mouth rounded perfectly. She dropped her gaze to the front of his shorts, which were tented. She exclaimed "oh" again. This time there was a purr to her voice. She ran a hand down the front of his shorts, cupping him through the fabric.

Flynn's groin tightened even further. Grabbing her wrist, he pulled her hand from him. "That's exactly what I'm taking about Katie." He tugged the sweatshirt over her head, dropping it to the ground. If it was possible to swallow his own tongue, Flynn would have at that moment. She wore a sports bra. It shouldn't have been sexy. But it was emerald green and highlighted her full breasts. Sexy as hell with her flaming hair all around her.

She returned the favor, grabbing fistfuls of his shirt and jerking it over his head. Her eyes were hot as she took in the planes of his chest and abdomen. Flynn was thankful for all the exercise he did. He wanted to be perfect for her.

Flynn ran one fingertip under the edge of her bra, teasing the heated flesh there. She sighed as her nipples pebbled under his touch. He dipped his head and teased the nipple of one breast through the material of her bra with his teeth. He blew on the dampened material, tightening the nipple further. Katie threw back her head and moaned.

He had to know if she wore matching panties. Flynn placed his hands within the waistband of her ruined sweats, drawing them down over her hips. One small centimeter at a time. His finger slid along the soft material underneath as he progressed.

Her head whipped up. "Are you trying to kill me, Flynn?" she muttered from between clenched teeth.

He chuckled in response. "Of course, not. I'm trying to make it better for you."

"If you want to make this even better Flynn, then touch me."

He obeyed her wish, pushing her pants down to her knees, leaving just a small scrap of cotton to cover her. Yep, they matched. He swallowed before sliding the material over her knees, taking care of the injured one. She lifted her feet, one at a time, to kick off the sweats. Flynn kissed her with the hunger that burned inside of him and walked her backwards until the backs of her knees met the mattress. Ripping his mouth from hers, Flynn pushed her down onto the bed.

He leaned over her and kissed her deeply. He traced the fingers of one hand down her abdomen to the center of her desire. Katie began to pant, a small delicious sound that drove Flynn crazy. She tossed her head back and forth on the bed while her hips writhed, silently begging for his touch.

Flynn stood up straight and kicked off his shoes, then slid off his shorts and briefs in one smooth move. Kneeling at the bedside, he trailed his hands up both of her legs, drawing out the sensation. Her skin was as soft as silk. He could have touched her for hours, but they were both growing impatient. Grasping both legs under the knees, he pulled Katie towards the edge of the bed. Flynn placed one of her legs over each shoulder.

He didn't have to touch her to know that Katie was ready for him. The emerald material was damp. His tongue grew thick at the thought of what she would taste like. "Baby, you're so beautiful." Katie answered by lacing her fingers in his hair.

Pushing aside the scrap pf material, Flynn slid his tongue home. She reacted immediately, jerking her hips off the bed to meet his tongue. "Yes," she growled in a strangled tone. Flynn pulled the panties down to give him better access. He gazed at her mound, the red curls darkened with moisture, and lowered his mouth again. This time, he inserted two fingers as well, driving her to the brink.

He could feel the muscles of her thighs quiver on either side of him as he plundered with his tongue. In and out he darted his tongue until he felt her nearing the breaking point. On the bed, Katie panted and writhed, as though fighting for control. Grazing his teeth over the small bud, Flynn felt her come apart.

Grabbing his wallet, Flynn found the condom he sought. He joined her on the bed, covering her trembling body with his own. "I'm right here, baby," he whispered in her ear. A fine sheen of sweat covered her body. Katie kept her eyes clenched. But the expression on her face was pure satisfaction. He felt pure masculine satisfaction at putting it there.

Flynn slid her bra up over her head and tossed it to the floor, freeing her breasts. Leaning in, he captured one tightened nipple with his mouth. He sucked on it before pulling his head back and blowing across the sensitive skin. He grew harder watching her nipple pucker in response.

Katie rewarded him with a fierce moan. "Please, Flynn, I need to feel you inside of me." She raised her hips to his pelvis to drive home her point. Flynn's erection felt like it would burst at any moment. The need was so great

"Well, since you asked so nicely," he joked.

But the laughter died in his throat when she opened her eyes. Katie sat up and flipped Flynn over onto his back. Grabbing the foil packet, she ripped it open with her teeth. She placed one soft hand around his shaft, sliding up and down ever so slowly. On the third pass, she traced one finger around the head of his penis, spreading the bead of moisture she found.

She laughed at his groan. "Not so easy to take, is it?" Not bothering to wait for his answer, Katie rolled the condom down his length. She straddled him, holding herself above him, poised to take him inside of her. Flynn reached up and cupped both breasts with his hands, teasing the already taut nipples. Katie moaned in response as she lowered slowly, taking his length inside of her. When he was completely encased, she smiled and clenched her internal muscles around his length.

"Good God, Katie," he uttered. He was close to the brink. Close to shattering into a thousand pieces. And far from caring if he'd ever be whole again.

"I take it you like that." She teased him as she raised her hips and lowered once again. She tossed her head, and her shining red hair cascaded over her breasts. The sight stole his breath.

"Like doesn't begin to cover it, Katie." Flynn reached up and brushed aside her hair, baring her breasts to his view. "You are so beautiful."

Her face flushed, whether with pride or embarrassment he wasn't sure. "I feel beautiful with you." She leaned in and ran her tongue down the center of his chest.

Her words and actions sent him spiraling higher. In one swift move, he flipped their positions. Katie locked her ankles behind his back, drawing him in even further. It was too much. He slid one hand between them and flicked her bud with a finger, sending her hurtling over the edge. Flynn was right behind her, tumbling in his release.

When he could breathe again, Flynn reluctantly withdrew from her. Getting up, he went into her bathroom to deal with the condom. He could only grin at his expression in the mirror. The smile that wouldn't end. His skin flushed with pleasure. He couldn't wait to rejoin Katie in her bed.

Chapter Nine

When Flynn headed into the bathroom, Katie rolled to her side, scooting under the comforter and pulling it up around her. What could she have been thinking? It's not like she could blame Flynn. She had taken him by the hand and brought him to her bedroom. Gentleman that he was, Flynn had given her more than one opportunity to back out. And did she? Oh no. Of course, not.

Katie closed her eyes and counted to ten in her head. She took a few deep breaths. In and out. She needed to gain control before he returned from the bathroom. But she no more had the thought when he padded back to the bed. The mattress dipped under his weight as Flynn crawled under the covers. Moving across the mattress, he slid up behind her, his chest pressing to her back.

Katie tried to not scream. What was wrong with her? This is what every woman wanted, a post coital cuddle. Every sane woman that was. But not her. She needed time and distance to deal with what she had started.

Flynn brushed the hair away from her neck before nuzzling it. "You're awfully tense. Is something wrong, Katie?"

"No." Her flat tone belied the word. Having sex with Flynn was a huge mistake. Nothing had changed. He was still a doctor. With whom she worked. Closely. They were still responsible for the community event that could make or break her graduate school admission. Where did that leave her? In one hell of a mess.

She felt him flip over onto his back. "Please don't lie to me, Katie."

A single tear slipped from under her eyelashes. She blew out a breath. "This was a mistake." The word sounded so much worse than it had in her brain. And it had sounded horrible there.

Flynn tensed next to her. "Really? Because it felt pretty damn good from my angle." There was the slightest bit of sarcasm in his voice. Katie could hardly blame him. Talk about your mixed signals. Flynn had every right to be pissed. But knowing that didn't make it any easier.

"I didn't mean that, Flynn." Her tone begged for understanding.

"I find that hard to believe, Katie. I've never known you to not say exactly what you meant. Ever." He blew out an aggravated breath. "I asked you if you were sure, Katie."

She felt the bed move again as Flynn got up. The rustle of his clothing followed as he got dressed. Because she wasn't a coward, at least not completely, Katie opened her eyes and sat up. She dragged the comforter with her, ensuring she was covered. She no longer felt beautiful.

"What I meant was that I knew what I was doing at the time, Flynn. I regret that choice now." Wow. Had she really said that? What was wrong with her? Someone needed to slap her. Or at least put some tape over her mouth before she said something even worse.

Flynn stopped in the middle of tying his sneakers. The hurt in his eyes was almost more than she could bear. "A *mistake*?"

"This," she gestured between them. "This was wonderful. But I don't want to give you the wrong impression. I'm not looking for a relationship with you, Flynn."

"Neither was I, Katie. But here we are." He finished tying his sneakers and straightened up. "So, what was this? A one-time only? A quick roll in the proverbial hay?"

Katie lowered her gaze, no longer able to meet his. "Yes," she responded in a tiny voice.

"I see." Flynn took one last look at Katie before walking out of her bedroom.

Katie stayed in bed until long after the front door closed behind Flynn. It would have been easier had he slammed the door. Anger, she could handle. But she had hurt his feelings; something she hadn't meant to do. It wasn't in her nature to be deliberately cruel. But her survival was at stake.

Throwing back the covers, Katie pulled on old gym shorts and a tank top. She winced at the pain in her knee but kept going. Stalking into the master bathroom, she grabbed cleaning supplies from under the sink. She turned her attention to the shower. She hated to clean. Today, it was a blessing. Furiously scrubbing the shower tile, Katie worked off some of her frustrations. The tiles and chrome gleamed with her effort. But the images of their sweat-slicked bodies entwined on her bed could not be washed away.

With a growl of frustration, Katie raced into her bedroom and ripped the sheets from her bed. No matter that she had changed them a few days ago. Even now, the scent of Flynn permeated the room. The scent of them. She threw everything into the hallway and then flopped down across her stripped bed.

What was she thinking? For months, the attraction between them had grown until it had taken on a life of its own. She knew when he entered the unit. She could sense him. Her body came alive when he was near. But she had resisted. Katie had her reasons, and they were good ones. So, did he. Funny how she didn't remember that when he was inside her.

Her skin flushed with pleasure at the memory of his hands on her body. On her breasts. His voice, roughened with emotion, as he whispered in her ear. She squeezed her eyes shut to block the image. But all that did was bring it to life in brilliant colors. Katie had resisted Flynn for months. Why now?

She wasn't sure why today had been the day. But it had been coming for a long time. From the first time she met him. In the back of her mind, Katie had been hoping that giving in and having sex with Flynn would quench the thirst. She laughed at her own ridiculous naivete. It wasn't a pretty sound. Touching him. Tasting him. Feeling him so deep inside her that she couldn't tell where she ended and he began, only made her want him again. But that wasn't happening.

Katie bounced off the bed and grabbed her cleaning supplies. There was another full bathroom plus a guest one that could use a little elbow grease. Katie would work herself to the bone. Otherwise, sleep would be hard to come by tonight.

*****

Leaving Katie in her bed was one of the hardest things Flynn had ever done. But he kept walking and didn't stop until he was in his car. That way he knew he would leave. Not that he wanted to. Flynn shook his head as he started his car. What had happened? She had kicked him out after incredible sex. Who did that? It was a first for Flynn. Yes, they had both agreed that a relationship between them wasn't happening. But that was *before*.

By the time Flynn drove home, he was no closer to understanding the enigma that was Katie Fitzgerald. She had caught his eye the moment they met. Yet, with a few notable exceptions, she held him at arm's length. For months, they had been dancing around each other. Katie had finally given into their incredible chemistry; only to send him packing the moment it was over.

Flynn dragged a hand over his face and sighed as he reached into the fridge for some juice. He had never lacked for female companionship. There were any number of women he could call right now who would be more than willing to go out with him. So why wasn't he calling them? An image of Katie under him in her bed, her brilliant hair spread across the pillow, popped into his head. That was why. He didn't want other women. Even though circumstances made them a better choice. Sure, they were pretty and bright. And several of them he found interesting. But they weren't Katie.

He dropped onto his leather couch and placed the half-drank bottle of orange juice on the coffee table. Kicking his shoes off, Flynn stretched out and thought about his situation. They had both been clear that this would not occur. Despite the fire that raged between them. No one was more surprised than him at what had happened between them. Except for maybe Katie. And yet it had happened.

He was already half in love with her. Which made this scenario even more impossible. But Flynn was a stubborn man. He wasn't willing to let her slip away. Not without a fight. Not when he knew how amazing they were together. There had to be a way to make this work. At least he hoped so.

****

Late Sunday afternoon, Katie pulled up to her parents' home for dinner. She and her siblings were all grown, two with kids of their own. Yet Maggie insisted on a family dinner at least once per month, more if their varied schedules allowed. Despite their hectic lives, it was rare for any of Katie's siblings to miss. Their numbers had grown over the years with significant others and then spouses and children in attendance. Only Donovan was married now, but Brendan also had the twins, six-year olds Abigail and Kerry. Much to Maggie's disgust and despite her endless matchmaking, the rest of them were still single.

Leaning into the trunk of her SUV, Katie grabbed the salad she had made for dinner. While she didn't see Flynn's Mercedes glide to a halt at the curb, she heard it. She knew it was him. Her siblings all drove trucks. His car was nearly silent and smooth.

Salad bowl in hand, Katie whirled around. "What are you doing here?" She flushed as the words left her mouth. Maggie would have her head if she heard. But the memory of his touch was still on her skin. She hadn't seen or heard from him since she threw him out after sex yesterday. Katie knew she would have to face him eventually. She just didn't know it would be less than twenty-four hours and with her whole family as witness.

As unflustered as ever, Flynn reached around Katie and closed the back of her SUV. In his other hand, he carried a bouquet of flowers. Her heart raced. She didn't want flowers from him. At least she didn't want to want them. Flowers meant they were in a relationship. They weren't. All they did was have sex. Once. The best sex of her life, but she wasn't telling anyone that.

"I can hear the wheels turning in your head, Katie. I'm here because your mother was kind enough to invite me at the wedding." He pointed the flowers at her. "And these are for her, not you." He answered the shock on her face with a smirk. "Nice to see you again, as well." Flynn continued to the front door.

Katie could only stand and stare after him. What was it about that man? He made her crazy.

Maggie Fitzgerald threw open the door. She exclaimed over the flowers that Flynn handed her. "I'm so glad you could make it, Flynn. I hope you brought your appetite! Come in!" She looked around Flynn. "Katherine Maureen, why are you standing in the driveway?"

Katie gritted her teeth before answering. "Coming, Mom." She got a better grip on her purse, keys, and salad bowl before heading up the driveway. Figures her mother would like him. Maggie continued to fuss over Flynn, leading him into her home while Katie brought up the rear.

"Thank you for inviting me, Mrs. Fitzgerald. I appreciate a home cooked meal. And don't worry about my appetite." He turned to stare at Katie as he continued. "I'm always hungry. Katie can vouch for that."

By the heat in his eyes, she knew he wasn't talking about food. Mumbling under her breath, Katie proceeded into the kitchen. She placed the salad in her mother's refrigerator, resisting the urge to stick her head in there as well. Too many witnesses. But being near Flynn raised her temperature. How was she ever going to survive this dinner? The wedding had been bad enough. But now that she'd slept with him, it could only be worse.

She heard the front door close, followed by the sound of her adorable nieces. Kerry and Abby sure made a lot of noise. Their high-pitched squeals rang off the walls. Maggie oohed and ahhed over their very existence. Conversation became next to impossible for the next few moments. Katie was happy for the reprieve. It gave her time to get her head together.

That thought had no more formed before Flynn sauntered into her refuge. "Hiding Katherine Maureen? I expected better of you." He raised one raven brow in question, but the look on his face was pure devil.

"Hardly," she answered with a haughty tone. "Some of us have work to do to get dinner ready." She turned her back to him and busied her hands with grabbing silverware from the drawer.

"I'm happy to help." Flynn's drawled words accompanied his warm breath on her neck. Because her hair was being its usual impossible self today, Katie had pulled it into a loose bun, leaving the skin of her neck exposed. Awareness of him danced across her sensitive skin. To save her sanity, Katie moved away from Flynn.

"No thanks. You're a guest. Mom would skin me alive. Why don't you go hang out with the boys? They're probably down in the basement."

"What's wrong, Katie? Why are you blowing me off?" His voice was no longer tinged with amusement.

Taking a deep breath, she turned to face him. "I'm not 'blowing you off.' I'm surprised to see you here. I wasn't prepared for that so soon after…yesterday." She gestured weakly with her hands, not finding the right words.

"You mean after having sex with me." His voice had both lowered and deepened, hitting her right in the gut.

She whirled on him, shushing him like a naughty child. Katie dragged him through the kitchen slider and onto the back deck. She shut it behind them. "Are you crazy? Why would you say that in there? Any of my many family members might have heard you."

"Would that have been the worst thing, Katie?"

Fire blazed from her green eyes. "Yes, Flynn, that would have been the worst possible thing. We aren't together. And as old fashioned as it may seem, my brothers, not to mention my father, are a bit overprotective. Do you want them to know what we were doing yesterday afternoon?"

Flynn's normally smiling face was blank. Except for the storm clouds gathering in his eyes. "Are you ashamed of me, Katie?"

Shock ripped through her. How could he even think that? "What? Of course, not! Yesterday is our business, not there's. If one person in my family suspects something, they'll all find out. You don't want that, Flynn. Mom will be suggesting names for our kids before you can blink."

Flynn's blue eyes were as dark as night. "So, let me get this straight. Sleeping with me, having sex with me, is okay. Being in a relationship with me isn't? Do I have that right?"

Katie dragged a hand through her hair as she blew out her frustration. "We've been over this, Flynn. Many times. We both have our reasons why this wouldn't work. Yesterday was, uh, unexpected. But nice. Don't get me wrong. I had fun."

"Nice? Fun? And I don't think it was unexpected. This attraction has built since the moment we met."

Katie noted the rise in his voice. Flynn wasn't happy. "Look, Flynn, this isn't the time or the place to discuss this."

He fixed her with a steely glance. "That's the first thing you've gotten right today, Katie." Without another word, Flynn walked back into the house.

Katie watched his retreating back. Anger reflected in the tenseness of his shoulders. She'd never seen him infuriated before. She had hurt his feelings; something she didn't mean to do. This was why she shouldn't have slept with him. There was no way she would ever get involved with another doctor. Another co-corker. She had plans and goals. She had already learned that lesson the hard way. Katie sat in a deck chair. She wanted to give him, and herself some time before she went back in the house.

*****

More than anything, Flynn wanted to leave. Just go home and skip the dinner. But he wouldn't do that to Katie's family. Mrs. Fitzgerald had been nice enough to include him. He wouldn't disrespect her by leaving.

Flynn was glad to find the kitchen empty. He needed a minute to calm down. Flynn paced the length of the room, not paying attention to the cheerful décor. "Nice?" She thought their time together yesterday was "nice"? Nice was an anemic word you used to describe a neighbor's flower garden. Or the weather. NOT what had happened between them yesterday.

An image of Katie, naked and wrapped around him, flashed through his mind. He smiled at the memory. Amazing. Stupendous. Electric. Those were more suitable words. Off the top of his head, Flynn could come up with a thousand words that were better suited.

"Hey man, there you are." Brendan, Katie's second oldest brother, filled the doorway. "What are you doing in the kitchen? Alone?"

Flynn mentally shifted gears. It wouldn't do to be remembering Brendan's sister naked. He forced a smile before closing the gap between them and shook Brendan's hand. "I was going to see if I could help." He would have liked to slap himself in the head. That was the best he could come up with?

The odd look on Brendan's face let Flynn know he wasn't buying it. "Uh, I didn't know you cooked."

"I don't, but I thought I could do something to help." Flynn made every effort to not squirm.

Brendan grinned. He waved an arm around the room. "This is Maggie's domain. Always has been. Mom barely lets the girls in here."

"Did I hear my name?" Maggie Fitzgerald bustled into the room, smiling as she came. "All good. I assume."

Brendan laughed. "As if there's anything bad to say, Mom." He leaned down and kissed her cheek.

"Oh, go on with you Brendan." Turning, she addressed Flynn. "Don't you believe a thing that comes out of this one." She smiled as she said it, the love she felt for her son glowing in her eyes.

"What can I do to help, Mrs. Fitzgerald?"

"For a start, you can call me, Maggie. Otherwise, nothing. You're a guest, Flynn. Why don't you join the rest of the guys in the basement? There's some game on I'm sure."

"Okay, Maggie, if you're sure."

"Hurry up man, before she changes her mind," Brendan joked as he pushed Flynn out of the room. Flynn followed Brendan down the stairs. The basement could only be described as a "man cave". The largest TV he had ever seen dominated one wall. A small bar sat in a corner. Two large, leather couches filled most of the room. Brendan's other brothers, along with their dad, were watching the Panthers play. The noise level discouraged any conversation. Apparently, the referee had made a call that was very unpopular with the Fitzgerald men.

Brendan threw himself down in an available spot as his father, Joe, spotted Flynn. The older man grinned as he got up and made his way towards him.

"Flynn! How are you? Nice to see you again."

The two men shook hands. Even though he knew what Katie's dad did for a living, he was impressed with the strength of his grip. "Great to see you again as well, Mr. Fitzgerald."

Katie's father laughed; a great, booming sound in the small room. "That makes me look around for my dad. Please, call me Joe. Come and sit. Tell me about the doctor business."

The hometown favorites scored, drowning out Flynn's reply. He joined the others in cheering, even though he was a long-time Falcons fan. When in Rome.

"The practice is going well, Joe. Sebastian and I are busy trying to increase our patient load. Prove ourselves."

"That's great news. Katie was telling me how hard you boys work. You don't want to burn out."

"You're right about that, Joe. I try to forget about work when I'm not there. But you know better than most how it is. Building Fitzgerald construction from the ground up can't have been easy."

Joe nodded and took a drink of his beer, watching Flynn over the rim of his glass. Flynn felt as though he might be under a microscope. "How are you liking Windsor Falls? Must be a huge change from Atlanta."

"Yes sir, it is. But I like the small-town life. People are friendlier. And everyone has gone out of their way to make sure that Sebastian and I are settling in."

"Like you and Katie."

Flynn's heart skipped a beat. Or maybe two. How could Katie's father possibly know?

Joe was looking at him strangely. "The community event coming up. Katie told us about it."

Relief flooded Flynn. "Oh. That. Of course, Joe. Not sure where my mind was for a minute." Flynn laughed, hoping Joe would as well and not notice his discomfort.

"Sounds like a great chance for you to get your name and face out there, Flynn."

"It is, of course. But, I'm also happy to give back to the community. Too many people don't realize they have a heart condition until it's too late."

Riley poked her head into the room. "Time for dinner." Flynn watched as she waited for her brothers and father to leave the room. Then she approached him. Her face was lit up with a sly grin. She was a dangerous one.

"Hello, Riley."

She put her arm through his and led him towards the stairs. "I thought I would take this moment to tell you that I approve."

Flynn's heart lurched painfully. "Good to know. May I ask of what?" He tried to keep his voice even, to not betray the anxiety he felt.

"Of you and Katie, of course." She beamed at him, clutching his arm to her. "You two are perfect for each other. You don't happen to have a younger brother, do you?" she joked.

"Sadly, I only have sisters. But to be clear, your sister and I work together. That's all. Your mother invited me to dinner at the wedding." They were half way up the stairs now. He didn't want to have this conversation where other members of Katie's family could hear.

Riley raced up two stairs and turned so that they were on eye level with each other. "Why? Katie's made it known she's 'on the market' again. And you two have some killer chemistry. So, what's the problem?" She looked him up and down with a serious look on her face. "You're not gay, are you?" She hurried up the stairs.

"What?" He continued after Riley.

"Not that there's anything wrong with that, of course," she hurried to say.

Flynn didn't know whether to laugh or cry. This family was a trip. "No, Riley, I'm not gay."

Unfortunately, they had reached the dining room when Flynn made that comment. At least a half a dozen pairs of eyes stared at him. There was a moment of silence before Katie's brothers burst out laughing.

Maggie Fitzgerald seemed completely unperturbed as she motioned everyone to sit. "Of course you're not, dear. Care for some mashed potatoes?" She motioned for him to take the empty seat next to Katie.

Everyone returned to taking a seat and reaching for different dishes. Flynn could feel Katie next to him, staring daggers at him. She had to be wondering about his strange declaration. On the other hand, he mused, she couldn't have any doubts after yesterday.

Dinner continued with a general roar of voices. The nine adults seemed to be having at least six different conversations. The four kids, two of Donovan's and Brendan's twins were eating at the kitchen table. Flynn enjoyed the noise and comradery. The Reynolds clan was just as boisterous.

Katie hadn't addressed him in the first fifteen minutes. She seemed quieter than usual. Flynn took matters into his own hands. He turned his gaze to her and waited until she glanced his way. "Is there a reason you're not speaking to me, Katie?" He slid his thigh along hers, hoping for a reaction. Her sharp intake of breath let him know she wasn't completely unaffected by him.

"I don't have anything to say to you. I certainly didn't ask to be placed next to you at dinner."

"No, I'm sure you didn't. That may have been Riley's doing. She thinks we're perfect for each other."

"What? Why?" Her green eyes widened as her mouth hung open.

"She thinks we have chemistry." Even now, Flynn saw Riley winking at them from across the table. "See what I mean?"

Katie turned to stare at her younger sister. Disgust lined her face. "Luckily for me, what Riley thinks doesn't matter."

"True." Flynn placed his napkin back in his lap after wiping his mouth. His hand wandered over to her knee, caressing it through the denim of her jeans. He felt her stiffen in surprise. "What you and I think counts, Katie."

Flynn was pushing his luck. He didn't care. He would make her see how good things could be between them. But Katie was as determined. She drew her leg away from his, dislodging his hand.

"You already know my opinion, Flynn. This isn't happening."

Challenge accepted.

"Riley, could you tell me why Katie doesn't like me? She's barely said two words since we started dinner. It's going to make working together on the health fair very difficult."

Once again, silence reigned at the table. All eyes focused on them. Out of the corner of his eye, Flynn could see the bright red color creep across Katie's face. This was probably a mistake, he mused, but she wasn't giving him a choice.

"I couldn't say," replied Riley. "Katie, why don't you like Flynn? He seems nice."

"That's enough out of you," scolded Maggie. "Flynn, is there a problem?"

"Other than the fact that your daughter won't play nice, no ma'am."

A strange choking noise came from his right. Flynn turned to look as Katie nearly spit an entire mouthful of water across the table. Luckily, she had grabbed her napkin just in time.

"Are you okay," he asked with a show of concern.

If looks could kill, Flynn would have dead on the spot. "I'd appreciate it if y'all would stop talking about me as if I wasn't sitting right here." Despite the high color and sparks coming from her bright, green eyes, Katie's voice was calm. Almost without inflection.

"You've done it now, Flynn," chimed in Donovan. "The quieter she is, the more she's pissed."

"Again, I'm right here." She addressed Donovan, who chuckled in response. Katie turned her gaze towards Flynn. "As for you, if you have a problem with me, please ask *me*." She got up, carrying her plate to the kitchen. Conversation resumed at the table, but people were still giving Flynn odd looks.

Flynn finished his delicious dinner. "Maggie, thank you for the wonderful meal. The roast was perfection. Far better than I could ever do." He stood up. "I'm sorry for the drama. It's probably best if I leave now."

"You're welcome, dear. And you're welcome here anytime. But no one leaves without dessert. Katie will be just fine."

Flynn grew up in the South, so he knew better than to disrespect the hostess. He sat back down. "I'd be delighted. Surely, I can help with the dishes."

Maggie laughed. "No, you may not. That's what I have children for." Taking their cue, Katie's siblings gathered their plates and left the dining room. The sounds of children laughing in the backyard was the only noise. Flynn sat with Katie's parents and a growing sense of unease.

Joe cleared his throat. Loudly. "Having an issue with our Katie, are you son?"

Flynn resisted clearing his. "Yes sir, I am." He got the idea that Joe was asking about something else.

Joe stared at him for so long that Flynn was afraid of what he would say next. When he spoke, it was a complete surprise. "Well then, prepare for a fight." Without any further explanation, he left the room.

Maggie came around the end of the table and sat next to Flynn, patting him kindly. "Our Katie is a very independent woman. Sometimes too much so. This event is very important to her. And that's all I'm going to say about that. You seem like a good man, Flynn. I wish you luck." She left the room, humming under her breath.

Flynn stayed at the table, confused by all that had happened. Things were never boring here. He shook his head.

"Just because my family likes you doesn't mean I'm going to go out with you. I make my own decisions."

Flynn turned to see Katie standing a foot behind him. He got up and turned to face her. "I wouldn't have it any other way. Your sister started this whole thing, Katie. I never intended to discuss it at dinner."

"Yet you did."

"True. Not my brightest move."

"You think?" Flynn could tell she was pissed. Katie was not one to hold anything back. Good or bad. He spread his hands in a gesture of surrender. "I'm sorry, Katie. I got carried away. In my defense, you have been giving off mixed signals." Flynn held his breath. That might have been the worst thing he could have said yet.

But the storm never came. Her face was blank. Fists unclenched. Her voice was monotone when she spoke. "You're right, Flynn. I said I didn't want to get involved with you, and I meant it." She closed her eyes, drawing in a deep breath. "And then I slept with you. That wasn't fair. To either of us." She turned around and walked out of her parents' home.

Flynn was stunned. He had expected an angry outburst. He would have preferred that to what he had witnessed. Katie was never so dispassionate about anything. What had he done?

Chapter Ten

Katie had only gotten as far as her car when she heard the front door bang. She didn't need to look to know it was Flynn. There wasn't anything he could say to change her mind. Yesterday had been an aberration. A one off. The fact that it had been delicious couldn't be a consideration. This was for the best.

His footsteps were closer and Katie tensed, prepared for whatever he might say. But there weren't any words. Flynn spun her around and placed his firm lips on hers. Backing her against her car, he positioned his hands against the windows on either side of her head. She could have moved at any time. He wasn't holding her against her will. In fact, other than his lips, he wasn't even touching her. Damn him. She could have resisted if he had been rough or demanding. But the feel of his lips against hers, and the heat that created, was too tempting.

Katie leaned into the kiss, groaning deep in her throat. Her fingers itched to touch him. With a will of their own, they buried themselves in his thick, soft hair, pulling him in even closer. In a small, dim corner of her brain, Katie knew this was a bad idea. But the rest of her was in a fog of sensation and had a different agenda. She took one step forward. Just one. Their bodies now pressed in all the important places. Yes. That's what she needed.

When she had accepted what she was doing, Flynn broke the kiss and rested his forehead against hers. His breathing was as ragged as hers.

"That's only part of why we could be so good together, Katie. Why do you want to throw that away?" Without another word, he walked to his car and drove away.

Katie stood there, fingers pressed to her tingling lips, and watched him leave. It wasn't any easier than watching him leave her bed yesterday. And yet this is what she wanted. Wasn't it? After David, she swore she would never get involved with another doctor. Ever. Not even the ridiculously sexy Flynn Reynolds. Especially him.

Katie dreaded dealing with the fall out. Her siblings could be ruthless. But she had rushed after Flynn without thinking. Her keys and purse were in the house. Plus, she wasn't going to slink away. Katie went into the house. She could hear the raucous noise coming from downstairs. The guys had resumed watching sports.

Hearing her mother's voice in the kitchen, Katie walked in that direction. She stood in the doorway, watching as her mother sang along to Colbie Caillat on her iPhone. Maggie swayed to the beat as she placed leftovers in a container. Shaking her head, Katie marveled at her mother's seemingly boundless energy. She grabbed a towel and picked up one of her mother's crystal glasses.

Maggie glanced over her shoulder. "Where's Flynn? He didn't leave, did he?"

"He did, Mom. Sorry about that. It's my fault."

"How is it your fault, Katie?"

Katie didn't answer right away as she considered the question. She didn't know how much she wanted Maggie to know about the situation. "We had a disagreement. Nothing new under the sun."

Maggie nodded her head and resumed dancing.

Katie was shocked. Her mother never missed an opportunity to give advice. And she needed some, even if she was too stubborn to ask. "No comments, Mom?"

Maggie finished what she was doing. "What would you like me to say, Katie? You're a grown woman with an education and a profession. You don't need my advice."

Katie's face crumpled. "Are you kidding me, Mom?"

Maggie sat at the table and motioned for her daughter to do the same. She took Katie's hands in hers. "Dear heart, you've always been a bit of a mystery to me. Riley has always been wide open, as our Connor was. You never have to guess what's on her mind."

Katie couldn't help it. Laughter burst from her. So much so, that she had to bend over and try to breathe as tears rolled down her face. When she could talk again, she addressed her mom. "Are you trying to tell me that I'm shy about speaking my mind, Mom? Because you might be the first person who has."

"Good lord, no! Katie, you are definitely the most outspoken of my children." She smiled at the confusion playing across her daughter's face. "But when it comes to personal issues, especially relationships, you clam up. Keep a close counsel. And there's nothing wrong with that. But I can't help if I don't know what's wrong."

Katie let out the air she was holding in one large whoosh. "Oh."

"It doesn't have to be today, dear."

In a very small voice, Katie addressed her mom. "I've decided to get out there again. Start dating. No big deal." The seriousness of her tone belied her words.

"Good for you, Katie. It's more than time. Young woman like you. Is this where Flynn comes in?"

"Sort of. I like him. A lot. But we work together. And he's a doctor. I can't go down that road again. Especially not now when I have so much at stake." She paused and then blurted out her plans for graduate school.

Maggie's whole face lit up. She jumped up and dragged Katie from her chair, hugging her until Katie was sure she'd crack a rib. "I'm so proud of you, Katie girl!" She kissed her daughter's cheek before sitting back down. "Tell me everything."

And Katie did. About graduate school. And the community event news. And finally, about how Flynn figured into it.

"Ah. This is about David then. I should have known." Maggie's normally sunny face darkened at the very mention of Katie's ex-boyfriend.

"This is not about David. That was more than two years ago."

"Oh, Katie, you're smarter than that. Of course, this is about David and how he hurt you. Why else would you be hesitating to get involved with someone like

Flynn?" Much to Katie's disgust, her mother patted her hand. And made little sounds of commiseration. Great! Now she was a charity case.

Embarrassment became frustration. Frustration became anger. Just as it always did with Katie. "You don't know Flynn like I do, Mom. He's not as perfect as you seem to think he is."

"Of course not, dear," murmured her mother from her place at the table. "Which of us is?"

Maggie's calm demeanor only added fuel to the fire. "Let me tell you about Flynn Reynolds. He's super smart and an excellent physician. He cares so much for his patients. And their families. And they love him right back." She paused to suck in some much-needed air. "Then there's the fact that he's drop-dead gorgeous. Women of all ages flirt with him, Mom. I'm talking little old ladies hooked up to all sorts of machines in the ICU. They put on lipstick when he's expected. Lipstick!" Righteous indignation was exhausting, Katie discovered. She dropped her head into her hands. "What am I supposed to do with that, Mom?"

Maggie placed a hand over one of Katie's, squeezing in a silent show of support. "You can hardly hold most of those things against him. Intelligence and looks are partly genes and mostly luck. Personality is all him, but it sounds like exactly what I would want if I needed a cardiologist. As for flirting with little old ladies…"

Much to Katie's shock and horror, her mother burst out laughing. Laughing! "Mom!"

Maggie wiped at her eyes, trying in vain to squelch her laughter. But it wasn't helping. "Oh, darling. Are you really concerned about Flynn cheating on you with Mrs. Foreman?"

The corner of Katie's lips quivered despite her mood. Mrs. Foreman was pushing a hundred and bore the self-imposed title of *widow* well. Allegedly there had once been a Mr. Foreman, but if there was, no one in Windsor Falls remembered. She dressed only in black and an air of unapproachability. She had lived alone in a tiny cottage a few blocks off the main drag in town as long as anyone could recollect.

She terrified the children in town. Only the bravest ventured to enter her yard for a lost ball or on a dare. And then only once. She seemed to have a sixth sense for when her private domain was under attack. Mrs. Foreman always responded with a loud voice, broom in hand. More than one kid had suggested that was her favorite mode of transportation.

A few months back, Katie had started a shift and found Mrs. Foreman lying in one of her ICU beds. Apparently, she did have a heart. Although not a very healthy one. The elderly woman answered Katie's assessment questions in monosyllables. Rapport was out of the question, despite her best efforts.

But the next morning, when Flynn walked in for rounds, a miracle occurred. Mrs. Foreman smiled. While Katie was picking her chin up off the floor, the impossible happened. A high, breathy giggle, reminiscent of a pre-teen girl floated through the air. Since the sound could not possibly have come from the strapping Dr. Reynolds, there was only one possibility. Indeed, there sat Mrs. Foreman, propped up by several pillows, batting her eyelashes at Flynn. All ninety pounds of her was leaning forward, hanging on the cardiologist's every word. If Katie had not been there to witness such a spectacle, she would have never believed it.

And Flynn, bless his Southern heart, had sat in rapt attention. He could flatter and cajole with the best of them. But damn him, he got Mrs. Foreman to agree to everything that Katie had suggested the night before.

Katie smiled at her mother. "No, of course I'm not jealous of Mrs. Foreman. But he's that way with *all* women."

"Exactly. If he was only friendly with blondes in their twenties, then maybe you'd have something to worry about, Katie. But, by your own admission, he's charming and personable with everyone. That's something different entirely."

Katie sighed, knowing her mother was right. As always. But it was more complicated than that. "This community event must go well. I need Ms. Nelson, the hospital's chief nursing officer, to write a glowing recommendation for me. That alone could be the edge to get into an NP program. I can't blow this."

"Then don't, Katie. It's that simple. Yes, you and Flynn must work together on this project to ensure its success. And ultimately yours as well. Do the work, make this event great, and then you move on."

Katie's shoulders slumped. Her voice was barely a whisper. "It's so scary, Mom. Allowing yourself to be vulnerable." Her normally bright green eyes clouded. "Do I really want to open myself up to that again?"

"That's a choice only you can make, darling girl." Maggie leaned in and brushed a bright, red swatch of Katie's hair behind her ear. "Just remember that the alternative isn't such a great option either. Sure, you'll be safe; but you'll also be very lonely." Maggie got up. She leaned down and hugged her daughter.

Later that evening, Katie walked into the Hole, scanning the crowd for her friend Kat. She spied her at the end of the bar, perched on a stool. Katie waded through tables to reach her friend. She stopped several feet away to watch another poor sap bite the dust. Kat was very dedicated to the bakery with little time for dating. When she did bother to date, she was very picky. This guy was probably nice, but everything about him screamed average. The fact that he seemed to be hanging on her every word sealed his fate. Kat needed someone to challenge her. Not agree with everything she said.

Kat turned and spotted Katie standing behind her. She turned to the man next to her. "See, I told you I was waiting for someone." She turned away from him, already forgetting his existence.

The man moved away, leaving room for Katie. She slid onto the barstool next to Kat and waved down the bartender. "Hey, Scott! Can I get a Corona please?"

The bartender, all six feet two inches of him, smiled in Katie's direction. "Anything for you, darling. Coming right up!"

Kat shook her head. "We're not in high school anymore, Katie. You're a confident, beautiful woman. Why don't you go for it?"

Katie laughed and then pointed to Scott. He was flashing his megawatt smile at a barely-old-enough-to-be-in-here blonde. "That's why. Scott's pretty to look at and fun to flirt with. But that's it. I don't want to be another notch on his bedpost."

"He could be another notch on *your* bedpost. It's all in your perspective." Kat took a sip of her white wine. "I'd say we're both overdue for an orgasm with a man attached to it."

Of course, Scott picked just that moment to return with her beer. His blonde eyebrows met his shaggy hair. He didn't say a word but smiled suggestively before setting down her Corona and leaving. Both women were silent for a heartbeat before howling with laughter. It was several moments before either could breathe well enough to speak.

"Come on, Katie, admit it. I have a point. We can only depend on our little battery-operated friends to do so much."

A flash of just what Flynn's hands, not to mention tongue, could do sent a wave of heat through Katie. She stopped short of fanning herself. She wasn't going to be bringing that up right now. But then she didn't have to.

Kat's eyes rounded as her mouth popped open. "Katherine Fitzgerald, what have you done? Or should I say, who have you done?"

Katie shushed her. Kat could be very loud when she wanted. She glanced around to make sure none of her siblings were there. Or worst yet Flynn.

"There's no point in trying to deny it, Katie. Your body language tells me everything but a name." She leaned closer, peering at Katie speculatively. "I might even be able to guess that. Would it be a certain, wildly handsome doctor we both know?"

She meant to deny it. With her dying breath. But, Katie couldn't stop the grin that was spreading across her face. She wouldn't say the words, so she nodded her head.

"Oh, my God, are you kidding me? And you didn't tell me? When did this happen? I'm going to need details. Lots of juicy details."

"Not here, Kat. Too many witnesses."

"Fine." Kat whirled around on her barstool. Without warning she grabbed her purse and Katie, taking both to a small table in the corner. "This is as private as we're going to get. Spill it."

Knowing Kat wouldn't stop, Katie took a sip of her beer for courage. "This is all because I decided to go running. I knew it wasn't good for me," she quipped. Katie told her friend about the incident in the park. And Flynn driving her home. "I swear, Kat, it just happened. One minute he was cleaning my knee, and the next we were all over each other."

"Now you're getting to the good stuff. Go on. Was he amazing?" She whacked herself in the forehead. "What am I saying? Of course, he was amazing. That man is dripping in sex appeal."

"Let's say he was much better than our battery-operated friends."

"Oh, come on. I need details. Hot, specific details. It's been a *long* time. Help a friend out here."

"That's your own fault, Kat. You could have any guy in here. You're too picky."

"I prefer selective. Particular. And you shouldn't talk. Prior to Flynn, how long has it been?"

"You're right, it had been much too long. Thus, the recent dating disaster with the gym teacher. I was trying to get back out there but not with Flynn."

"True. You did try. Why not Flynn? I know you have good reasons, and it's not that I don't agree with you on that." She stopped and took a drink of her beer. "But, Katie, men like Flynn Reynolds do *not* come along every day. Trust me! Isn't there some way to make this work?"

She shook her head. Her green eyes clouded with remorse. "No, Kat, I don't think there is. I'd be risking too much. I need to focus on this event and getting into graduate school. Until then, no getting involved with someone who can risk all that for me."

"Okay. Fair enough. But what about Flynn? Now that you guys have gone there, where does he fit into your neat, little plan?"

"He doesn't. That was a one off. An aberration. That won't be happening again."

Kat's face said exactly what she thought about that, but she didn't argue. "If you say so. You may never get back this chance." She glanced at her watch and stifled a yawn. "Well, time for me to go. The life of a baker is oh so glamorous."

Katie knew her friend's crazy hours regularly cut into her social life. "I'm on my way out anyway, let's go."

The two friends walked outside. Katie stopped to zip up her fleece. Nights were getting chilly. She hugged Kat. "Thanks for meeting me tonight. You're my favorite sounding board."

Kat smiled in return. "Always!" Her normally cheerful expression turned serious. "Remember what I said, Katie. Don't settle. Life is short."

Katie watched as her friend walked down the street. The bakery, and her apartment, were only a block away. She stood there a moment, breathing in the crisp mountain air and thinking about Kat's advice. She was right. She, better than most, knew how fragile and unpredictable life could be.

An old, familiar melancholy settled over her as she thought about Connor. He had been the heart of the family. All their lives had changed when they lost him in a tragic accident. Connor would never have settled.

She shivered a bit in the night air. Katie got into her car and waited for it to warm up. Before she could lose her nerve, Katie pulled out her phone and hit one of the saved contacts. She gnawed on her lower lip while the call connected. By the third ring she had almost talked herself out of this. And then he answered.

"Hello, Katie."

Two simple words, yet her heart rate jumped even as her palms grew damp.

"Hi, Flynn." She cleared her throat. "You're probably wondering why I'm calling you."

"Considering how we left things, yes." His usual light-hearted banter was absent.

Okay, so he wasn't going to make this easy for her. Why should he? "Uh, true. Sorry about that." So much for brilliant conversation. "I'm sorry I bothered you."

"Do you want to come over?"

She heard herself agreeing even as her mind screamed "NO."

"I'll text you my address. See you soon, Katie." The call disconnected, leaving a confused Katie staring at the silent phone in her hand. Before she could even begin to wonder why she had agreed to such a thing, her text alert sounded.

Katie recognized the address, which was only a few short blocks from where she sat. Knowing this was a bad idea but not caring, Katie backed out of her parking space and headed towards Flynn's home. She tried to slow her breathing, which was coming in short, rapid puffs. Butterflies danced in her stomach. The thought of being alone with Flynn was unnerving her.

What was she doing? She had reasons, sound ones, for why Flynn was a bad idea. She needed to remember them when she was with him, not just alone in her car. But she also needed to work with him, now more than ever. They had to find a way to put what had happened behind them. Move forward.

Too quickly, she arrived at the address. Turning off the car, she took a moment to settle herself and looked at the house. A soft sigh escaped her lips. Of course, he would have a great house, she groused. The older Craftsman was large and a bit the worse for wear. But she had great bones. Great potential.

The front door opened, and Flynn was back lit from the soft light inside. Even though she couldn't see him clearly, her mouth went dry. She knew, remembered, what he looked like. All of him. No, she scolded herself. She had no idea what she was doing here, but it wasn't for *that*. In a moment of panic, she considered driving away. But she wasn't a coward. She straightened her shoulders.

Chapter Eleven

Flynn tried not to smile as he watched Katie wage a silent war with herself. Considering how they had left things, she was the last person he expected to hear from tonight. He had surprised himself by inviting her over. Even more so to hear her accept. A smile won out, lifting the corners of his mouth. Things would never be boring with Katie.

At least she seemed as conflicted as he felt, Flynn thought, as he watched her get out of her car and shut the door. Her remote lock was the only sound as she approached him. She sailed right past him and into his house without so much as a word.

Amusement floated through him as he shut and locked the door. He turned, and she was nowhere in sight. "Katie?" he called out to the empty room.

"Up here," came her reply from a distant part of the house.

Anticipation tightened his groin. She was upstairs somewhere. He had moved in recently and was only using two of the rooms upstairs. One for his bedroom and the other for a home office. Interesting. Maybe she wasn't as over this as she tried to tell him.

Flynn headed to the stairs. At the base of them sat a pair of boots, one tipped over and both kicked off hastily. His breath hitched in his chest. Taking the stairs two at a time, Flynn grew hotter with each garment he passed. She couldn't have much else on. He paused in the doorway to his room, struck by the scene that greeted him. The only light was that which filtered in from the bathroom. Katie sat, propped up on several pillows, his sheet tucked around her breasts.

His heart forgot to beat as Flynn stared at her. Glorious red hair fanned out behind her, and the pale silk of her skin shone against the navy of his sheets. He felt himself harden at the mere sight of her. Words were beyond him.

"Why are you still standing all the way over there?"

Why indeed? He didn't understand what was going on with them, but he wasn't stupid. He had Katie in his bed. Naked. That's all he needed to know. "Good question."

Flynn closed the distance between them with three long strides. He shed his clothing as he went. With only his boxers left, Flynn slid onto the bed and gathered Katie in his arms. A shudder rippled through her at his touch. His body replied in kind.

He'd probably regret it, but he had to ask. "Katie, what are we doing?"

"Would it matter if I told you I have no idea?" One well-placed hand stopped him from answering. He sighed as she slid her hand under the band of his boxers. Her smile was pure female as she closed her fingers around his growing erection. "No talking." To drive home her point, Katie leaned in and seared his mouth with her own.

He was good with that. Flynn closed his eyes on the pleasure that poured over him and kissed her back. All the pent-up frustration he had felt over their situation exploded in an instant. She ran one finger down the length of him and back up again, stopping to tease the responsive head of his penis.

He closed his hand around hers to slow things down a bit. "Keep that up, and this will be over before it starts."

Katie opened her hand, releasing him. She raked her nails across his lower abdomen. "Is this better?"

Flynn sucked in a harsh breath. "Not much."

She smiled and placed her hot mouth on his neck, kissing and nipping as she made her way down to his chest. She pushed him until Flynn fell back against the pillows, half under her. He smiled at her actions. He had always known she would be a firecracker in bed, as she was in life.

She seemed determined to drive him mad. All thought left his head, along with blood, as she dipped her tongue into his belly button. The muscles of his abdomen tightened when her warm breath blew across it. She glanced his way one last time before pulling down his boxers and settling her mouth around his penis. The sight of her red lips surrounding him almost sent him over the edge.

Desperate for control, Flynn squeezed his eyes shut and gripped fistfuls of sheet. She released him, and he took a deep breath. But the reprieve was fleeting. She flicked the tip of him with her tongue.

A low, guttural sound ripped from his throat as he grabbed her by the upper arms and flipped her beneath him. "My turn," he muttered before laving one tightened bud with his tongue. When he had thoroughly wetted it, Flynn blew across the sensitive flesh. Her moan was his reward. Turning his attention to the other breast, he gave that nipple the same treatment.

Katie moved restlessly beneath him. His smile was wicked. "Not so easy to take, is it?"

She answered him with her hips, rocking her pelvis against his. Flynn gritted his teeth for control. Reaching over her, he grabbed a condom from the bedside table. Katie opened her legs wider as he sheathed himself. He tore his underwear the rest of the way off and settled himself between her thighs. Damp, red curls at the core of her were a welcoming sight.

Flynn entered her slowly, drawing out both of their pleasure. Her muscles stretched to receive him until he was buried within her. He paused there for a moment, looking into her bright, green eyes. He felt a connection with this woman. Had the very first time they met. "Katie," he murmured as he began to move within her. Flynn pulled back, almost entirely out of her, before plunging back in. He repeated the movement until he could feel her muscles tense with the need for release.

"Yes, Flynn, like that." Her voice was a breathy moan that sent him even higher. Katie raked the nails of both hands down his back. She closed her eyes and arched her back until there wasn't any space left between them.

"Open your eyes, Katie," Flynn commanded. "I want to watch as you come."

Katie did as he asked. She looked right at him, and Flynn could feel her start to come apart from the inside out. She moaned his name. Her nails tightened on his back. The sensation pushed him over the edge. He groaned aloud as he came. Flynn gave one more long thrust before collapsing half on top of her. He rolled to his side to take his weight from her, pulling her with him.

"That was not my intention when I called you," Katie muttered into his chest. Her meaning was clear nonetheless.

Unease snaked through Flynn. They might still be connected physically, but he could feel her distancing herself emotionally. He withdrew and got up to take care of the condom.

*****

Katie watched Flynn walk into the bathroom, enjoying the view. He was the most beautiful man she had ever seen, although she was sure he wouldn't like that word. She pulled up the sheet around her and curled on her side with her back to the room. Regret coursed through her.

What she wanted to do was pound her head against his bedroom wall until her good sense returned. Why did the best sex of her life, possibly in anyone's life, have to be with the one person who was the most wrong for her? Why had she even called him?

If nothing else, Katie was as honest with herself as she was with others. She was here because she wanted to be. The chemistry between them was a living, breathing thing. She had believed that sleeping with Flynn would quench that burning desire. At least slake it. But she had been wrong. Oh, so wrong.

So here she was, back for round two, and no closer to being over him. Katie needed to be very careful. She could fall hopelessly in love with him with very little prompting. She could also derail all her plans. That thought clenched her heart in an icy fist and sent her scrambling for her clothes. That's when she remembered her impromptu striptease. Her clothes were strewn from here to the downstairs. Great! She pulled the sheet free and managed a make-shift toga.

"I'm a little surprised you're still there."

In her haste to leave, Katie hadn't heard Flynn come back from the bathroom. She straightened up and turned to face him. "I have to go." But she didn't move, just stood there with a death grip on the sheet.

"Why?" His tone was soft with a hint of hurt in it; enough to spark her remorse.

Katie stood frozen to the spot, unsure how to answer. "This was a mistake, Flynn." She didn't meet his eyes.

"I know," he admitted. "And yet it felt right to me."

Katie moved to the edge of the bed and sat. Her voice was barely audible when she spoke. "Nothing has changed. We both still have good reasons for not pursuing this." She gave a small smile. "Tell me again what those were." Her voice was thick with unshed tears. There would be plenty of time for those later.

She tensed as he walked around the bed towards her. Wariness turned to disbelief as he kept going. She sat there, not sure what to do. After a few moments, Flynn returned, carrying her clothing. He sat them next to her without a word.

"Thanks," she muttered. She turned her back to dress and heard him do the same. When she turned back, Flynn was wearing an old pair of shorts and tee shirt. The faded gray cotton of his shirt molded to his shoulders and chest in a way that weakened her knees. She sat down to put on her boots, averting her eyes. This was tough enough already.

The mattress dipped next to her and his musky scent enveloped her. Not fair. "Katie, why won't you look at me?"

"Because it's too hard. If I look at you, I'll want to stay."

"Then stay. You know that I want you to."

"I want to. More than I've ever wanted anything. But, that's not what this is, Flynn." She gestured between them. "This is sex. Not staying over. Not actually sleeping together. Not having dinner." She exhaled roughly. "Just sex."

"Are trying to convince me or yourself?"

That brought her head up. And her Irish temper. "I'm being clear, Flynn. You were right. We have a wicked chemistry. That's why I'm here. Do you have a problem with that?"

He smiled, but it never quite reached his eyes. "Nope. A beautiful woman calls me and wants sex. No strings. No, I don't have a problem with that, Katie."

Being disappointed when he said exactly what she wanted to hear was ridiculous. Still, her shoulders drooped a bit. "Fine. If we're clear. We have a committee meeting tomorrow morning. You should be my coworker. Not someone I slept with."

He nodded. "I can do that if you can."

The challenge was enough to get her moving. She stood up and kicked the rumpled sheet out of her way. "I'll be going then."

"I'll walk you out." She began to protest but Flynn stopped her with a glance. "I was raised right Katie. I'll walk you to your car."

She let it go and preceded Flynn down the stairs. Emotions raged in her head, but Katie wasn't going to acknowledge any of them until she was home. Alone. Away from Flynn and the effect he had on her. Even now, when she should feel sated, Katie had to fight the urge to throw herself back into his arms.

They walked out into the night. The temperature had dropped. Katie shivered as she pulled her fleece around her. She stopped at her car. "Well, good bye, Flynn. I appreciate the fact that we both agree this should remain between us." More than anything she didn't want to be the subject of gossip at work. Again. That had almost been the worst thing about David's betrayal. The gossip and the pity had been almost unbearable.

"So, no taking out a full-page advertisement in the Windsor Falls Gazette?"

She gave him a look that she used to stop unruly patients in their tracks. He smiled in return. Damn him. "I don't want things to change at work."

His smile dimmed. "Neither do I, Katie. I have as much to lose. And Sebastian has a stake in this as well. Building our practice means people believing in us. Taking me seriously. I can't afford a bad reputation in Windsor Falls. As archaic as it sounds, sleeping with a co-worker doesn't help my position."

Once again, she couldn't help but feel she was hurting him. "If that's a problem for you, Flynn, we can stop this right now."

Flynn hauled her against him, fitting her body exactly to his. The kiss was insistent with a hint of anger or maybe frustration. Her bones melted into his until they felt like one. She wondered idly how she had ever felt cold. A delicious warmth was pooling in her belly and parts south. She heard a low groan of satisfaction and wasn't sure if it came from her or Flynn. It didn't matter.

Flynn released her. "Drive safely, Katie." He took her keys from her tremulous hands and unlocked her door. Katie got in and put on seatbelt before he closed the door. He stood there while she drove away.

*****

When her SUV was out of sight, Flynn went inside. He walked into the kitchen and grabbed a beer from the fridge. He should feel relaxed, to say the least, but he felt the exact opposite. He stalked around the first floor, beer in hand, wondering how this had happened. Again.

His phone rang, breaking his reverie. The caller ID flashed Quinn's name. "Hey Quinn, what's up?"

"Hey, man. I have some free time and was wondering if you're available to talk about the house projects."

Besides being a local firefighter, Quinn also ran a small painting business on the side. Flynn had neither the time nor the desire to do it himself. He was happy to throw some business Quinn's way.

"Absolutely. Come on by. There's a cold beer with your name on it."

Quinn laughed out loud. "I won't say no to that. Be there in a few."

Flynn disconnected the call and walked back into the kitchen to grab a beer for Quinn. This was the first house that the realtor had shown him, and he had fallen in love with it. Not wanting to grab the first property he'd seen, Flynn had dragged Elizabeth to at least a dozen others. Last summer, when her mother's illness had brought her flying home from California, the two had become fast friends. He had recognized a kindred spirit in the emergency physician, much to the chagrin of her new husband, Sam. When he brought Elizabeth to see this house, she agreed it was perfect for him.

The doorbell rang. Beer in hand, Flynn answered the door. "Hey man, thanks for coming over." He shook Quinn's hand and gave him the beer. Flynn liked the other man, although he didn't know him well. They were close in age, and Flynn appreciated Quinn's sharp mind and wit.

"Thank you," Quinn responded, gesturing with the chilled bottle. While he took a drink, Quinn walked in a slow circle, taking in the view. He gave a long, low whistle. "Excellent choice, Flynn. She has beautiful bones."

"That's exactly what I thought. Hearing it from a professional like you makes me feel even better about it."

Quinn laughed. "I'm not sure 'professional' is the right word, but I know some things."

It was Flynn's turn to laugh. "Yeah right. Joe Fitzgerald told me he would hire you in a second if you weren't a fulltime firefighter."

Quinn grinned. "Wow! That's a huge compliment coming from him, but I love being a firefighter. I started doing these jobs on the side a few years back to make some extra cash. Found I liked it too."

"So, what do you think about this place? Where do I start?"

"Some fresh paint would make a world of difference in here." He pointed with his beer bottle. "You never know what you'll find under that old wallpaper. Since it's dark, I didn't get a chance to see the exterior. There's still some time before winter weather if you need that done."

"That's a definite."

"Figured it would be. If I'm not mistaken, this place has been empty for a while. Have any colors in mind?"

"I was thinking earth tones to go with the surrounding area. Maybe green or red."

Quinn shook his head in agreement. "That could work. Especially being so close to the mountains."

The two men moved into the living room and took a seat. Flynn's eyes moved to the spot at the bottom of the steps where Katie had left her boots earlier. That led to thoughts of other pieces of her clothing lying on the stairs. The events of a little while ago, and yesterday, had blown his mind.

Quinn snapped his fingers. "Hey, Flynn, where'd you go?"

Flynn dragged his mind back to the present and smiled sheepishly at his friend. "Sorry. Just wool gathering, as my grandmother used to say."

"Looked pretty serious from here. Something wrong?"

"No, but thanks." He took a drink of his beer, wondering how much to tell the other man. He certainly couldn't name names. "It's a woman actually."

Quinn gave him a knowing look. "Anyone I know?"

Flynn dodged that for the moment. "Let me ask you something. What would you think if a woman offered you casual sex? No strings attached."

Quinn, who wasn't exactly known for long-term relationships, answered immediately. "What's there to think about? Go for it."

He wasn't exactly surprised by Quinn's response. "But what if I like her? Could see a future with her?"

"And she doesn't feel the same?"

"She's offering a physical relationship only. No emotions. No dating. No long-term commitment." He shook his head. "It doesn't feel right to me."

Quinn leaned forward in his seat. "You and I want different things, Flynn. I wouldn't have a problem with that arrangement. Sounds like you do."

"I'm on the wrong side of thirty-five, Quinn. Without sounding too much like a woman, I do want to get married and have a family. I'd rather not be fifty when I did so." Quinn's expression closed, and Flynn had no idea what his friend was thinking. "Don't you want those things someday?"

"No," His eyes were as flat as his tone.

Since they didn't know each other that well yet, Flynn let it slide. "I'm not sure that entering into a purely physical relationship with her is a great idea."

"You could always send her my way."

Flynn's teeth ground at the thought of Katie getting involved with Quinn, or any other man.

"From the look on your face, I'm guessing that's a no." Quinn laughed and then took a sip of his beer.

Flynn did the same, taking the few moments to gather his thoughts. It didn't work. Someday, Katie was going to meet someone. She would get married and have kids. But not with him.

"So, colors for the exterior. Is this something you have time for before the weather turns?"

If Quinn was curious about the abrupt change in conversation, he was wise enough to not mention it. "Generally, we don't get snow until December. The temperature should remain in the low sixties for another week or two. I don't have anything else scheduled right now, so I could start this week if you wanted."

Flynn grinned from ear to ear. "Great! Thought we'd have to wait until Spring for that."

Quinn stretched and rose from the couch. "I'll put together an estimate for you. I have some color charts in the truck. Be right back."

Flynn carried the two empty beer bottles to the kitchen. He rinsed them before placing them in the recycling bucket next to his garbage can. By the time he finished, Quinn was at the dining room table with two, large books.

"You're going to need to narrow that down a bit for me."

Quinn glanced up at his voice, grinning. "Don't worry. Most of the choices are way off what you mentioned."

"Whew. I'd be up all night poring over that whole thing."

Quinn pointed his finger to the middle of a page. "This may be what you want. Keep the books. I'll get you the estimate tomorrow. The color doesn't affect the price." He grinned at Flynn. "Don't worry. I'll be sure to give you the doctor discount."

Flynn clapped his friends on the shoulder. "Great! I'm sure whatever you come up with will be fine. I'll win it back at poker anyway."

Pure disbelief flitted across Quinn's face as he snorted aloud. "Yeah, right. There's always pool. If Katie isn't playing."

Flynn tried to not blanch at the mention of her name and walked him to the door. "I'll pick a color by tomorrow. Thanks for doing this, Quinn." He glanced around the house. "There's so much to do, but this is a great start. Now, I can feel like I'm getting somewhere."

"We definitely are. I can do the interior whatever the weather, so we have time for that. You'll feel relieved once you pick a color for the exterior. That's the hardest part for you. Other than parting with all that money."

"How hard can it be? I might just close my eyes and point."

Quinn laughed. "Get your booty call to help you. Women have better taste."

His friend's laughter trailed after him as Quinn got in his truck and left. Flynn shut the door. Unease snaked through his gut. The last thing he considered Katie was a booty call. And yet that's pretty much all she was willing to give him.

Flynn knew he would have to make a choice at some point, but he wasn't at that point yet. He needed to find a way to make a relationship with her work, without risking all they both had to lose. His professional reputation meant a lot to Flynn, but she might be worth the risk.

Chapter Twelve

Katie headed into the hospital for the committee meeting on Monday morning, yawning as she went. She was normally a great sleeper, but images of Flynn had taunted her all night. Sleep had not been her friend. Now she had to sit across from him in a meeting and pretend she didn't know how his hands felt on her body. Yeah right.

Katie took a sip of coffee form her travel mug as she opened the door to the conference room. She was a bit early and the first one there, so she flicked on the lights and entered the empty room. She set up her computer trying to keep thoughts of Flynn from her mind. Since she couldn't sleep, she had thrown together a quick power point presentation. It outlined what was in place and what still needed doing.

A few people drifted in, nurses that Katie knew. She greeted them by name and thanked each for coming. Memorial might be a huge medical center, but it was more like an extended family for those who worked there. She glanced up from her laptop as she heard another person enter thinking it must be Flynn.

"Good morning, Katie." Ginny Nelson, the director of nursing, popped in the conference room. "Thought I'd stop in to see where we are with everything. All ready to start?"

Katie swallowed her nervousness and plastered a bright smile she didn't feel on her face. "Yes, Ma'am, we are. Just waiting on…"

"I'm here, ladies." Flynn entered the room at a run, taking a seat near Ginny. He turned to Katie. "Sorry I'm late. I had a new patient who was more complicated than I had been told." He flashed his dimple at Ginny, and Katie tried to not throw something at him.

"Not at all," gushed Ginny. "We haven't started yet."

Katie couldn't believe her ears. Or her eyes. The tough administrator never smiled at anyone. But she smiled at Flynn. "Glad you could make it, Dr. Reynolds. Shall we get started?"

Katie tried to not grind her teeth in frustration. "We have exactly thirteen more days until the Heart Health Fair. I know that you're all as excited as I am. I'd like to start by reviewing where we're at and what needs to happen to make this day a success."

Katie shared her power point with the attendees, reviewing numbers for last year's event. When she finished, she turned the lights back up. "As you can see, we've enjoyed enormous success in the past. The event has grown every year so far. This year, we can do even better. The key is making sure the people of Windsor Falls know about it. And that means bumping up our exposure. I've spoken with legal and public relations." Katie grabbed her briefcase from the floor. She pulled a colorful poster from within. "They've approved this for immediate release. If we post them in local businesses, we can get the word out these last two weeks. I've also arranged for interviews with the local newspaper and television news station. These will take place in the days leading up to the event. Flynn, as a cardiologist, I think you'd be a great face of the event." Katie held her breath. She hadn't discussed this with him ahead of time. She was throwing him under the bus. No doubt about it.

But her fears were unfounded. "I'm happy to talk with the press, Katie. I'm very passionate about community health, as you know."

Katie took a breath and waited for a reaction. Annie, her enthusiastic coworker clapped. "That's a great idea, Katie. I'd love to help you distribute those." Bless her, Katie thought in relief.

Ginny stood and nodded in Katie's direction. "Sounds like you have everything under control, Ms. Fitzgerald. Though, I'd like to suggest something. I'm sure this year's event will be a rousing success. But it might be better to have both of you in the interview, Katie. After all, nursing is a highly-respected profession. People trust nurses. That, combined with Dr. Reynold's expertise, will be the thing we need to push this over the top."

Katie suppressed a groan. This was not what she needed on a Monday morning without sleep. More opportunities to be thrust together with Flynn. But she smiled and thanked Ginny for her suggestion, not daring to look in Flynn's direction. She could almost hear the gloating.

The meeting broke up, and everyone filed out. She thanked each person and reminded them of their last-minute responsibilities. When only Flynn remained, Katie collapsed into the closest chair. She leaned her head back and closed her eyes.

"That went well." His voice was shockingly close. Katie cracked one eye to find Flynn sitting next to her. "See, I can be professional." His voice grew rougher. "Even if I was thinking about yesterday through most of the meeting."

Her face flamed, and Katie leapt out of the chair. When the table was between them, she responded. "See, Flynn, that's why you and I won't work. It's too complicated, separating our personal from professional lives."

"Complicated yes, but was it that difficult?"

"It is for me. I didn't sleep well last night." Understatement of the year, but she could have bitten her tongue for telling him. "I worried about people thinking there was something between us. I can't go back and forth like this, Flynn. Can't shut it off when we're working." She covered her face with her hands. "I'm sorry. I thought I could. I have too much at stake here." Her voice had dropped to a whisper.

Flynn stood. "I get it, Katie. I'm not happy about this, but I understand."

He left the room, and Katie felt as though he had taken all the oxygen with him. She sat down and sniffed back tears. She didn't have time for tears. In two weeks, she could cry all she wanted.

Several days later, Katie grabbed her stethoscope from her locker. She was starting her third shift in a row, and sleep had been elusive today. And the day before that. The whole week had been a loss. And she knew exactly who to blame. The fact that she had barely seen Flynn since the meeting had nothing to do with it. Memories of the taste of him, his skin against hers were enough to keep her awake. Even when she slept, her dreams were so vivid, so hot, that she awoke in a bothered state. Slamming the locker door with a satisfying bang, she headed out into the unit. On a positive note, she and Annie had managed to get all their posters hung in local businesses. They had also stopped to talk with the owners about the event. Katie was sure this would give them the boost they needed.

The patient board mocked her as Katie walked onto the unit. Four open beds. There was no way this would be one of their less busy nights. At least she hadn't seen Flynn all week. His partner, Sebastian, was covering the hospital. The temptation to jump him again was easier to handle when she wasn't near him.

The day shift nurses had relief written all over their faces. Along with more than a little fatigue. Never a good sign. Katie huddled with Jackie, getting report on her one patient this evening. She listened while also surveying the unit. Everything seemed stable for now.

When Jackie finished, and had practically ran off the unit in her escape, Katie settled in. Since she only had one patient this evening, it would give her time to also catch up on some last-minute details. The event was getting closer every day.

She scanned her patient's electronic record for new orders. Finding none, Katie went to check on her. Mrs. Abrams was an elderly lady with pneumonia and several underlying chronic conditions. Katie had taken care of her several times. She was a widow in her eighties whose only daughter lived in Seattle. Her loneliness was evident in her eyes as Katie assessed her. She spent some time catching up with Mrs. Abrams as she did, promising to come back later when she had more free time.

Katie enjoyed spending time with Mrs. Abrams, but it also made her melancholy. She was in her mid-thirties and still single, without a prospect in sight. Unless you counted Flynn. Which she most certainly did not. She didn't miss David. Not after what he had done to her. But she missed the idea of him. The companionship. The years of her life she had devoted to him that she would never be getting back.

Not for the first time, embarrassment trickled through her at the thought of her ex. She was so sure they were right together. That he was "the one." But David had been busy finishing his medical training and didn't want to get married right away. And David was focused on David. And his needs. Meanwhile, Katie's biological clock had ticked. Loudly.

Frustrated with herself for wasting even one more second of her time on that man, she pushed thoughts of David from her mind. As she finished charting her assessment findings, they received report on two patients being transferred to the unit. One coming from the ED and the second from the OR. She took the information and assigned each to two of her nurses.

The patient from the ED was a cardiac case, a gentleman in his sixties with unstable chest pain. She noticed he was being admitted to Flynn's service. That meant she would either be seeing or hearing from Sebastian soon. Katie breathed a sigh of relief that Flynn wasn't covering the hospital this week. She needed time and distance from him. And the ability to fight her attraction to him. Something that included her bones not melting every time she saw him. Yeah, she thought bitterly, good luck with that one.

Katie remembered the first time she saw Flynn. She had heard they were getting a new cardiology practice at the medical center but hadn't met any of the doctors. Naturally, she was in the middle of a code, sweat pouring down her face as she did chest compressions. Not a great first impression. Not that she cared. Afterwards, she introduced herself to Flynn and Sebastian. Both were handsome, but her attraction to Flynn had been instant and out of control.

Katie had sworn off dating another doctor. And Flynn, with his impeccable clothes and manners, was a prime example of why. Charm oozed from his pores. Within days, news of the "delicious" new cardiologists had spread like wildfire. Female co-workers, not to mention some of the male ones, were all eager to meet the new team. Not Katie. She'd already been down that road. Been the topic of gossip. No thanks.

But she had felt something that day. There was an energy about him. When she shook his hand, tiny electric shocks spread up her arm and all throughout her body. That was all the warning she needed. Up until last week, she had managed to be professional but cool with him. At least when he wasn't pissing her off. Which was often. Then she was professional but spitting fire. But even then, she found ways to keep her distance. To not touch him.

Katie needed to get back out there, she thought. Meet a few nice guys. Get to know them. Find someone she could have a relationship with and not risk her heart too much. That wasn't asking much, right? The gym teacher, was it Bill or Jim, wasn't a great start. But at least she had put herself out there. No more hiding. She would meet someone. She would get married, and she would finally have a family of her own. Being the favorite Aunt was great, but Katie had always wanted kids of her own. By now, her biological clock was in overdrive.

The thought was still floating around in the ether, when Katie went on Flynn alert. That's how she thought of it. That crazy reaction whenever Flynn was within fifty feet of her. She peered over the screen of her computer to find the man himself standing there. He grinned at her, looking way sexier than was fair in a pair of rumpled navy scrubs.

"You," she said, heavy on the shrew with a little accusation thrown in for good measure. She couldn't help it. He showed up unexpectedly, just as she was thinking about her biological clock. "What are you doing here?"

If anything, Flynn's smile broadened. "Miss me, did you?"

Gathering every etiquette lesson she had ever learned, Katie reigned in her feelings. "No. Not at all. I expected Sebastian."

"Disappointed?" Flynn leaned in a bit, resting one well-muscled forearm on the counter that separated them.

Katie licked her dry lips. She would be professional. She would not think about what the rest of his body looked like. Or tasted like. "Of course, not. I thought he was on call all week. I saw him yesterday."

"Sebastian's on a date. First date, I think."

"Oh. Good for him. Anyone I know?"

Flynn's dark brow rose. "Not sure. I didn't ask as I'm not his mother. Jealous?"

She hesitated before answering, hoping her voice was neutral by now. "No. Just curious."

An amused chuckle escaped him. "What's going on in that pretty head of yours, Katie? I can hear the wheels turning from here."

She flushed as she remembered what she had been thinking earlier. "Nothing that concerns you, Dr. Reynolds. Pam will be taking the patient you're admitting. You can chat with her." Katie gathered her coffee mug and what was left of her dignity. She headed to the staff lounge for a necessary dose of caffeine.

*****

Flynn chuckled. Her posture was so rigid, he was afraid she might snap her spine. "Yep, she can't live without me," he commented to himself.

"Keep telling yourself that, Doc."

Flynn turned at the voice. Pam was standing there, smiling at him. Not particularly a nice smile, he noted. More of a wolf bearing its teeth. "I will, Pam. She's crazy about me. You'll see."

"One of you might be crazy, but it's not Katie." Pam moved in closer and glanced around her, as if checking her surroundings. She lowered her voice. "Katie is a friend of mine. A good one. I don't know what's going on between you two, but I don't want to see anything happen to her. Again. She's already had enough crap from a man."

Flynn could see she was being serious and replied in kind. "Katie and I are coworkers. And I'd like to think we're friends. I'd never hurt her, Pam. I swear. She wouldn't let me anyway. She keeps me mostly at arm's length."

"Mostly, huh?"

The tips of his ears turned a dull red. "That's neither here nor there, Pam." He cleared his throat and hopefully his embarrassment. "I care about Katie. I know what she has riding on this upcoming event. I'll do whatever she needs to make it a success. Any suggestions?"

Pam stared at him for so long that Flynn tried his hardest to not squirm. When he was sure he couldn't stand it another moment, she finally spoke. "I may be older, but I'm not senile. Nor blind. I can see the chemistry between you two. Nothing you can do about that. I like you, Flynn. You're kind with your patients and respectful to nurses, which is more than I can say for some. If you have her best interest at heart, then be persistent. Figure it out. Don't take no for an answer. Katie needs someone to care about her. Care for her. Maybe, you're the right one." The teeth were back. "But there's nowhere for you to hide if you hurt her."

He nodded in acknowledgement. "That's it? Be persistent?"

Pam turned to face Flynn again. "Should I draw you a map? You're bright. Figure it out. Now, can we talk about your patient?"

Flynn took his cue. He respected Pam. She was a brilliant critical care nurse and an asset to the hospital. Plus, she cared for Katie. All good things in his book. He filled her in on Mr. Johnson's worsening angina and promised to enter his orders. Pam nodded and walked off to admit his patient.

Flynn sat in front of a computer and logged in to do what he had promised. When he was done, he checked results of one of his patients. He perused them, pleased with what he saw. Flynn leaned back and closed his eyes, thinking about what Pam had said. "Be persistent." He thought he had been. Without much success. While the sex between them was amazing, Flynn wanted more of her. Her time. Her company. But how could he accomplish that without risking either of their positions at work?

"Young man, come here please." Flynn's reverie was disturbed by the shaky voice of an old woman. Looking around, he noticed he was the only one there. He must be the young man. That amused him. Flynn got up and walked toward the room opposite of where he had been sitting.

"How may I help you?" he asked as he entered the room. The patient, a little old lady with white hair, was sitting up in the hospital bed. The raspy quality to her breathing alarmed Flynn. Her skin was almost translucent. She wore an aura of frailty. Her attitude, however, did not.

"Young man, you can stop staring at me like that. I'm not fixin' to die just yet." The rattling cough that came out of her belied her words. But she held direct eye contact with Flynn. "What's your name?"

"Dr. Flynn Reynolds, ma'am. And you are?"

"I'm Mrs. Abrams, but you can call me Eugenia. And I shall call you Flynn. Pull up a chair, Flynn."

Because he respected his elders, Flynn did just that. "Tell me about yourself, Eugenia."

Mrs. Abrams's eyes lit up. "You are a charmer, aren't you Flynn? You don't want to hear about an old lady like me. Tell me some juicy gossip about this place."

Flynn chuckled in response. Leaning back in the visitor chair, he began to tell her stories he had overheard.

*****

Katie came back from the lounge, steaming cup of coffee in hand. She breathed in the delicious scent of the Jamaican blend one of her co-workers favored. Jasmine was from the island nation and loved the coffee of her home. Still too hot to drink, Katie could at least enjoy the smell of it.

She stopped at the sound of silvery laughter coming from her patient's room. Craning her neck, she saw Flynn seated at the old lady's bedside. Mrs. Abrams wasn't his patient. But then again, by the looks of things, this was more of a social call. Katie tried not to smile. The last thing she needed was yet another reason to like him.

A half hour later, Katie grabbed the Albuterol treatment ordered for her patient. She was surprised to see Flynn still seated at the elderly woman's bedside. Mrs. Abrams was resting, eyes closed, against her pillows. The white of her hair blended in with the pillow case. Katie was not pleased with the sallow nature of her skin tone. Pneumonia could be fatal for older people, especially those with serious underlying health issues. Patients like Mrs. Abrams.

She tapped Flynn on the shoulder. Keeping her voice low to not awaken Mrs. Abrams, she murmured to him. "What are you doing in here, Flynn? Don't you have enough of your own patients?"

Flynn turned to look at her. His dark blue eyes were warm and inviting, causing Katie's stomach to clench. As usual. "Just keeping her company."

Katie's heart flopped in her chest. That wasn't fair. How was she supposed to distance herself when he did things like this? "Oh. That's nice of you."

Flynn shrugged his broad shoulders. "She's a lovely woman. And very lonely. I get it." The last part was said so softly that Katie almost missed it. Flynn talked often of his parents and sisters. He must miss them. Even though they drove her crazy at times, Katie couldn't imagine living hours away from her family. Flynn had enjoyed eating dinner at her parents' house. She could cut him some slack.

"You're more than welcome at the next Fitzgerald family dinner. Maggie loves to cook for a crowd. Besides, Elizabeth and Sam will be back from their honeymoon by then. Give you two a chance to catch up." Katie kept her voice neutral. She had been about as excited at the bourgeoning friendship between him and Elizabeth as Sam was. But Elizabeth only had eyes for Sam.

"That's a good sign, young man, when she wants you to meet her family."

Both Flynn and Katie turned towards the bed. She had almost forgotten about her patient, lost in thoughts of Flynn. He was a distraction she didn't need at work.

"Out you go, Dr. Reynolds" muttered Katie. "Mrs. Abrams has a date with a breathing treatment."

Flynn stood up, picking up Mrs. Abram's wrinkled hand. He bowed over it, bestowing a kiss. "It was a pleasure to meet you. I leave you in very capable hands. Feel better soon."

Katie watched in amazement as color suffused her patient's cheeks. Flynn strikes again, she thought. But she couldn't be mad when Mrs. Abrams looked healthier than she had all shift.

"See you later, Katie," Flynn murmured as he left the room.

"Now that is a handsome man. My Maurice, God rest his soul, was never what you'd call a looker." She had a distant look in her eye as she reminisced. "But he was a good man. Love of my life. And could he dance!"

"Sounds like a keeper, your Maurice."

"Oh, he was. I loved that man from the second we met. There was a connection between us that has never broken. Even now when he's been gone over fifteen years." She placed a shaky hand over her thin chest. "I can feel him still. Here in my heart."

Katie turned her back to wipe a tear from her eye. She loved getting to know her patients and their families. She turned back to Mrs. Abrams. "Now, I have your breathing treatment for you as promised." Katie poured the Albuterol in the chamber of the pipe and handed it to her patient. She hooked it up to the wall oxygen port and turned it on. The aerosol emitted from the pipe with a soft hiss, and Mrs. Abrams placed the mouth piece between her lips.

"I'll be back in a few minutes when that's finished." Katie left the room, knowing that her patient would chat with her if she stayed. The treatment wouldn't be as effective if that happened. She went to the computer and added a note to Mrs. Abram's chart. Then she made a quick round, making sure everyone was doing okay.

Returning to Mrs. Abram's room, Katie took the nebulizer from her and rinsed it in the sink. When she finished, she used her stethoscope to listen to the woman's lungs. "That sounds a bit better, Mrs. Abrams. How are you feeling?"

"Not bad for eighty-two, dear. Not quite ready for the boneyard yet." She laughed at her own joke but coughed. Her thin frame shook with the effort.

Katie handed her some tissues and patted her on the back. "Never thought you were, Mrs. Abrams. You're going to outlive us all."

"Tell me about your young man, dear."

Katie shook her head. "Dr. Reynolds isn't my 'young man' Mrs. Abrams. We work together."

"Is that what you kids are calling it these days?" Her voice might be raspy, but Mrs. Abrams got her point across.

Katie gave Mrs. Abrams her sternest nursing face. "We're not here to discuss my personal life."

Mrs. Abrams smiled. "Oh poo. Mine is so boring. You can call him whatever you want, Katie, but I see the way he looks at you. I wouldn't ignore a man who looked like that and looked at me like I was the best thing on the menu."

She couldn't help it. Katie burst out laughing. "Thanks for the advice, even if you're way off base." She squeezed the older woman's hand affectionately. "Flynn and I are colleagues. And friends I guess."

"But friends with benefits. Right? Isn't that what all you young folks call it. Or maybe a 'bootie call'?" Her cackle brought on another bout of coughing.

The last thing she was going to do was admit that she had had smoking hot sex with Flynn to her geriatric patient. "It's complicated. He's not what I'm looking for."

Mrs. Abrams took a drink of water and then laid her head back against the pillows. "Then you, Katie, are a fool. That's the problem with young folk today. You think you have all the time in the world. I'm here to tell you that you don't." Her voice faded out as her eyes drifted closed.

Katie pulled the covers up, smoothing them before turning to leave. She smiled at Mrs. Abrams' advice. Katie knew that more than most, losing Connor as she had more than ten years ago. Life was short. And there weren't any guarantees. Which was why she was moving on. Putting herself out there. But not with Flynn.

The evening passed without any more sightings of him. That was a good thing she reminded herself sternly. Yes, he was eye candy. And a delicious one at that.

And he was without a doubt the best sex she had ever had. But he was all wrong for her. She just needed to remember.

At two in the morning, Katie sat in the employee lounge with her feet up. She ate a salad and wished it was a cheeseburger. Or pizza. She was also reading the latest nursing journal. The advances in critical care nursing came at a dizzying speed, and she made it a point to keep up. She loved her job but was looking forward to a change. Graduate school would be grueling but worth the struggle.

A distant alarm broke her concentration. She leapt out of her chair, the forgotten journal fluttering to the floor. She knew that sound. One of their patients was in trouble. She reached the nursing station in time to see Pam coming out of Mrs. Abram's room, shaking her head. The alarm had stopped shrieking. Katie knew what that meant.

She made her way to her patient's room, each step heavier than the one before. Mrs. Abrams looked peaceful, as though she had fallen asleep. But there were already traces of blue in her skin tone; a tell-tale sign that oxygen was no longer coursing through her veins. Katie picked up her hand and sighed. This was the part of the job she hated.

Mrs. Abrams, like many of her elderly patients, had signed a Do Not Resuscitate order, or DNR. The DNR ensured that she would receive the necessary treatment for her pneumonia but also prevented "extreme measures" in the case of a cardiac arrest. There would be no code team for Mrs. Abrams. Katie respected her patient's wishes, but losing her was still difficult.

Now she had a grim phone call to make to the daughter in Seattle. Another aspect of her job that Katie despised. It would take at least the next hour for the necessary tasks. Because of her advanced age, there wouldn't be an autopsy. Someone from a local funeral home would be here to take away Mrs. Abrams. There was a ritual to death that Katie found comforting.

She needed caffeine and chocolate before she started. Katie headed back into the lounge to grab a cup of tea and a Snickers bar. So, what if they contained a billion calories? For once she didn't care. She stood in the employee lounge, chewing slowly with her eyes closed to savor the first, delicious bite. The only sound was the faithful Keurig pumping out hot water for her tea. The door opened softly as reality intruded.

"I'm fine, Pam," Katie said in a tired voice. She sniffed back threatened tears. Crying for her patient would come later. When she was alone in her shower.

"Then why are you hiding in here, eating a candy bar?"

Katie almost choked on a bite of said candy bar. Her eyes sprang open. "You're not Pam." Her Flynn radar had failed her.

"Never said I was." Flynn came further into the room, stopping within reach of her. He seemed uncertain about touching her. "How are you really, Katie?"

She looked at his arms, roped with muscle, and wanted nothing more to stand within them. To lean on him for just a moment. Rest her head on his chest and her troubles at his feet. But that wasn't her style. No man was an island, but Katie Fitzgerald didn't seem to know that. "Why are you awake?" She knew she sounded ungracious, but she didn't care. She had a thin control of her emotions. His being nice to her might send her over the edge.

Chapter Thirteen

Without saying a word, Flynn closed the small distance between them. He wrapped her in his arms. He felt her resistance in the stiffness of her body. "Don't be mad. Pam told me what happened. You don't always have to be so strong." His whispered words must have gotten through to Katie as her body relaxed and seemed to melt into his. Her arms snaked out, encircling his waist. She pressed her face into the cotton of his scrub top. They stood there, wrapped in each other's arms, neither speaking. The sound of her quiet sobbing filled the room.

Each tear that fell to his shirt burned him. Each sob was a dagger to his heart. It was more than Flynn could bear. He stroked her hair and whispered to her. "I know, sweetheart. Losing patients never gets any easier." He kissed her hair and murmured to her.

Her tears slowed, and Katie made a small sniffing sound. Flynn leaned back and tipped her face up to his. "What is it about this room that always makes you cry? Should I get ready to duck?"

His question had the desired effect. Katie burst out laughing, even as the last of her tears shone on her lashes. "I promise to not throw a mug at your head."

Flynn laughed as well. "Do you remember why you threw that mug?" His voice had grown husky at the memory.

The green of Katie's eyes darkened to jade. "You kissed me for the first time. And when I asked you why, you said 'I wanted to replace the sad memory with a good one.'"

"It's still true." A woman's tears always terrified him. A by-product of living with his sisters all those years. But Katie's tears were different. They hurt his heart.

"Mrs. Abrams' death is a sad memory," she whispered.

He needed no further encouragement. Flynn lowered his mouth to hers. He had good intentions. To comfort her. Take away her sadness. Instead, it took away his breath. Heat exploded between them the minute their lips touched. She groaned into his mouth, and Flynn took advantage. Moving his tongue along hers, he stoked the flames higher. Katie responded by sliding her hands up under the edge of his scrub top. Her fingers scorched him wherever they met his flesh.

Flynn broke the kiss. He took a large step back, breaking her hold on him. He was relieved to see that she was looking as flummoxed as he felt. "There's nothing I'd like more than to follow that kiss to its natural conclusion. But we're at work. No reason to set tongues wagging. That's the last thing either of us needs."

Katie smoothed a shaky hand down her scrubs. "You're right of course." The chill in her voice belied her words. "This is exactly the issue, Flynn. We can't be doing this at work. We can't do it at all. It's getting too hard to keep things in check with you." Katie sighed. "How many times are we going to have this same conversation?"

Flynn, let it go. "You're right. It's late, and I'm exhausted. I'll be catching some winks in the on-call room if you need anything." He thought about dropping a soft kiss on her forehead but knew it was the wrong choice. He turned and left the room.

*****

Confusion battled with frustration as Katie watched the door close behind him. This was exactly why things couldn't go on the way they were with them. She walked to the sink to splash cool water on her face. Catching her reflection in the mirror hanging above it, she grimaced. Her skin was blotchy. Her nose red. She had never mastered the art of the graceful cry.

She took a deep, steadying breath and left the lounge. The unit was calm. Someone had dimmed the lights in Mrs. Abrams' room. Katie could barely make out the outline of the old woman's body on the bed. A ripple of sadness wound through her. She sat down at her computer to make the dreaded call to her patient's daughter.

Pam slumped into the seat next to her. She placed a hand over Katie's on top of the phone. "I took care of it already."

Gratitude shone on Katie's face. "You didn't have to do that. But I'm so glad you did." Making that call is horrible. Doing it at this hour is even worse. "Thank you, Pam. I owe you one."

"You could make it up to me by telling me what's going on with Dr. Cutie Pie." She pulled at the neck of her scrub top, pretending to fan herself.

Never a good liar, Katie averted her eyes. "Dr. Reynolds? We're friends." She busied herself by documenting on Mrs. Abrams' chart. "More like co-workers."

Pam wasn't so easily fooled. "Huh. I notice you only call him by his title when you're trying to avoid something. Like the truth. And I'd love to have a 'friend' like that. Does Flynn happen to have a much older brother? Uncle?"

A snort of laughter escaped Katie. Guilt followed behind it as she glanced at her deceased patient's room. But humor was one way people in her field kept it together in the face of tragedy. She sighed. "It's complicated." She continued typing. She loved Pam, but she didn't feel up to discussing the situation with Flynn.

Pam hugged her. "I'm sure it is, honey. But life's short. A man like Flynn isn't going to be single forever." With that last word of warning, Pam walked away.

The doorbell to the unit rang, and Katie glanced at the monitor. A tall, thin man stood at the door, a stretcher at his side. She hit the button to open the door and went to greet the him. Tim worked for a local funeral home, coming to retrieve bodies when needed. He was a quiet almost painfully shy man but very respectful of the dead. Katie admired him for this.

"Good morning, Tim. Thanks for coming."

Tim tipped his head in her direction. "No problem, ma'am. Just doing my job."

Katie smiled. "Well, I appreciate it. Mrs. Abrams is in here." She pointed to the dimly lit patient room. "I'll grab the paperwork."

When she returned, Tim had already transferred Mrs. Abrams' body to his gurney. He was carefully securing the straps. "Here's everything you need. There's only a daughter in Seattle. We've notified her, and she has the number for the funeral home."

Tim released the brakes on the gurney. "Thank you, Katie."

That was the extent of their conversations every time. She stepped aside as he wheeled Mrs. Abrams out of the room. Katie followed him to hit the button for the door as he left. When he turned the corner towards the elevator, Katie went back to her desk. Documentation took up a large amount of her time. She resented the time it took, even as she understood its importance.

Katie finished charting and closed out Mrs. Abrams' chart. The rest of the shift passed without incident. Katie was thankful for that. Losing patients was a part of what she did. Now, all she wanted was a hot shower and her bed. Not necessarily in that order. It had been a long shift, and she was exhausted.

Pam joined her at the elevator. "Coming to Bob's for breakfast with us?"

Katie shook her head. "Thanks, but no. I have a date with my pillow." A huge yawn escaped her. "Besides, the last thing I need is Bob's. I won't fit in my scrubs."

The door opened, and the two women got on. Pam, who described herself as "pleasantly plump," pointed a finger at Katie. "Yeah, right. You're perfect as you are, Katie. I can never understand why you're so hard on yourself."

Katie laughed, more than a bit self-consciously. "Don't let these scrubs fool you. They hide a lot of sins. And Bob's buttermilk pancakes. Plus, the holidays are coming, and that's always good for another five or so pounds."

Katie was more than grateful when the elevator had reached the ground floor. Katie took off and continued out to the parking lot. Fatigue dogged her steps. She was almost to the safety of her car, when she spotted a man leaning against it. The warmth seeping into her body told her what she already knew. It was Flynn.

"Wanted to see how you were this morning."

Without turning to face him, Katie clicked open her door with the remote control. "Fine. Exhausted. Going home to sleep." She sighed and her shoulders drooped. She turned to face him. "It was a bad night, as you know." In for a penny, in for a pound she thought. "Speaking of last night… thanks."

"Maybe with some feeling next time," he commented.

He was right. She was not being very pleasant. But leaning on anyone had never been her style. Leaning on a man even less so. Flynn was dangerous. He had held her and let her cry, never once complaining. Katie knew she could get used to that. And therein laid the problem. Depending on Flynn was a bad idea.

"I know you have patients to see. And I have some sleep to catch up on. I'll see you around, Flynn." She slid in behind the wheel, and Flynn closed the door. When he had taken a step back, Katie started her car and drove away. She didn't look back. He was far too tempting.

*****

Flynn headed into the medical center, ready to start his day. But thoughts of Katie followed his every step. They were good together. He knew this. As did she, even if she was too stubborn to admit it. Holding her while she cried had brought them closer together. Or so he thought. Katie seemed to view it as a weakness.

He was off this weekend and so was she. Flynn had taken the effort to check her schedule. If only they could spend some time together, away from work. And not in the bedroom either. As much as that appealed to him, they needed to get to know each other better. Work on their friendship.

Flynn arrived at his office and greeted the front staff. He smothered a yawn as he made his way back to his office.

"Late night?"

Flynn turned to see Sebastian coming from the staff lounge, two large coffee mugs in his hand. "Yes, but not in an enjoyable way. You'll be my best friend if one of those is for me."

Sebastian grinned and extended one steaming mug towards Flynn. "I'm already your best friend, but here you go."

Flynn blew on his coffee and inhaled the delicious aroma. "Thanks, man. Speaking of late nights, how was your date?"

His friend's face scrunched into a grimace. "Don't ask."

"Didn't get to play doctor then, huh?"

"The doctor part was the problem. She was all too happy to play doctor. As in Dr. & Mrs."

Flynn barked out a laugh. "Wasn't this a first date?"

"Yes." His expression darkened. "There won't be a second."

Flynn clapped him on the back." I know, man. It's not easy meeting the right woman. One who isn't interested solely in the occupation or bank account." They had grown up together and were from a similar, privileged background. Both had dated women more impressed with their bank accounts than them. Sebastian took it more personally.

"You seem to be having a lot of first dates lately." Sebastian was his oldest and best friend. But that didn't stop him from needling him from time to time. It was a guy thing.

Sebastian nodded. "That works for me. You know I'm not interested in the long haul anyway."

While their backgrounds were similar, their families differed. Sebastian's parents had a terrible marriage followed by an even worse divorce. Both had married again. Several times. Flynn could understand how this had left his friend rather jaded.

Flynn covered another yawn by taking a swallow of steaming coffee. "Well at least you're out there having fun. Or trying to."

Sebastian grinned. "That's true. Need me to fix you up with someone, Flynn?"

"No thanks, buddy. But we could grab a burger tonight." He yawned into his coffee. "If I'm not asleep by six."

"Absolutely." Sebastian checked his watch. "Time to get busy. I'll see you later."

In his office, Flynn placed his mug on his desk and then took a seat behind it. He groaned aloud as he perused the printed schedule left for him. He had a busy day planned for him. Great for the practice. Not so much for his lack of sleep.

On a whim, he Googled De Luca's Bakery. He had ten minutes before his first patient of the day. Enough time to set his plan into motion. He dialed the number listed for the bakery and waited.

"Good Morning, De Luca's. How may I help you?"

"Hey Kat, this is Flynn Reynolds. Do you have a minute?" He made a face at the noise in the background. This was probably a busy time for Kat.

"Hey, Flynn. For you, always. What's up?"

He smiled into the phone. Kat was a sweet woman. Just not his type. No, his type had to be prickly, difficult red heads. Or at least one specific one. "So, let me start by saying I am not a stalker."

Her laughter drifted through the phone. "Well, that's good to know. So, this has something to do with Katie then."

"That obvious?"

"Only to me. How can I help?"

"I'm trying to get to know her better. Spend some time with her."

"And how's that going for you?"

Flynn let out a sigh. "Not so well, actually. I'm wondering if you had any ideas. After all, you are her best friend."

"That I am. And because of that, I'm also her fiercest protector. Although her big, brawny brothers come in a close second. I have to tell you, Flynn, that if you hurt her, I'm coming after you."

He might have sixty pounds and more than half a foot on Kat, but he wouldn't mess with her. "Understood. And I'm glad. I like knowing Katie has someone in her corner."

"She has a lot of someones, Flynn." There was a moment of silence. Kat had lowered her voice when she spoke again. "Do you know anything about David?"

Flynn's gut tightened at the mention of another man. He'd always suspected someone had hurt Katie. Now, he had a name. "No, Kat, I don't."

"Well, that's Katie's story to tell you. Or not. But I will say that he wasn't a good thing in her life. And she's very cautious with men since him. Especially men with whom she works."

"I am aware of that."

"But I like you, Flynn. You seem like a good guy. What are you doing tomorrow?"

Flynn hesitated at the question. "Uh, nothing."

Kat laughed once again. "I wasn't asking you out, Flynn. Tomorrow is the Windsor Falls annual scarecrow contest. It's in the town square. There's live music and booths from local vendors. The bakery has one, and Katie always helps me out."

"I knew there was a reason I always liked you, Kat. What time does it start?"

"It starts at nine a.m. and goes all day. Katie will be there pretty much the whole time."

A knock sounded at his door. "Two minutes, Dr. Reynolds."

"Kat, I have to go. Time to start earning a living. But I'll see you tomorrow. And thanks."

"You're welcome. Don't make me sorry about this."

The smile disappeared from Flynn's face. "You have my word, Kat."

"All right then. One more thing. This conversation never happened." She was gone before he realized.

Flynn placed his phone in his pocket. Now he had at least the beginning of a plan. If he and Katie spent some time together away from work, she could see he wasn't a bad guy. He grabbed his stethoscope and went out to see his first patient of the day.

Chapter Fourteen

Saturday dawned bright but chilly. Katie rubbed her hands together as she got out of her car behind De Luca's Bakery. She breathed in deeply. The crisp air tickled her lungs. Fall was one of her favorite times of the year. And the Windsor Falls Annual Scarecrow Contest was one of her favorite events. She laughed as she thought about last year's event. The residents of her town were ridiculously competitive. At everything. There was no telling what this year would bring.

"I'm here," she called out as she entered through the back of the bakery.

"Thank God," came Kat's exuberant reply. Katie caught a brief glimpse of her friend behind a teetering stack of pink De Luca's Bakery boxes that Kat was carrying. De Luca's enjoyed a thriving business every day. But on days like this, when there was a town event on their doorstep, it was all hands-on deck. Katie had been helping with her friend's family business since she and Kat were in middle school.

She let out a yelp, as strong arms surrounded her from behind. Turning her head, she spied Kat's younger brother, Antonio. She twisted in his arms and gave him a hug. "How's my favorite brother from another mother?"

"Not bad, Katie, not bad."

"Great! And how's your lovely, pregnant wife?"

"Still lovely. Still pregnant."

"Don't believe a word he says. I'm fat. I'm uncomfortable. And I haven't seen my feet in months. Do my shoes at least match?' Kat's sister-in-law, Angela, waddled into the room. That was the only way to describe how she was moving now that she was in the last few weeks of her first pregnancy.

"Nonsense, Angela. You're as beautiful as ever." And it was true. Even with a very distended abdomen, Angela was beautiful, inside and out."

"I'd hug you if you could get your arms around me, Katie. Bless you for lying."

Katie placed a sympathetic hand on the other woman's shoulder. "That was not a lie. And it won't be long, now. You'll be skinny again in no time and have a beautiful little girl as well."

"Your lips to God's ears, Katie. I love being pregnant, but I'm also over it. I'm hot. All the time. I pee like every thirty seconds. And I have the worst heartburn in modern history. Yep, I'm done."

Antonio placed an arm around his wife's shoulders. "And through it all, you're still the sweetest woman in the world."

Angela's face softened as she smiled at her husband. The two stared into each other's eyes as though everyone else in the bustling bakery had disappeared. Katie's heart cramped a bit. That's what she wanted. What she thought she would have with David. But if she was honest, even when things were good between them, she had never looked at him with her heart in her eyes.

"Ready to go?"

Katie jumped a bit at Kat's question. She hadn't heard her friend approach. "Sure. What can I do to help?"

"Grab some of these boxes and bags. Dad's already setting up the booth. I came back for these." She pointed at stacks of small bakery boxes and bags.

"That I can do." It was a running joke between the best friends that Kat got all the baking talent. Katie had never baked so much as a batch of cookies that hadn't ended up resembling a lump of charcoal. It was a personal offense to Kat, who had begged her for years to stop trying.

The two shuttled the various boxes and bags out the front door and across the street to the town square. Katie glanced around. There were tents and banners of assorted sizes and colors. Most were familiar, but she spotted a few that seemed new this year. The event grew each year, drawing spectators from surrounding areas as much for the various craft vendors as the scarecrows.

"Ciao, bella," boomed Kat's dad in way of a greeting. Katie walked up to him and kissed his cheek.

"Good Morning, Mr. De Luca. Are you ready for today?" De Luca's was always one of the more popular booths, and hundreds of people would stop by before the day ended.

"Of course, Katie. I'm always ready to make some money." He laughed out loud at his own joke.

Katie glanced at the various Fall themed baked goods for sale. There were pumpkin tarts and pumpkin mini cheesecakes, cranberry scones and cinnamon muffins. Mr. De Luca liked to create items to match the theme of the day. She particularly liked the scarecrow-shaped cut out cookies. They were decorated as elaborately as the scarecrows that lined the square.

"That won't be a problem today, Mr. De Luca. This all looks fabulous!"

Kat's father beamed. He sent a pointed look at his daughter. "See, Ekaterina, at least someone appreciates what I do."

Katie winced at the look on her best friend's face. Although she was sympathetic, this was an age-old battle that Katie did her best to avoid.

"I never said I don't appreciate what you do, Dad. As you well know. I think..."

"I know what you think, Ekaterina." Mr. De Luca's face flushed an angry red. He didn't even let Kat finish her sentence. "You think the 'old ways' aren't good enough. You want to turn De Luca's into some snooty, high-end place. Well, that's not who we are. At least not while I'm still drawing breath."

Kat grabbed her father's arm and walked him around the side of the van. Katie could still hear the tone of what they were saying but didn't understand the Italian they had lapsed into. She couldn't help but grin. Kat's Italian family was as volatile as her own Irish one. They all loved each other, but that didn't mean they agreed all the time. Or ever. Katie's brothers were known to get into a scrap over things. And not just when they were kids. But fifteen minutes later, the air cleared, and everything was fine again. The same was true of her and her younger sister, Riley. Although their fights were verbal, they could be as vicious. Still, she wouldn't trade her family for the world.

Katie continued to adjust the display, shifting this, tweaking that, until the display was perfect. Katie hoped that Kat and her father worked it out soon. The festivities would be starting soon, and a crowd was already starting to gather.

She waved and yelled good morning to the Bakers in the next booth. Sally and Joe Baker ran a local coffee shop, Cup o' Joe. For years, their coffee booth was next to De Luca's bakery. A match made in heaven, especially on chilly, fall mornings such as today. Any moment, early morning scarecrow enthusiasts would swamp both booths. Kat walked around the front of the bakery van, dashing tears from her face. The storm clouds that remained in her eyes told Katie everything she needed to know.

"I take it he didn't see your side of things. I'm sorry, Kat."

The other woman sniffed and smiled. But it didn't reach her eyes. "He's never going to get it through his thick skull, is he Katie? I'm not trying to make De Luca's into something it's not. All I want to do is expand the range of it a bit. But God forbid we change anything at all." She broke off into rapid Italian, mostly under her breath. Katie was glad she didn't speak the language.

"People are arriving, and I didn't want to have to hold down the fort by myself. So, let's do this."

This time, Kat's smile reached all the way to her eyes. Katie knew she loved the family business, even if she didn't agree with her dad all the time. Families. She linked her arm with Katie's. "Let's."

The Mayor of Windsor Falls made his opening remarks, kicking off the event. The first wave of customers arrived, and the two women were busy for the next hour. As fast as Katie replaced baked goods on the tables from the racks in the back of the van, hungry customers snatched them up. She was grabbing more pumpkin cake donuts from the back of the van when the fine hairs on the back of her neck stood at attention.

"What do you recommend?" came Flynn's deep voice from the crowd.

Katie turned away from the van, both hands gripping a tray of cookies at a precarious angle. "Uh, everything is delicious. What are you in the mood for?" The words were still hanging in the air, and she wanted to bite her tongue.

Flynn's raised eyebrow told her that he had also gotten the unplanned double entendre. His blue eyes crinkled with his smile. "Something sweet. Maybe a little spicy. You pick."

Never one to back down from a challenge, Katie perused the tables. She chose a pumpkin tart. Placing it on a napkin, she handed it to him. "This might be what you're looking for. Three dollars please." Warmth spread through her hand when his fingers touched hers.

Flynn took out his wallet and handed over a five. "Keep the change." He bit into the pastry. "Wow. Excellent choice, Katie." His voice was deep and rumbled from his chest. His bright blue eyes never left hers.

Katie closed her mouth when she realized it was hanging open. She restrained herself from checking for drool. Whatever was happening between them was palpable. And not what she wanted. Thankfully, she was busy here and would be safe from his charms. And her own impulses.

Kat joined them. "Flynn, I guess this is your first time, huh? What do you think?"

"Well, I just got here. Figured I'd start with breakfast first." He looked around them. "I saw a couple of very impressive scarecrows on my way here. Can't wait to see the rest."

"You won't believe it, Flynn. I don't know if you've heard but folks in Windsor Falls take competitions seriously. It's more about the bragging rights than the actual prize."

"I've heard. I can only imagine what I'll see."

"Lucky for you, Katie's all done. I'm sure she'd love to show you around." She turned and smiled at Katie. "Wouldn't you, Katie?"

Katie's cheeks heated. "Oh, I couldn't. I'm helping you guys. It's tradition."

"Nonsense, Katie. The initial rush is over. Dad and I can handle things." She motioned to her father to get his attention. "Hey, Dad. You're okay if Katie takes Flynn to see the scarecrows, aren't you?"

Mr. De Luca nodded. "Of course." He approached Flynn with his hand extended. "I didn't know Katie had a suitor. Hi, I'm Marco De Luca. Pleased to meet you."

Flynn shook the offered hand. "Hi, Mr. De Luca. I'm Flynn Reynolds. I'm a huge fan of your bakery. In fact, I've had to add some time to my work-out regimen because of it." He patted his flat stomach for emphasis.

Kat's father burst out laughing, patting his less than flat stomach. "I should take a page from your book, son. As you can see, I don't have an exercise regimen."

"You should make an appointment to see Flynn, Dad. He's a cardiologist."

Mr. De Luca waved a hand at his daughter. "This one. Always worrying about something. I'm as healthy as a horse."

"Sure, Dad. A middle-aged horse who doesn't exercise and eats poorly. Not to mention the cigarettes."

Her father's face diffused with dull red. "I'm as fit as a fiddle, thank you." He turned to Flynn. "Kids these days; no respect for their elders."

Flynn shook his head. "I'm sure Kat is worried about you." He took a card out of his wallet and handed it to Mr. De Luca. "I'm happy to see you anytime. Give me a call."

Mr. De Luca placed the card in his shirt pocket. "Thanks, Flynn. I'll think about it." He turned to Katie and leaned down to kiss the top of her head. "Go, Bella. Have fun. We can handle this."

Before she knew it, Kat had removed her apron and spun her to face Flynn. He took her hand and led her out of the booth. So much for avoiding Flynn.

Not having much of a choice, she let Flynn lead her away from the booth. Her small hand was all but engulfed in his, and sensations ran from it all the way up her arm. His skin was warm and felt way too good against hers. This was the kind of thing she could get used to. Which was exactly why she pulled her hand from his. Katie pointed out the first scarecrow as an excuse.

"Oh, my goodness. It's the whole crew from *The Wizard of Oz*." Katie approached to get a closer look. Dorothy, Tin Man, Cowardly Lion, and of course the Scarecrow himself were all there. She pointed to Dorothy, who was carrying a small basket. "There's even a small Toto in the basket."

Flynn grinned at the small rendition of Toto made of straw. "I'll be damned. You're right. I would have never thought of that. I thought scarecrows were just, well, scarecrows."

"You haven't seen anything yet." She led the way around the square, careful to not touch him again. It was all about self-preservation.

They spent more than an hour looking at all the entries, debating each one's chances in the judging. Katie and Flynn differed on who they thought would win first place. They did agree on one thing. The scarecrow depicting Stephen King's *Children of the Corn* was perhaps a bit too much. They examined it before walking away, shaking their heads.

"That was a bit blood thirsty for me," commented Katie as they turned a corner of the square. She shuddered. "The blood on that sickle looked real. I may have nightmares tonight."

Flynn slung a protective arm around her shoulders. "I'm willing to keep you company. Chase off any bad dreams."

He made a loud oof noise as her elbow connected with his abdomen. "I'm more than capable of taking care of myself, thank you very much."

Flynn rubbed his stomach. "That's a mean elbow you have there. I can only imagine what your right hook feels like."

She laughed. "Hopefully, you'll never find out." She gasped and pointed to the next scarecrow. "Wow! This may be my favorite yet."

The Windsor Falls fire department had the next booth. Quinn and his friend, Jack, were talking to a group of small kids about fire prevention. Katie noticed that more than one mom was checking them out. Both were gorgeous. Yet Katie didn't feel any of the intense things for them that she did for Flynn. Figures.

Their scarecrow depicted a window with a ladder leading up to it. A firefighter made of straw was climbing up the ladder. In the window was a female scarecrow holding a baby scarecrow, complete with footed pajamas. Very realistic flames framed the window.

As they approached, the group broke up. Children headed back to their respective parents. Flynn approached his friends, clapping Quinn on the back.

"Hey man, fantastic job." Flynn gestured at the display. "I hope they survive," he joked.

"Don't worry. We always save the day. By the way, what do you think of our progress? We should finish up in another day or so. Then the real fun begins. Picking the interior colors."

"Yeah, like that's the hard part. What about my aching back?" joked Jack.

Katie looked from Flynn to Quinn. She addressed Jack. "What 'fun' are you guys talking about?"

"We're painting the exterior of his house." Jack looked up at the sky. "Weather should hold until we finish."

She turned to Flynn. "What colors did you choose?" The fact that Flynn hadn't told her about the project disturbed her. But Katie dismissed it quickly. After all, they weren't anything to each other. Why would he?

"Uh, forest green and burgundy for the shutters and trim. I wanted to keep the feel of the mountains, even though I live in town."

She nodded. "Sounds lovely. I'll have to drive by when it's done."

"You're welcome anytime, Katie."

The two firefighters were friends of her brothers. She could feel their speculative stares This was the side of small town life she didn't care for. "Flynn and I work together," she mentioned by way of explanation.

"Oh, I forgot. I thought maybe Flynn was holding out on us," joked Quinn. "Good thing, Flynn. I wouldn't envy you telling the Fitzgerald boys you were dating their sister."

Katie could see the almost imperceptible stiffening of Flynn's posture. If she hadn't been standing next to him, she might have missed it.

His voice had an edge to it when he spoke. "I guess that's why you don't 'date'. Aren't you more into hook ups, Jack? Can't imagine there's a whole lot of meeting families."

Quinn laughed, punching Jack on the arm. "He sure got your number."

Katie didn't know Jack that well, only through her brothers' stories. She had always gotten the vibe that he was a player. But for some reason, there was an undercurrent between he and Flynn. Not a good one.

"Funny, Reynolds. We'll see how much you're laughing when I take all your money at the next poker game."

The words were friendly, but his tone was anything but. Katie placed a hand on Flynn's arm. "Nice seeing you guys. Good luck in the contest."

Flynn waved goodbye as well and followed Katie to the next display. When they were out of ear shot, he turned to her. "That wasn't necessary," he muttered.

"I enjoy a good pissing match as much as the next woman. But this isn't the time or place. What's up with you two anyway? I thought you and Jack were friends."

"We are. But that doesn't mean I care for his attitude toward women."

Katie stopped, wide eyed, and stared at Flynn. "Really? I thought all men would pat him on the back for that."

"There are very few things that 'all men' agree upon, Katie. You can't make generalized statements like that." He moved on to the next entrant without a backward glance.

Katie stared at his retreating back. What just happened? She was only teasing him, but he seemed to take it very personally. Hmmm… Katie jogged a bit to catch up to Flynn, who was perusing the library's scarecrow. The placard read Don't Judge a Book by Its Cover. A stereotypical librarian, complete with granny glasses balanced on the end of her nose, perched on a counter stool. She appeared to be reading a large tome by William Shakespeare. But on closer inspection, there was a romance novel tucked inside of the larger book.

She threw back her head and laughed out loud. Flynn turned toward her, a smile on his way too handsome face. "Now that's what I like to hear. You have a beautiful laugh."

She was glad he seemed to have shaken off the bad mood. "I'm sorry for what I said back there, Flynn. You were right. That was a sexist and generalized statement that I shouldn't have made. I'm sorry that I hurt your feelings. I was joking."

He looked at her for so long, that Katie felt Flynn was trying to figure something out. "It's not what you said. It's how that statement reflected on me." He ran an agitated hand through his hair and blew out a large breath. "I always feel like you're condemning me for sins I haven't even committed. That's not fair to me."

"That's not what I was doing, Flynn. It was a joke. A poor one, mind you, but a joke nonetheless."

"If you say so." He turned back to look at the display again.

Katie could see the tension creep back into his shoulders. It had started with Jack, but she was to blame now. She stepped next to him and laced an arm through his. "This one is my favorite. The library was always a favorite place to visit when I was little. Still is. Even with technology and e-readers, I love the feel of a book in my hand. The smell of it."

"That may be the very first personal thing you've ever told me about yourself, Katie." His smile warmed her more than the sun.

"No way. That's not possible. We've been working together for almost a year."

"Exactly. You tell me things all the time. About patients or the hospital, Windsor Falls, your family. But you don't tell me about yourself. You don't let me in, Katie."

"Oh," she replied in a small voice. He was right. She was so busy protecting herself from him, or anyone that could hurt her again. "I don't mean to."

"I know, Katie. That's what makes it so hard." He walked away, leaving her with that thought to chew on for a while.

Chapter Fifteen

Flynn walked away from Katie, wondering what he was doing. How many times did he have to remind himself to not go there? And yet here he was. Trying to spend time with her. Trying to be her friend. Somedays he wanted to kiss her right in the middle of town square and let the chips fall where they would. Today wasn't that day.

Flynn stopped and stared at the mountains in the not so distance. The Blue Ridge Mountains were a sight to behold, with their seemingly endless peaks and valleys. He loved growing up in Atlanta, but the natural beauty of Windsor Falls was breathtaking. Seeing the mountains, that had been here long before him and would be eons after he was gone, gave him perspective. Reminded him to breathe.

He turned to find Katie, but she was nowhere in sight. Flynn headed back to the bakery stand, eyes scanning the crowd as he went. He didn't see her, but Kat was there, working the crowd.

"Hey, Kat. Have you seen Katie recently?"

Kat looked puzzled. "I thought she was with you."

"She was. I must have lost her in the crowd."

A smug smile spread across Kat's face. "What did you do?"

Flynn held up both hands in entreaty. "How do you know I did anything?"

Kat laughed. "Because you're here looking for Katie. Not the other way around."

"Oh." Flynn's eyes dropped to his shoes. He was a very intelligent man. But for some reason, women kept beating him at every turn. His sisters would have a field day with this.

"Her car's behind the bakery. You might want to check there."

"Thanks, Kat." He started to walk away but turned back. "Why are you helping me?"

Kat's smile was purely feminine. And more than a bit mysterious. "I'm not. I'm helping Katie."

"Got it."

Flynn started in the direction of the bakery, heading down the block to get to the rear of the building. The foot traffic in town was crazy today, but he figured that was a good thing for local merchants. By the time he reached De Luca's, Katie's car was gone. Flynn stood there for a moment, perplexed. He decided to head home.

He fought the crowds again to where he had parked his car. As he drove home, he hit the number for his sister Allison on his speed dial. He needed advice.

"Is that my favorite brother finally remembering to check in?" came her disembodied voice.

Flynn shook his head at the old joke. "Well, as I am your only brother, then I guess so. How are you, Ally?"

"I'm great, Flynn. What's new with you? Tired of living in the sticks yet?"

A dry chuckle rumbled from his chest. "Windsor Falls may not have its own ballet and symphony, but that doesn't mean it's without its charms. If you ever came to visit, you would know that."

"Touché little brother. Kidding."

"No, you're not, but I forgive you, Ally. Only because I need some advice."

"Uh oh. What have you done now?"

Flynn shook his head. Women always stuck together. "I'm going to ignore that, Ally. I met someone." The silence on the other end was deafening. "Ally? Are you still there?"

"I'm here. It took a moment to wrap my head around the bomb you just dropped. Who is she?"

"Her name is Katie Fitzgerald. Why so stunned? I haven't exactly led a monk's life."

Her chuckle made him smile. "No, but then you've never said, 'I met someone.' Ever. And you've never asked for my advice. Even though I have so much wisdom to give, little brother."

"That much is true. At least the part about never asking for advice. Can't say about the wisdom."

"Funny. Now spill."

Flynn caught her up to speed, leaving out the juicier parts. That was a conversation he was never having with his sister. Ever. "She's a critical care nurse at the medical center. So of course, I see her at work often."

"Okay, that's a start. Why do you need advice? What have you done?"

"Hey, now. That's the second time someone has asked that today. Why do you think I did anything?"

"Because you have a Y chromosome. And we all know what that does to a person. So, again, what did you do?"

"I'm falling for her. Hard."

"Oh, Flynn," Ally whispered into the phone. "Why is that a terrible thing? Wouldn't I like her?"

"Everything's wrong. The timing. The scenario. We work together, Ally. And neither one of us can afford to screw this up. There's too much at stake." He sighed. "But you'd love her. She's very much like you."

"So, she's perfect!"

Flynn barked out a laugh. "For me. Except the part where she wants nothing to do with me. And I need to focus on my career."

"Prove to her that you're not like whoever hurt her. Be yourself, Flynn. At the risk of swelling your head even further, you're adorable. She'll come around. The rest of it will fall into place."

Flynn grimaced at Ally's choice of words. "Puppies are adorable. I'm a grown man. I'm not adorable. And it's not that easy, Ally. There are so many things at stake here."

"Well, not when you're grumpy." At his growl of frustration, Ally sobered up. "All I'm saying is that she needs to see you're not like whoever hurt her. Give her time. But if she's that important to you, then don't give up. And I never said it would be easy. But if she's worth it, then that won't matter."

"Okay, Ally. Sorry about that. She's got me all tied up in knots."

"The best ones always do. Let me know how it goes." She clicked off before Flynn could say another word. The conversation had taken most of the way home, not that Windsor Falls was very big. He turned onto his block and did a double take. There, in his driveway, was Katie's car. He pulled in next to it, and got out. Katie was nowhere in sight. He found her on his patio, neck craned, looking up at his house. Quinn and his crew had already completed the back.

"Like the color?"

She hesitated before answering but didn't turn to face him. "Yes. Yes, I do. Fits in well with the surroundings."

"That's what I thought. What are you doing here, Katie?"

She dipped her head before turning to face him. "I came to apologize. I was a bitch, and I'm sorry."

"I need you to tell me about David."

Her eyes widened, but she didn't answer.

"Can I ask what he did to make you not trust me? Or yourself."

Katie's chest rose and fell as she took a deep breath. Flynn's heart ached for the pain that flashed through her eyes.

"He broke my trust. He lied to me. He chose her over me."

She spoke the last part so softly, that Flynn almost didn't hear it. Almost. He covered the space between them in a few long strides. "So, he was a fool." Her soft laugh was half sob. Ever so carefully, Flynn reached out to touch her. He stroked a hand over her brilliant hair.

"Oh, Katie, I would never hurt you like that. Would you tell me about it?"

She nodded. And shivered. They were standing in the shade on his patio, and the late fall temperature was chilly. Flynn gathered both of her hands in his and rubbed them together for warmth. Without a word, he tugged her along with him and went inside.

Flynn led the way into the living room. With a single flick of a switch, a fire sprang to life in the gas fireplace. "Might not be as masculine as building a fire, but it works," he joked. He took her coat and Katie stood right in front of the fireplace, rubbing her hands together.

When he came back from hanging up her coat, Katie was wandering around the living room, taking it all in. She turned to him with a shy smile on her face. "I didn't get to see much last time I was here."

Warmth spread through him at the memory. "Would you like a tour?"

"No thanks. Not right now." She walked over to the brown leather couch and sat. Patting the seat next to her, she gestured for him to join her. He did so, taking care to be close but not touch her. It was difficult to think when he touched her.

Katie stared at some spot over his shoulder. "David was an internal medicine resident at Memorial. We met the very first day of his training. I vowed I was never going to get involved with a doctor. Especially not one at work. But David was different. Or so I thought." She closed her eyes, and Flynn reached out to squeeze her hand in support.

Opening them again, she offered him a tremulous smile. "It's not what you think. He didn't deliberately hurt me. Or cheat on me. He had told me about his ex-girlfriend, Lisa, before we ever got together. He just didn't tell me that he was still in love with her. They had dated all through medical school, and then she dumped him when they graduated. They were going their separate ways for residency, and she wanted a clean break." She broke off. "Could I get a drink of something, please?"

Flynn jumped up, heading for the kitchen. "Of course."

He returned a moment later with a bottle of water. Flynn placed it on the table in front of her and retook his seat next to her. He watched as Katie took a long sip, almost half the bottle. She replaced the cap before continuing.

"This isn't difficult to tell because I still love him. I don't. But it's hard to remember what a fool I was."

"That wasn't foolishness, Katie. You loved him."

She shook her head in agreement. "Yes, I did. But I was foolish as well. I didn't see the signs. Or maybe I did, but didn't want to."

At his look of confusion, she continued. "After the first year we were together, he moved in with me. It made sense. Why have two rents, right? We talked about getting married. One day. But he didn't want to do anything until he completed his training. I didn't agree, but he was adamant. So, I went along with it."

"He grew quieter that last year of his residency. I put it down to the long hours he was keeping. I wanted to start planning our wedding, but I could never pin him down." She gave a short laugh. The sound was harsh and lacking in humor. "I told you I was an idiot. All the signs were there. I just didn't want to see them."

Unease wound its way through Flynn. He already knew there wasn't going to be a happy ending to this story, but he hadn't been prepared for the pain in her voice. He squeezed her hand again. He had asked her to share this with him. "Go on. Tell me the rest. What happened?"

"He left," she said in a voice devoid of any emotion.

"When?"

"Right after finishing his residency. A medical group at the hospital had offered him a position. David told me was going to take it. I thought we were finally going to start our lives. But he was just waiting to restart his life. With her. In Oregon. That's where she was. Apparently, she called David one day. Told him she had 'made a mistake.' Just like that, he was gone."

"Wow." Flynn knew that one little word wasn't enough, but it was all he could think to say. The betrayal must have been shocking. Slow, red-hot anger built in his belly. He wanted to find this David and teach him a thing or two, with his fists, about respecting women.

A bitter sound exploded from her. "All that, and all you can say is 'wow'?"

Flynn gathered her in his arms. "I was thinking about flying to Oregon and finding him. Having a chat."

She shook with laughter in his arms. "Noble and more than a little intriguing. But not necessary. I'm over him."

"And that might be true. But you're not over the betrayal. And here we are, having a relationship we both decided we shouldn't have. Yet we can't stay away from each other. We can make this work. But not without trust. I'm not David. I would never do that to you. And until you know that, understand that, we don't stand a chance." He gripped her a little tighter, willing away the chill that spread through him despite the fire.

Katie wiggled out of his arms. She gazed into his eyes. "You're right. I can't make any promises, Flynn. It's hard to trust again."

She closed the gap between them and placed her lips on his. Flynn grew hard at her touch. It was like this with her. Every time. Nothing made sense. Nothing had changed. But she was in his house. In his arms. And kissing him. There was nothing to debate.

He took over the kiss, slanting his head and applying a deeper pressure until she opened her mouth on a pant. He took advantage, plunging his tongue in to claim hers. She moaned, and he pushed her backwards until she was flat on the couch with him on top of her. Flynn rested his weight on his forearms on either side of her to not squish her.

But Katie had other ideas. She raised her hips to meet his. "Closer, Flynn. I need you closer. Please."

Her words burned into him, drove his desire higher. Grabbing the bottom of her sweater, Flynn pulled it up over her head, Katie lifting to help. He lowered his mouth to the sensitive skin at the corner of her jaw, kissing a hot trail down her neck to the edge of her bra. Flynn slipped the edge of one finger under her bra, tracing a path along the swell of her breast. When she started to undo the front clasp, Flynn shook his head.

He got up and swooped her off the couch, causing her to let out a gasp. "There's not enough room on this couch for what I have planned for you." Striding up the stairs, he carried Katie into his bedroom. Flynn tossed her on the bed, landing next to her. Grabbing both of her wrists in one hand, he raised them above her head to the bars of the headboard. "Hold on," was all he said.

Katie did as he asked, grabbing a bar in each hand. "I want to touch you, Flynn."

"Later," he muttered in her direction. Returning his attention back to her breasts, he pulled down one cup, freeing it. The nipple, already puckered, was a rosy pink. Flynn touched his tongue to the very tip, circling it. Then he covered it with his mouth, sucking on her.

Katie moved restlessly on the bed, her hips writhing. Flynn lifted his head long enough to turn his attention to the other breast. This time, he undid the front clasp of her bra, freeing both breasts. He cupped each in a hand, delighting in the feel of them. "You are so beautiful, Katie. I love the way you respond to me."

Katie threw her head back as he drew the other nipple into his mouth and sucked that one. He grazed it with his teeth, enough to cause a reaction but not pain. She moved faster on the bed, raising her hips in silent entreaty.

"Patience, Katie, patience." To give her a taste of what she craved, Flynn undid the button clasp of her jeans. He slid them down her thighs, far enough to give him better access. There was something exciting about touching her while she was still partially dressed. He toyed with the lacey edge of her panties, sliding his finger under but not all the way. He tangled it in the curls there. He lifted his head to glance her way. "Is this what you wanted?"

"Yes," she muttered through gritted teeth. "Keep in mind, your turn will come."

He grinned at her. "I should hope so."

Flynn slid his hand all the way into her panties, pleased to find her wet. "You're ready for me, baby." One finger moved within her, circling her center.

Her breath was harsh and fast. She tossed her head from side to side. "Yes, Flynn. Right there."

Flynn sat back on his heels to look at her. She was beautiful, with her creamy, fair skin and freed breasts. Her abdomen was gently rounded. She always thought she needed to watch her weight, but Flynn thought she was perfect just as she was.

He peeled her panties and jeans down her legs and tossed them on the floor. She moved her legs apart, telling him what she needed, and that action alone nearly made him lose control. Flynn jumped off the bed and shucked his clothes in record speed. Grabbing a condom from the bedside drawer, he quickly sheathed himself. He rejoined Katie on the bed.

Katie lifted her head. "Hurry."

Flynn smiled in return. He slid a finger into her to make sure she was still ready. She was. He moved his finger in and out several times, foreshadowing what was to come.

"You're killing me, Flynn."

Her throaty laugh was all the encouragement he needed. "I'm right here." Slipping between her legs, Flynn positioned himself at the juncture of them. The head of his penis touched her center. She raised her hips up to meet him, and he slid home. He stopped for a moment to savor the feeling. She was a hot, wet, silken glove surrounding him. Drawing him in. There was something about being with her, like this, that felt like home.

Flynn began to move, slowly at first, and then faster. In and out. The friction was almost too much to bear. Katie's eyes glazed with passion, need. He could feel that she was at the brink. He covered her mouth with his own, drinking deeply. Their tongues dueled, sliding over each other.

He knew the moment she came. Her whole body stiffened, and she called out his name. As she flew over the precipice, she tightened around him, ensuring that he joined her. Flynn collapsed onto the bed, careful not to crush her.

Sometime later, they both lay on their backs, side by side. Each breathing raggedly. "Flynn, that was, uh. That was something. Words escape me."

He peeled off the used condom and tossed it in the trash can next to his bed. The bathroom seemed like miles from where he lay. "It definitely was." He instinctively knew she wasn't ready to hear what he wanted to say. That he was falling in love with her. That he wanted to be here, with her, forever and damn the consequences. He was willing to take the risk. He wasn't so sure of her.

Instead, he reached to the end of the bed for the comforter. Pulling it up around them against the chill of the room, he tucked her in next to his side. It was still only afternoon, but clouds had rolled in. The light coming through the curtains had dimmed, throwing the room in shadows.

Katie rolled to face him. She brushed aside the hair that had fallen over his forehead. "This wasn't supposed to happen, you know. You're not in my plan." She sighed as she said it, as if admitting some difficult truth, and buried her face into his throat.

"Plan? I didn't know there was a plan. Care to share with the rest of the class?"

She giggled against him, causing a vibration that echoed throughout his body. "I want what my parents have, Flynn. They've been married for over forty years. They've built a life with each other. They're each other's best friends. I want that. And children."

Katie was finally opening to him. He didn't want to blow it. He chose his words with care. "Who says you can't have that?" His lungs burned with his held breath as he waited for her answer.

"I'm already in my mid-thirties, Flynn. I wasted three years on David and then more being angry and scared after he left. That's why I tried dating again. To meet someone. Someone who wasn't you."

Ouch. That bruised more than his ego. He kissed the tip of her nose. "And yet, here you are."

"Here I am." Unease snaked through him. She didn't sound happy about that.

"Is there somewhere else you'd rather be?" Please say no, he begged her silently.

"No."

Flynn released the breath he wasn't aware he had held.

"But I didn't plan this. You are all wrong for me. I tried so hard to resist you."

"I know, but that didn't work." He mentally crossed his fingers. "Are you sorry?" Having regrets?"

"No," she answered quickly. Perhaps a bit too quickly. "I'm afraid of losing myself again. David took over my life, and I swore I'd never let that happen again."

Flynn raised himself up on one elbow and gazed at her. "Katie, what have I ever done to make you think that's what I'd want from you? Have I ever asked you to change? Be something that you aren't already? I like you Katie, as you are. Funny. Bright. Irreverent at times. Sassy." He punctuated each with a kiss on her lips.

She made a face. One that conveyed her disbelief. "Sassy? And by that you mean pain in the ass, I suppose."

"I always say what I mean, Katie. You should know that by now. You are sassy. And I like it. You challenge me, both professionally and personally. I'm a better man."

"About that. I may not be working there much longer."

Her words were a torrent of icy water washing away his mellow mood. Flynn's heart raced. Fighting the panic, he tried to keep his voice as neutral as possible as he turned towards her. She played with the end of the sheet, twisting it in her hands. It was a dead giveaway.

He covered her hands in his. "Tell me what's going on. Are you leaving Windsor Falls?" His voice wasn't as calm as he would have liked, but it didn't matter. He couldn't lose her now.

"I'm going back to school to be a nurse practitioner. When I start the program, I'm dropping back to PRN. I want to do this right, and that means devoting myself to it full time. Even though it will be a financial squeeze."

He realized then that he had not responded to her announcement. He smiled and pulled her in for a hug. "Are you kidding me? That's great! You're going to make a wonderful NP." He could feel her smile in return against his shoulder.

Katie pulled back and searched his face. "You mean that. Don't you?"

"Yes, of course, I do. You're already a brilliant critical care nurse. This is the next logical step. You're going to be fabulous!"

"It's all very new. Well, not really." She laughed at her own mixed up statement. "What I mean is that I've wanted to do this from the time I graduated from nursing school. But first, I needed to get some real-world experience. And then, I, uh… Well it didn't seem so important for a while." She dropped her eyes, not meeting his.

Foreboding and something akin to rage built in his chest. "Let me guess. David didn't support your dream. Even felt threatened by it." It wasn't a question, and Flynn didn't need an answer.

She chewed a bit on her lower lip. A sure sign she was either concentrating or worried about something. "Got it in one."

"You know I'm not him. Don't you?"

"Of course." But she didn't meet his eyes. And once again her answer was a bit quick. And forced.

The dread became acid, and it was bathing his stomach. "What's the real problem with becoming an NP, Katie? Sure, school will be difficult. But much less for you than others. You're very bright, and you have years of critical care experience."

She worried her lower lip again. It bothered him because it was a sign of her distress. But then he remembered what her mouth could do to him. Had done to him. He suppressed a groan.

"I need, want, to do very well. This means everything to me. And for that to happen, I need to work PRN at most." Katie balled up an edge of the sheet and then smoothed it out again. "That means getting a roommate. Just what every woman in her mid-thirties wants." Sarcasm dripped from her last words.

Flynn's gut twisted at her obvious distress. Which is why he said the worst possible thing. "Your parents would help out."

Color suffused her porcelain skin. Her green eyes snapped with fire. "Of course, they would, Flynn. As would Donovan, even though he and Nora are paying college tuition. That's the last thing I want."

"I see," Flynn responded, even though he didn't. He'd never had to think about money in his life. It wasn't important to him, in the way only people who had lots of it could claim. He could write her a check for her entire degree, her mortgage even, and not blink an eye. But Katie Fitzgerald was proud. If she wouldn't accept help from her family, she certainly wouldn't from him. He could make this so much easier for her, and it was killing him to not offer. But that wasn't what she wanted. What she needed. For whatever reason, Katie needed to do this by herself.

Katie scooted to the far edge of the bed, taking the sheet with her. She wrapped it around her like a shield and then got up to gather her clothing. She walked into the bathroom, presumably to get dressed.

Feeling ridiculous still sitting there naked, Flynn got up and did the same. He had more meaningful conversation with Katie today than ever before, and yet he wanted more. He wanted her to know that she could depend on him. For anything. But she was like a frightened deer, skittish and easily spooked. He had to be careful.

The bathroom door opened, and Katie appeared, fully dressed. And looking like she was ready to bolt. Flynn wasn't. "How about some dinner? I have exactly two dishes in my repertoire. Scrambled eggs and spaghetti." His tone was light despite the tension in the room.

Katie smiled, but her eyes darted to the door. "I'm going to head home. If you don't mind."

There was a bitter irony to this scenario, Flynn thought. How many first dates had he been on in the past few years? How many times was he eager for the evening to be over? Now, he finally finds someone he wants to spend more time with, get to know, and she wants to go home.

"No, of course not." He gestured to his opened bedroom door and followed her out and down the stairs. They stood at the front door. Neither said anything. The part of him left over from caveman days wanted to swoop Katie up and carry her back to his cave. Or in this case, his bedroom.

Instead he opened the front door. "I'm glad you stopped by, Katie. And I had a lot of fun today at the scarecrow display. I wonder who won."

Katie laughed. "I'm sure it's already posted on the town website. People take their bragging rights seriously in Windsor Falls." She tucked her purse strap over one shoulder, playing with it as she did.

"Maybe I'll enter next year. How about a scarecrow doing CPR? Would that be too grim?"

She held up two fingers slightly apart. "A bit? But if you're feeling competitive, there's always the ice sculpting or Christmas decorating contests. They're coming up in December."

Flynn pretended to give it thoughtful consideration. "Sounds too dangerous and too complicated. I'll leave those to the pros."

She moved closer to the edge of the porch, bouncing her keys in one hand. She started down the few stairs but turned to face him at the bottom. "So, I guess I'll see you at work."

"You definitely will."

Flynn turned and went back inside. Pulling out his phone, he called Brendan. The call was brief. He went upstairs to take a shower.

Chapter Sixteen

Katie drove straight to the bakery. She parked in back and knocked on Kat's apartment door. Please be home, she thought. Her thoughts were more jumbled than ever, and she needed some girl time, conversation, a little wine, and carbs. Oh yeah, there would be wine and carbs.

She shifted her weight from one foot to the other, waiting for Kat to answer. She needed Kat. She'd knock one more time, for good measure. If Kat didn't answer, then she'd go home to lick her wounds. She was in mid-knock when the door was yanked open from within. Katie lost her balance and almost landed on her friend.

"Goodness, Katie, what's wrong with you?"

"I don't know," she responded in a half laugh, half sob. Katie ran up the stairs to Kat's apartment, leaving her bewildered friend holding open the door.

Kat took the stairs two at a time, rushing in her haste to make sure Katie was okay. "What's going on? Did someone die?" Good Catholic girl that she was, Kat made the sign of the cross. Katie was on the couch, hands over her face, sobbing.

"Oh no. I was only kidding. Did someone actually die?" Kat sat next to Katie and gathered her friend into her arms. She rocked her gently, whispering soothing words.

After a few moments, Kat dropped her hands to her lap. She took in a ragged breath. Without lifting her gaze from her shoes, Katie muttered "I slept with him. Again."

"Is that all?" Kat squealed. "I thought something terrible had happened." She bent over to search Katie's eyes. "It wasn't terrible, was it? Please tell me that's not why you're crying."

"Kat," Katie yelled with as much righteous indignation as she could muster. "Is that all you ever think about?"

"No, of course not! I think about new recipes for the bakery as well."

Katie laughed a little at that. "Those are the only things?"

"Hey! You're getting lucky. I'm still getting my orgasms flying solo. I can't even remember the last time there was another human being present."

"That's not true, Kat. There was what's-his-name last summer."

Kat cocked her head and appeared to be thinking hard. "Oh. Right. My one and only one night stand. And that was Memorial Day weekend, not even technically summer." Her face scrunched in displeasure at the memory. "And that was hardly worth counting." She placed a hand on Katie's shoulder. "What's the problem?"

Katie sat back, kicked off her shoes, and drew her legs underneath her. "I'm going to need some reinforcements if we're going to talk about this."

Kat nodded and walked into the kitchen. "Start talking," she threw over her shoulder.

"The sex is amazing, Kat. That man has mad skills. But sleeping with him isn't the hard part. I spent most of the day with him. We talked. He laughed at my jokes. I told him about David." She looked up at Kat as she came back to the couch. Her eyes were bleak. "He gets me, Kat."

"The bastard," joked Kat. "We'll have him shot at dawn." She placed a dish of her latest creations on the table and poured two glasses of wine, passing one to Katie. "Sorry. Couldn't resist. But seriously, you told him about He-who-shall-not-be-named, and he was kind? Understanding? So, where's the problem?"

Katie took a bite of chocolate goodness and washed it down with a large sip of her wine. "Oh, yummy! What is this?" She took another bite. "I could die right now and be fine with that." Katie licked chocolate from her lips. And moaned.

'Not to change the subject, but that is my newest experiment. Chocolate glazed, raspberry cream puffs. Do you like?"

Katie grinned, licking chocolate from her fingers.

"I'll take that as a yes. Good! Now back to why we're mad at Flynn for being perfect."

Katie reached for another pastry, even though she shouldn't. "That's just it. There's nothing wrong with him. He's smart, honest, caring, funny."

"Let's not forget sexy as hell," suggested Kat from the other end of the couch.

"He's sex on a stick. He's so sexy there should be a warning label on him. Like at an amusement park."

Kat snorted and swallowed her wine too quickly. "You mean like 'Do not ride if you have a heart condition or back problems'?" This sent them both over the edge, and they laughed until mascara ran down their faces.

Finally, Katie sat up straight, arms wrapped around her ribs. She grabbed a napkin and wiped her face, laughing again at the black smears on it. "I needed that."

"Okay, Katie. What's really got your panties in a twist?"

Katie sprang off the couch and began to pace. She wobbled a bit as she did. "I like him too much, Kat. He makes me laugh. And he values my opinion. And my heart." She stopped pacing and ran a hand through her hair. "My heart flips and flops when he's near. I can't have that, Kat. I can't." She sat down with a thud.

"Oh, Katie, you're afraid."

"Of course, I'm afraid. I trusted David. Was planning a life with him. David broke my heart."

Kat looped an arm around her friend's shoulders and squeezed. "Did he really? Break your heart?"

Katie turned to her, eyes wide. "What? Of course, he did. You were there. You saw how much he hurt me."

Kat nodded in agreement. "Yes, Katie, I saw how much David hurt you. But did he break your heart?" She grabbed Katie's hands in her own. "I never said this before. Maybe I should have. I think he hurt your pride. And your trust. But, honestly, Katie, I don't think he broke your heart."

Shock set in. Kat was right. She had loved David, but his leaving her was more about breaking her trust than her heart. "Wow." Katie reached for her glass and took another large sip, draining the last of it. Kat took it from her hands and refilled it while Katie sank into the couch cushions. She turned her head to look at Kat. "Why are you telling me now?"

Kat shrugged her slim shoulders. "It was time." She handed the glass back to Katie and took a sip from her own. "Actually, it's past time. And there's more."

A bitter laugh escaped from Katie. "Am I ready for more?" She reached for her third cream puff, vowing to hit the running trail tomorrow. "Okay, now I'm ready."

"Keep in mind, I'm saying this because I love you." At Katie's nod, she continued. "David was a stronzo. That's Italian for turd. He was very critical of you. Your family didn't like him, and family is everything to you. He wasn't good enough for you."

"Geez, Kat, tell me how you feel."

"I did. Pay attention." She swatted Katie with a throw pillow. "Did I say anything that wasn't true?"

Katie gnawed on her bottom lip. "Well, no. But you never told me any of that before. You knew my family never liked him?"

"Yes. He wasn't good enough for you. He didn't treat you as he should have. David was all about David. His needs. His residency."

"Well, residency isn't easy."

"I know that. But, it was *never* about you, and it was *always* about him. Your needs never came first in the relationship. Did he ever encourage your dream of being an NP? Even once?"

There was no way to refute what her best friend was saying. So, she didn't. "You're right. How could I have not seen it?"

"Oh, Katie. We're all blind at times when it comes to relationships. You wanted it to work, so you made the effort. But you shouldn't have been the only one trying."

Katie sighed and took another gulp of her wine. Her head was starting to swim a bit. She grinned. "You're right. I'm fabulous. And he was an ass; even though he didn't have one." She burst out laughing, falling over on the couch.

"Oh, my God. What did you say?" Kat joined in the laughter.

When Katie could breathe again, she sat up right. "I might be drunk." She looked at her empty glass. "Yep. Drunk. But that doesn't change the fact that David had a skinny, little, non-existent butt." She sighed, a happy, drunk smile on her face. "Flynn has a great butt."

This sent both women off into more peals of laughter.

*****

As usual, The Hole was crowded on Saturday night. Flynn made his way through the throng to the bar and waved at the bartender. A clap on his back made him turn in the opposite direction.

"Hey," shouted Brendan over the din. He drained the last of his beer and set the empty bottle on the bar as the bartender arrived.

Flynn pointed to it and held up two fingers. The bartender, Scott, nodded and went to grab the beers. Flynn turned back to Brendan. "Where's the rest of the crew?"

"Donovan is on a date with his wife. Aidan, Quinn, and the others are playing pool. I came out to look for you."

"Thanks for coming. I needed to blow off some steam."

Brendan laughed. "Sure thing. It's not like you had to twist my arm, Flynn."

Flynn had called Brendan right after Katie left. A few beers with his friends was what this doctor needed. Katie had his gut tied in knots. Part of that was knowing that his friends, her brothers, weren't aware of any relationship between the two. He had to fix that. Tonight.

Scott returned with two, cold beers. "Thanks," yelled Flynn as he handed over some bills. "Keep it." Scott nodded and headed to the next thirsty customer.

Flynn handed one to Brendan and followed him to the pool room. The other Fitzgerald sibling was in a heated battle with Quinn at the table. "Who's winning?"

Aidan sent the eight ball into the far corner pocket, lifted his head, and grinned. "That would be me." He held out a hand to Quinn. "I believe you owe me twenty bucks."

"Yeah, yeah," Quinn mumbled. He slapped a bill in Aidan's hand. He drained his beer. "I'll be right back." He leaned his cue stick against the wall and headed for the bathroom.

Brendan and Aidan were setting up for the next game. Flynn figured this was the best time. He cleared his throat and took a sip of his beer for courage. "I need to tell you both something."

Both men turned towards him. Brendan raised an eyebrow. "What's up, man? You look pretty serious."

There was no painless way to say this. They would either be happy. Or pound him into the ground. "It's about Katie."

Aidan took a step closer, a menacing look on his face. "Is it that resident again? I'll take care of it this time."

"No. She hasn't had any more trouble with him, at least as far as I know. She might not tell me, though. I pissed her off last time by stepping in on her behalf."

"It's about you and Katie. Am I right?" This was from Brendan. His tone was bland, not giving Flynn any clue to his feelings on the subject.

Aidan looked blankly at Flynn. "There's a you and Katie?"

"I'd like there to be. I'm not so sure she would."

Neither of Katie's brothers said anything for a few moments. Sweat begin to trickle down Flynn's spine. These were his friends. He didn't want his feelings for their sister to come between them.

Finally, after what felt like an eternity, Brendan broke the silence. "I speak for both of my brothers when I say this. We like you, Flynn. You're a good guy. And if you and Katie end up together, great." He stepped closer and lowered his voice. "Of course, that won't stop us from killing you if you hurt her."

He didn't laugh, and Flynn took him at his word. He nodded. "I have sisters, so I get it. I care very deeply for Katie, and I would never hurt her." He shook his head. "In fact, if anyone gets hurt from this, I'm pretty sure it'll be me."

Aidan picked up the chalk and rubbed it on the tip of his stick. "You're probably right. Katie got burned in her last committed relationship. She's not big on trust right now."

"I know. David sounds like an ass."

The two brothers exchanged a glance. Brendan grimaced at the mention of David's name. "She told you about him?" Disbelief rang in his voice.

"Yes. Today."

"Huh," exclaimed Brendan. "She usually doesn't talk about him. With anyone."

"I take it you weren't a fan?"

Brendan made a harsh sound in his throat. "Hardly."

Aidan nodded in agreement. "He was a self-centered prick who thought he was more important than Katie. Needless to say, that didn't go over well with us."

Quinn came back from the bathroom by way of the bar, a fresh beer in his hands. "What did I miss?"

Aidan turned to him. "We were talking about David."

"That jerk? Why?" He turned to Flynn. "That was before your time. Total asshole who broke Katie's heart." He grimaced. "She wouldn't let us kill him."

"Much to our disappointment," added Brendan.

Aidan nodded in agreement. "Actually, he was gone before any of us knew. One day he and Katie were making plans, then his ex-girlfriend beckoned from Oregon. And that was all she wrote." He took a sip of his beer. "Would have been nice to pound his face into the ground."

Quinn nodded. "I'm not even her brother, and I wanted to hurt him."

Flynn gripped his beer bottle harder than necessary as he took a sip. He took a healthy gulp. "Then there's another part to this conversation that you need to hear, Quinn."

Quinn swiveled to face him. "Oh, yeah?" His brown eyes were sharp and didn't miss a thing.

"I'm interested in Katie. More than interested. I'm involved with her."

Both Brendan and Aidan stared at him. Brendan took one step closer, drawing himself up to his over six feet in height as he did. "Involved? You didn't mention that before."

Flynn had the grace to flinch. His face had turned a dull red. "Katie is a grown woman. I didn't feel it was necessary to ask your permission first. But in the interest of our friendship, I'm telling you now."

All three men stared at Flynn. Hard. Aidan spoke first. "What are you not saying, Flynn? Are you and Katie, uh…?"

Flynn put down his bottle and held out his hands. "What I'm saying is that I have very strong feelings for Katie. What I am not saying is the extent of our relationship. With all due respect, that's none of your business."

Silence reigned. Uncomfortable silence. Finally, Brendan spoke. "You're right. I'm not happy about it, but you are." He glared at Flynn. "Remember what we said earlier. Hurt her, and you're toast." All three men nodded.

"If I hurt her, then by all means. Do your worst." Flynn took a long pull of his beer. He feared, deep in his heart, that Katie would be the one to hurt him.

After an uncomfortable moment, Flynn gestured to the pool table. "Now, who wants to lose some money?"

Brendan stepped up, grabbing a cue. "You can try." His grin was full of testosterone and confidence.

*****

Sunshine peaked through Kat's blinds, hitting Katie square in the face. Pain lanced through her whole head. She groaned and rolled over, pulling the blanket over her face. She realized that she wasn't in her own bed and sat up, causing her stomach to roll. Note to self. No sudden movements. She placed her aching head in her hands. Katie would have moaned, but it wasn't worth the pain that would cause.

"Kat?" No answer. She grabbed her cell phone from the floor and squinted at the numbers. Eleven o'clock? Kat must have gone to work. How, Katie wasn't sure. They had stayed up very late, dissecting their past relationships. There had been a lot of wine as well. At least she had drunk a lot of wine. She wasn't sure how much Kat had. After the third or so glass, it was all a blur.

Katie looked around the room, turning her head carefully. The tiny living space was as neat as a pin, without any traces left of last night's debauchery. She stood slowly, testing the waters. The room stayed still. Her stomach made a loud, gurgling noise. Katie couldn't be sure if it was from hunger or nausea. But food was out of the question. That was one thing she was sure of. She had one, or maybe seven, too many cream puffs last night.

The memory of eating all the delicacies made Katie cringe. She was usually very careful with desserts. Being short, and curvy, meant that Katie was always watching her weight. Flynn never once mentioned her weight. Unlike David, who had been naturally wiry, bordering on thin, and very critical of her weight.

The more she thought about it, the angrier she got. David had forever been needling her about her eating. Did she *need* that second piece of pizza? Had she run today? Her blind date had never stood a chance. The last thing she needed was another man telling her to eat less or exercise more. But Flynn, who was a cardiologist for Pete's sake, had never even so much as hinted to her about her weight. That should probably tell her something.

Her stomach gurgled again. This time she listened to it. Maybe a plain bagel from downstairs would help. Nothing better than some carbs to soak up the damage from last night. Katie couldn't remember how much wine she had consumed. Not a good sign.

She stepped into her shoes and walked into the bathroom to survey the damage in the mirror. Ugh! Her hair, sticking out everywhere, was a nightmare. She wet both hands and slicked it into place as well as she could, pulling the whole mess into a ponytail. Then she splashed water on her face, erasing the black tracks of mascara. She took one last look in the mirror and grimaced. But that would have to do.

Katie grabbed her purse and locked the door before heading down to the bakery. The De Lucas had seen her looking worse at some point. Since she and Kat had practically grown up in each other's houses, she wasn't going to worry. Thankfully, there was very little danger of running into Flynn at this hour on a Sunday. So, of course, he was the very first person she saw upon entering the bakery.

*****

Flynn narrowed his choice of the delicacies in De Luca's display cases as Katie walked in from the back room. Her clothing was wrinkled and a bit disheveled. Her face was devoid of any makeup. She looked beautiful.

"Hello, Katie." Flynn wanted nothing more than to take her in his arms. But the scowl on her face ensured him that was not the wisest choice.

"Flynn." She nodded in his direction before disappearing back into the employee area.

A few moments later, Kat came out, trying to not grin. She walked right up to Flynn. "What can I get you this morning, Flynn?"

He looked at the swinging door over Kat's shoulder. "Is she okay?"

"Yes, of course. Why wouldn't she be?" The bell over the front door tinkled as an elderly couple strolled in. "I'll be right back to take your order."

"Mr. and Mrs. Bradley, good morning. The usual?" The elderly couple nodded, and Kat went to work filling their order.

Flynn toyed with going back through the swinging door but thought better of it. If Katie wanted to talk to him, she wouldn't be hiding back there. He had no idea what was going on but had to respect her wishes.

Kat finished with the couple and held the door for them as they left. She rejoined him at the counter. "Made a decision yet?"

"I'll have the cranberry scone, thanks. If you wanted to throw in telling me what's wrong with Katie, that'd be great."

Kat raised an eyebrow and grabbed the scone. Placing it in a bag, she returned to Flynn. "If she wanted you to know that, I'm sure she'd tell you." She raised her voice before continuing. "Not hide in my kitchen."

Flynn tried to not laugh. "You're a good friend, Kat." He took a five from his pocket and tossed it on the counter. "Please tell her I'm here if she needs anything." He grabbed the bag and headed out the door.

Flynn wasn't half way to his parking spot when Katie caught up to him. He glanced down at her. She was wearing sunglasses that hid most of her face and covered her eyes completely.

"Don't even think about taking off my shades. I'd hate to have to kill you," she grumbled. Katie took a large bite of her plain bagel.

"No jam? Cream cheese?"

Her lips curled in a disgusted expression. "Only if you feel like holding back my hair." She took another bite and kept walking.

Flynn kept abreast of her, taking a bite of his own scone. "Ah. Have a bit too much to drink last night?"

Her only reply was a scowl.

"I can give you a tried and true cure if you want. But I should warn you, it contains a raw egg."

Katie threw her bagel in a trash can. "Are you trying to make me hurl?" They had reached the corner, and she stopped. Turning to face him, she scowled at him again. Flynn was sure lesser men would have cowered.

"If you didn't want to feel like this, you should have paced yourself. And stopped earlier."

"Thanks, Dr. Reynolds. I'll remember that for next time." She placed a hand on her stomach. "Not that I'm ever drinking again. And anyway, it's your fault."

Because he wasn't stupid, and had been the only boy in the family, he kept from laughing. He did give her a curious glance. "How, exactly, is your hangover my fault?"

Katie put her hands on her hips and tapped her foot. "If you had stayed in the category of friend/coworker, like you were supposed to, I wouldn't have drunk way too much wine last night."

Flynn knew that probably made sense to Katie. Him? Not so much. But then a slow smile creeped across his face. "You like me."

Katie shook her head. "Of course, I like you. I never would have slept with you if I didn't like you." Her tone suggested he might not have been that bright.

"But you like me, Katie. You might even have the tiniest crush on me." He whistled a happy tune just to watch her response. Saints preserve him, but he loved to see her all riled up.

She stomped her tiny foot. Even in a boot, it made no noise at all. "What are you, three?" She was a quivering ball of indignation by now. "I'm going home, taking a long, hot bath, and forgetting I ever met you." She stomped away before he could respond.

But that didn't stop Flynn. He called out to her "Do you need me to scrub your back?"

Two teenage boys walking by gave him a thumbs-up. Flynn knew that Katie had heard him, based on the even stiffer posture of her back, but she didn't stop.

Flynn turned and walked back to his car, whistling all the way. The sun was shining; he had seen Katie today. Life was good. He had to think of something to kill some hours. Quinn and his crew were hard at work finishing the house. He wanted to stay out of their way. He'd take a drive; see some more of his new home town and the gorgeous mountains surrounding it.

Chapter Seventeen

Katie aimlessly traced a pattern through the bubbles that encased her. She rested her head back on the inflatable bath pillow and sighed in contentment. She had filled the tub with water that was just shy of boil-off-your-skin. Enya sang softly into her ears. The new age, Celtic singer had a haunting quality to her voice that never failed to relax Katie. Usually.

Katie sighed and tried to relax. But how could she when her mind was racing? Thoughts of going back to school and Flynn dueled for winner in the most annoying category. But going back to school was a good thing, even if it meant her life was about to get complicated. Yep. Flynn won.

And why should she waste time thinking of him? He was essentially a bootie call. But the mere thought of him sent flutters curling through her belly. And other places. No denying that. The problem was that Flynn was so much more than that to her. She cared about him. More than she should. But he was also a complication she didn't need right now. Flynn was trouble. To her heart. To her peace of mind. To her plans.

She sank lower in the tub as she considered the unfairness of that statement. Flynn hadn't done anything wrong. He had shown interest, and she had rejected him. And damn him, he had respected her wishes. Then she had to show up at his house and throw herself at him. Several times.

She tried to relax as she listened to the soothing words of "Evening Falls." Katie closed her eyes again and concentrated on relaxing one muscle group at a time. It was a technique she had learned in nursing school and often taught to her patients. But an image of Flynn, his hair tousled from their lovemaking, blazed behind her eyes. He was a beautiful man, even though he would balk at that word.

But it went so much deeper than that. He was dedicated to his patients. From the respect with which he treated them to the many small acts of kindness she had witnessed. And he didn't take himself very seriously. That was a big one for her. David had thought he was the center of the universe, to the exclusion of all else. Including her. In truth, David had done her a favor when he left. Of course, it hadn't felt like that at the time. Far from it. But he hadn't been good for her.

She had watched what an unhappy marriage had done to her brother Brendan. He had married a spoiled oil heiress after a whirlwind courtship. He thought he was in love with her. She wanted to spite her overprotective father. The result was they had divorced almost as fast as they married. The reality, as it turned out, wasn't as great as the fantasy. Gillian didn't want kids. Something she withheld from Brendan until after she was pregnant.

He had returned from Texas with her infant nieces over six years ago. And while Brendan was a brilliant single father, Katie knew it wasn't easy for him. That wasn't what Katie wanted. She dreamed of a family, always had. But there were two parents in that family.

Flynn loved kids. He talked about his nieces and nephews all the time. He would make a great father. No doubt. But Flynn was too much for her. Wasn't he? Too handsome. Too charming. Too much of a risk to her heart.

But what if he was just right, whispered a small voice in her brain. What if she took a chance on him? Trusted him with her heart? Would he hurt her like David had, shattering her trust once and for all? Was going for everything you ever wanted worth the risk?

The water had grown tepid, and Katie washed and rinsed before getting out of the tub. Wrapping herself in a thick, green towel, she swiped a hand down the bathroom mirror to see her reflection. She studied the woman in the mirror. She was fearless at work. So why was she being such a coward now?

Maybe, she should face this thing head on. Ask him out. See where this thing between them went. There must be a way to separate their professional from personal lives. Katie had always gone after what she wanted in life. Why was she afraid now?

Before she lost her courage, Katie called Flynn. The call went right to voicemail. She hung up without leaving a message and then cursed out loud immediately. Now she had to either call him back to leave one or text him. She chose the latter. Less scary. Katie chewed on a hang nail as she considered what to say.

Was hoping you'd like to have dinner. Tonight. Let me know.

There. She did it. Took the first step. That's when the panic set in. Katie finished drying herself off and squeezed the extra water out of her hair. She threw on sweats and headed downstairs to think about this some more.

No big deal. Women asked men out all the time. Right? And she and Flynn had already had sex. Several times. How hard could this be? Her stomach did flips to answer her.

She wandered into the kitchen. She was hungry, she reasoned. She hadn't even had more than a few bites of her bagel earlier. She opened the fridge door, but it was bare. Unless you counted questionable Chinese food. She couldn't remember when she had ordered it, so the questionable part was whether it would poison her. Not wanting to take the chance, Katie grabbed the carton and pitched it in the garbage. She shrugged into an old North Face jacket and grabbed her keys and purse. Her mom always had food.

By the time, Katie reached her childhood home, her stomach was grumbling audibly. Only her mother's car was in the driveway, for which she was thankful. She needed to ask her mother for some advice. Without an audience.

Maggie greeted her at the door, a huge smile on her wide face. "There's my darling girl. Come in, come in." But she held Katie at arm's length, looking her up and down. "Katherine Fitzgerald, you're practically skin and bones. Come in before you faint."

Katie followed her mother in, laughing all the way. "Only you would say I was skinny, Mom." She shrugged out of her fleece. Her mouth watered at the incredible scent coming from the kitchen. "But I am starving. Got anything for your favorite daughter to eat?"

Maggie clucked her tongue. "You know I don't have favorites, Katie. This must be your lucky day. I have a big pot of stew simmering on the stove."

Katie knew it was more than luck. Maggie always had a pot of something 'simmering on the stove.' But she wouldn't point this out. She was too hungry.

"Go wash your hands young lady," scolded her mother as Katie reached for a bowl. She left the room as her mother muttered something about 'savages' under her breath. Katie walked back into the kitchen and smiled. Her mother had a bowl of stew and a basket of her famous buttermilk biscuits waiting for her on the table. She walked up to her mother at the stove and hugged her.

"What would I ever do without you?"

"Luckily you don't have to find out anytime soon," her mother joked in response but hugged her back.

Katie sat down at the table and grabbed a biscuit. Biting into it, she moaned in appreciation. "These never get old, Mom."

Maggie smiled and ruffled her daughter's hair. She took the seat opposite of Katie. "Whatever it is, just tell me Kathleen. You'll feel better."

Katie stopped her spoon half way to her mouth. She shot her mother a look before continuing. She closed her eyes to savor the taste of the stew. Only then did she reply. "I don't know what you're talking about, Mom." This was an old game with them. She would pretend to not know, and Maggie would get it in one.

"It wouldn't have anything to do with a certain handsome doctor, would it?"

"You are a witch, aren't you?" She threw up her hands.

Maggie laughed. That was another old joke between them. "It's been many years since you thought I was a witch, Katie." Reaching across the table, Maggie patted her daughter's hand. "I had you all convinced that I had 'powers' that enabled me to know everything you were doing and thinking. I miss those days."

"It always was more than a little scary how you could know everything we were trying to hide from you."

"There's nothing supernatural about it, Katie. That's a mother's intuition. And right now, that same intuition is telling me that you're thinking way too hard about something. Then there's the palpable tension between you and Flynn."

This time Katie put down her spoon. "What tension?" She thought back to the last family dinner and the wedding. She had been careful to control how she acted around Flynn with her whole family in attendance.

Maggie shook her head. "Oh Katie, really? There was enough electricity between the two of you to light Windsor Falls. Did you think you kept that a secret?" She stroked the back of Katie's hand. "I guess I'm wondering why you even felt you needed to."

Katie's shoulders sagged. "Oh, Mom. It's so complicated. I can't get involved with another doctor. Not to mention, co-worker. I can't go through that again."

Maggie got up and came around the table, taking the seat next to her daughter. She placed an arm around Katie's shoulder. "Honey, being a doctor is the only thing that Flynn has in common with David. After that, there's no comparison."

"Let me guess, you never liked David either." Katie rolled her eyes at her mother's expression. Maggie couldn't lie to save her life. "Why didn't you ever tell me?"

"It wasn't my place, Katie."

Katie threw up her hands. "Are you kidding me? That's never stopped you before."

Maggie sighed. "Yes, I tend to be outspoken. Especially when it comes to my children." She smiled at her daughter. "Where do you think, you got it from? David was a nice enough guy, Katie, and you seemed happy with him. At least in the beginning. But he never put you first. That says a lot about a man. When he left, I wasn't terribly surprised. Nor sad."

"You never said anything, Mom. How am I supposed to avoid these mistakes if you're not pointing them out to me?"

Maggie laughed. "Oh, my dear, that's not my job. Your father and I raised you to think for yourself. Be your own person. And those 'mistakes' as you called them are what life's all about. You can't appreciate the wonderful things life has to offer if you never have anything to compare to."

Katie picked up her biscuit, breaking off small pieces of it but not eating any of them. "David wasn't a mistake. More of a learning experience."

"That's right, honey. David was one of the many experiences that make up your life, shape who you are. It's not about what happens to you, but how you react to it. How you bounce back."

Katie ate a few spoons full of her stew. She chewed thoughtfully. "I feel as though I've been asleep for a long time. When David left, without any warning, the carpet was ripped from underneath me. How had I not seen that coming? I was such an idiot!"

Maggie made a soothing sound. "No one saw that coming. Maybe not even David. But it doesn't matter. He wasn't the one for you, Katie. You're better off without him. That being said, it doesn't mean that his betrayal hasn't been hard on you. You trusted him. You were going to build a life with him. That's not an easy thing to get over. But it's time."

"Past time if we're being honest, Mom. I actually went on an almost date last week." Katie told her mother about the mishap with Bill the gym teacher. Both women laughed until they cried. It was funnier now then that night for sure.

Maggie wiped her eyes on a napkin. "He asked you your weight? On a first date? In a bar? Did he have a death wish?" She collapsed in laughter once again, unable to speak.

"Yes, he really did. Then I played pool with the boys and separated Flynn from some of his hard-earned cash." She smiled a bit ferociously. "Poor man never saw it coming."

Maggie clucked her tongue again. "So, we're back to Flynn, huh? Funny how that works. Care to tell me about him now?"

"Oh, Mom, where would I start? He's the first guy I've even noticed since David. But he's a doctor. On my unit. Even before David, I swore I'd never get involved with one. And look how that turned out."

"So, all doctors are off limits?"

"Yes." But even to her own ears it sounded weak at best.

Maggie got up, taking Katie's empty bowl to the sink. "Besides the fact that he's a doctor, what are your other objections to Flynn?"

Katie put her head in her hands. "There isn't a list, Mom. He's just too much. Too handsome. Too rich. Too charming."

"Wow, those should be punishable by death," Maggie suggested.

Katie shook her head. "The worst is the work thing. I was the subject of gossip and pity, and worse, after things ended with David. People whispered, and then stopped talking altogether when I entered a room. I can't deal with that again. And I need this event to run smoothly next week. He's too much of a distraction."

Maggie placed the soup bowl in the dishwasher and turned to her oldest daughter. "Or maybe, just maybe, you like him too much."

Once again, her mother hit the bullseye. In a very small voice she replied, "I don't want to get hurt again."

"Of course not, Katie. No one does. But what's the alternative? You were never the type to settle."

Katie gnawed on her lower lip. "He does something to me, Mom. Affects me. Makes me crazy."

"Makes you feel something." Katie nodded and Maggie smiled at her kindly. "I know you're being careful because of David. And I don't blame you. But don't miss your opportunity at happiness because you're being cautious. From what I've learned of him, Flynn is a great guy. Take a chance."

Katie ducked her head and grinned sheepishly. "Well, that's kind of why I'm here."

"Oh, so it wasn't only for the stew and chat?"

"Not entirely, although I do appreciate both. I need a recipe. Something easy."

Maggie stared at her daughter. "You're going to cook? For Flynn? When?"

"Uh, tonight."

Her mother threw her hands in the air. "And you're telling me now?"

"It's kind of last minute." Of course, Flynn hadn't even answered her text yet, but she wasn't telling her mother that.

Maggie bustled over to the corner and grabbed an ancient looking box off the counter. "This belonged to your Grandmother Rose. I learned everything I know from her. Tried to teach you girls, but we all know how that turned out."

Katie laughed. Her mother was an amazing cook. Her grandmother had been too, from what she could remember. Rose had died when Katie was very young. Maggie had tried, many times, to pass along her skills to her daughters; to no avail. Thankfully, Nora was a fabulous cook. Donovan had chosen well. "You tried Mom. You get an 'A' for effort."

Maggie mumbled something under her breath as she thumbed through the recipes in her box. "A ha. This should work." She handed over a well-worn card to Katie.

Katie looked at it, as one might a copperhead, and took it from her mother. "Pork roast?"

"It's simple and delicious. No reason to get fancy." Maggie grabbed a piece of paper from the table and jotted down a few things. "Here. This is your grocery list. The prep is not long, thirty-five minutes tops. And most of that is peeling potatoes and carrots. You do have a peeler, right?"

"I know where to buy one."

Maggie muttered again before opening a few drawers. She placed some items in a recycle grocery bag. "Now, go to the store, and follow Grandmother Rose's recipe. Exactly. Oh, and I would suggest a good red wine."

Katie smiled. "That part I can do." She leaned in and kissed her mother's cheek. "Thanks, Mom. For everything."

Maggie kissed her back. "You're welcome, honey. Good luck!"

Katie took the bag off the counter and left. She stopped at a grocery store on her way home, buying everything from her mother's list plus a good bottle of red. She sure hoped Flynn answered her soon.

Katie whirled through the downstairs, tidying her house, when she heard her phone chime. Her text alert. She glanced around, spotting her cell phone on the kitchen counter.

Sorry. I was out of range. Just got this. I'd love to have dinner. Where and when?

Katie hesitated, thrown by the butterflies in her stomach. What was the matter with her? This was Flynn. They'd already had sex for goodness sake. Twice. *But you've never invited him over for dinner* a small whisper in her head mocked. True. But there was a first time for everything. It was dinner, not a life-long commitment.

I thought I'd cook. Seven?

There wasn't any hesitation on his part. *Perfect. I'll bring dessert.*

The butterflies were in full flight now. Flynn Reynolds *was* dessert. He was certainly mouth-watering.

See you then.

Katie hit send and looked around her. She still had some work to do straightening up. And she wanted to change the sheets. You never knew. Then there was the actual cooking. Her mom had promised a short prep time.

She flew around the house, straightening up and then headed into the kitchen. Katie took out all the groceries she'd bought and put them on the counter. Then she emptied the bag from her mom. She was momentarily flummoxed. The recipe had looked so simple in her mother's kitchen. Now, not so much.

The prep time was closer to seventy-five minutes. By the time she had the roast, along with sliced veggies, in the oven, she was running out of time. Katie had already preheated the oven at three hundred fifty degrees. But when she glanced at the clock, she knew there would never be enough time. She bumped the temperature up a little to hurry it along.

Then she ran upstairs to her bedroom. Stripping as she went, Katie jumped in the shower for the fastest one ever. Her cleaning blitz, not to mention cooking, had worked up a sweat. She was in and out in mere minutes. She rushed around, getting dressed and putting on a bare amount of make-up. The doorbell rang before she could even find a pair of shoes. But then, they weren't going anywhere. She didn't need shoes.

Something smelled a bit off as she ran down the stairs, but Katie put it out of her mind as the doorbell rang a second time. "I'm coming," she called out as she reached it.

She was panting by the time she pulled open the door. "Hi," she murmured breathily. Maybe Flynn would pass it off as sexual tension.

"Are you okay?" His voice held a hint of concern.

So much for that thought. "Fine. I was upstairs when you got here." She noticed the brightly colored flowers in his hand. Her smile stretched from ear to ear. "Are those for me?"

"Only if I can come in." He held the flowers out of reach. She noticed a bright pink box from De Luca's in the other one.

Katie's face flooded with color. "Of course! Where was my brain? Please, come in." She backed up and made space for him to enter, following him in and shutting the door behind her. She took the flowers he offered, grinning. What woman didn't want to get flowers from a handsome man? As she did, she noticed the smell was stronger now. What was that?

Flynn tilted his head and sniffed. "Is something burning?"

"The roast!" Katie dropped the flowers and ran to the kitchen. The smell was very strong in here. Katie grabbed the oven door, pulling it open. Black smoke poured into the room. Several colorful words left her mouth. She turned off the oven and fanned the smoke with a towel. Of course, the smoke alarm chose that minute to erupt in a screeching noise. What else?

Flynn stepped up, grabbing oven mitts from the counter. "Can you open the back door please?" He grabbed the pan with the offending pot roast, now a blackened lump, and carried it out to the deck.

Katie followed him out onto her deck. Flynn placed the pan on her table. He turned to her, his handsome face very serious. "It's a goner."

*****

Flynn held his breath. This was a total disaster, and he probably shouldn't have made a joke. But the situation was funny. Like something out of a sit-com. He hoped Katie saw it that way.

There was a sound coming out of her that could have been anywhere between a sob and a growl. But when he looked closer, her shoulders were shaking. Katie's hands flew over her mouth, but laughter burst from her.

Flynn joined her. The two stood there for several minutes, howling with laughter. Finally, Katie wiped her eyes. "Thank goodness for waterproof mascara."

Flynn glanced at the ruined roast. "How do you feel about pizza?"

"I love…I love…pizza." She could barely get the words out before laughter spilled out of her once again.

Katie led the way back inside. Flynn propped open the door and opened some windows in her kitchen to get rid of the smoke. Katie waved a towel at the smoke, clearing it. Finally, the smoke alarm stopped.

Flynn pulled out his cell phone. "I'll order delivery." Katie nodded. "What would you like on yours? Are you more of a plain pizza or loaded with toppings kind of gal?"

"I'll have anything but anchovies. Never could get past the fishy taste."

"Agreed. Any place in particular?"

Katie moved to a side drawer and pulled out a menu. "This is where I usually order," she said as she handed the menu to Flynn.

As he dialed and ordered, Katie grabbed the wine from the fridge. She held up a nice red. He gave her a thumb's up before turning his attention back to ordering. Finishing up, he placed his phone on the table. "Should be here in thirty-five to forty minutes. Can I get that for you?" He gestured to the bottle of wine in her hands.

"Please." She handed over the bottle. "Opener is in the drawer behind you. I'm going to rescue the flowers."

Flynn watched as she left the room. Tension radiated from her in waves. He hated that dinner had been ruined, but only because it made her unhappy. He was fine with pizza.

Katie came back in, clutching the flowers. Lowering her face into the brightly colored bouquet, she inhaled. "I love them. Thank you very much." He watched as she raised up on tip toe to grab a vase. He would have helped, but Flynn was too mesmerized by the sight of a sliver of bare skin on her back where her shirt rode up.

He walked up behind her and placed a hot, open-mouthed kiss on the back of her neck. When she squealed in surprise and turned around, Flynn took her in his arms. "Who needs pizza?" he growled into her opened mouth as he covered it with his. Her lips were as soft as he remembered.

Katie was holding the vase in one hand and flowers in the other. She placed both on the counter behind her and wrapped her arms around his waist. Her eager hands roamed over his back. Flynn leaned in, closing any gap between them. There could be no question of his arousal. Katie leaned into the kiss for a moment before stepping back, out of his arms.

When she opened her eyes, Flynn was happy to see she appeared as dazed as he felt. A slow smile spread across her face, lighting her dazzling green eyes. "Who needs pizza?" She echoed his earlier sentiment.

He smiled at her, brushing the hair off her face. "I don't, but they're on the way." He lifted the wine bottle and opened it. Her hands shook slightly as she arranged the flowers in a vase.

"Flynn, I'm so sorry about dinner. I never should have tried to cook. As you can see, I'm terrible at it."

Flynn put down the wine bottle and took her hands in his. "Katie, I'm so touched that you made the effort. Just the fact that you wanted to means more to me than you know."

"I had my grandmother's recipe. My mom gave it to me. Assured me it would be easy." She dropped her gaze to the floor.

Flynn's heart soared. Katie had told her mom about them? About him? That had to be good news. "It's the thought that counts. I'd be happy to cook for you sometime. We could even take cooking lessons together."

She raised her eyes to his. "You know how to cook?"

He grinned. "I do. At least a few things. I'm better at following recipes than trying on my own. I can also sew on a button and waltz. My mom, not to mention my sisters, made sure of it."

"Wow. You'll make someone a good wife someday."

He grabbed her, drawing her in and nuzzling behind one ear. He growled into it. "That's a bit sexist, don't you think?" He kissed her in the sensitive spot behind her ear before backing up. "I'll make someone a good *husband* one day. Not because I can cook and sew a button, but because I'm a good person who would never hurt the woman I loved."

*****

Their gazes collided, and for a long moment, Katie forgot to breathe. Then she sucked in a lungful of air. And then did it again. Every time she was around Flynn, she forgot to breathe. Luckily, it was an automatic thing, or she would have been long dead.

Maybe, she thought with a grain of hope, her mother was right. Maybe Flynn was someone she could trust with her heart. But how could she be sure? She gnawed her lower lip. Her mother had never given her bad advice before. She should go for it. Be brave. See what happened.

"Where are your wine glasses, Katie?"

She pointed to a cabinet. Taking the wine bottle, Katie walked into the living room. She placed it on the coffee table and then flicked a switch for the gas fireplace. The temperature had been steadily dropping throughout the day. The fire would feel nice.

Flynn joined her, carrying the glasses. "When are you working again, Katie?" He sat and poured them both a glass of the red.

She took a sip of the wine. "Mmmm. I may not be able to cook, but at least I can pick a decent wine. I took a few days off, in preparation for the event on Saturday. So, I'm only working tomorrow night. Which reminds me, we have to discuss the publicity for the event this week."

Flynn nodded and pulled out his phone. "Let me put the schedule in here, that way I'll know where to be."

"Tomorrow at nine in the morning, one of the local TV news stations is coming out to interview us at the hospital. Shouldn't be more than thirty minutes, start to finish. Then on Wednesday, a reporter from The Gazette will be there. They've agreed to run a piece about it, human interest and all that. That'll be at the hospital at noon. Do those work for you?"

Flynn finished typing in his phone and set it on the coffee table. "I'll make sure they do."

The doorbell rang. Flynn jumped up to answer it. "Your dinner, my lady." With a flourish, Flynn set the box on the coffee table. Decadent, savory smells wafted from it. Flynn's stomach rumbled loudly. "Easy to tell I skipped lunch."

Katie put a piece of pizza on a plate and passed it to Flynn. Then got one for herself. Taking a bite, Katie moaned as she swallowed. Flynn sat still, holding his plate, as he watched her enjoy her pizza. She moaned again and then licked her lips. Katie looked up and caught him watching her. She set her plate down and wiped her mouth a bit self-consciously. "Uh, I really like pizza."

"I could tell. Please don't stop on my account." Flynn took a large bite. He sat back, chewing. His eyes never left hers.

Katie sighed and then took a sip of her wine. "I don't eat pizza very often, so this is a treat."

He took her plate from her hand and placed it on the coffee table. Flynn threaded the fingers of one hand into the hair along the side of her face. He leaned in. "I'm going to kiss you now, in case you hadn't guessed." And he did just that.

Katie's mouth formed a smile that was quickly covered by Flynn's. Nibbling at the corners of her mouth, he sent trickles of delicious sensation throughout her body. She would never be able to get enough of him was her last conscious thought. She placed her hand over his erection, and rubbed back and forth with enough pressure to get his attention.

"Should we take this somewhere else?"

Katie raised her head from his. Her eyes were alight with a wicked gleam. "Do you want to waste all that time going upstairs?"

"Maybe later," he muttered. Flynn's hands swept up underneath her sweater, whisking it off her. He put his mouth over her breast, and even with her bra still on, Katie twisted underneath him. She thrust her body up at him, silently begging for more.

Flynn started to undo the front closure on her bra, but Katie covered his hands. She slid out from under him and stood next to the couch. After throwing several, large pillows on the floor before the fireplace, Katie took his hand and pulled him up from the couch. "It's my turn to play." Her voice was thick with desire.

She led him to the pillows. Katie turned to him and started working on the buttons that lined the front of his shirt. He started to pull it out of his jeans, but she stopped him. "I've got this, Flynn."

When she had undone all the buttons she could reach, she bunched his shirt in her hands and pulled. Her fingers brushed against the skin of his lower abdomen causing Flynn to suck in his breath sharply. Katie stripped the opened shirt from his torso and started in on his belt. "Darling, if you keep up this pace, I'm never going to make it."

"I guess you'll have to concentrate then," she whispered in his ear.

Flynn lowered himself to the throw pillows at the slightest touch from Katie. She undid his belt and reached for his zipper. Katie slid a hand into his opened jeans and palmed him over his underwear. He closed his eyes and groaned. She raised her head to look at him. "Imagine how good it will feel when these clothes are out of the way." He flattened his hands on the floor as if to keep them from grabbing her.

Katie chuckled when she saw him do this. "Problem?"

He shook his head and opened his eyes to look at her. "No problem. Just trying to do what you asked when I really want to strip you naked. With my teeth."

Her eyes widened slightly as her pupils dilated. Instead of answering, Katie withdrew her hand and then slid it in again. This time under his layers of clothing. She slid her hand along the length of him, forcing another groan from deep in his throat. Flynn closed his eyes again and threw back his head. "Yes, baby," he muttered through clenched teeth.

"I thought you might like that," Katie purred.

Katie let go of him to push his jeans off his legs. Flynn dug his heels into the ground and lifted his hips to help her. When everything was lying in a pool at his ankles, Flynn flicked them aside with his foot.

"I'll take it from here," she teased. "Lie back and enjoy." Flynn sank into the oversized cushions on the floor. The fire sent shadows and light flickering over his body. Katie lost her breath at the site.

He opened his eyes and looked at Katie. "There's something sexy about the fact that I'm naked and you're still mostly dressed. But, eventually, we'll have to do something about that."

"We'll get there," Katie whispered as she swiped his nipple with her tongue and then pulled back to blow on it. The nipple hardened immediately. She gave the same attention to his other nipple. Flynn began to move under her, straining to be closer.

She laughed and raked the nails of one hand across his abdomen. His muscles quivered beneath her seeking fingers. Katie slid down his body, trailing wet, hot kisses across his skin. When she got to his erect penis, she slowed. Smiling up at Flynn, she touched her tongue to the tip of his penis.

Flynn groaned. "Katie, you're playing with fire."

"I know," she answered and lowered her mouth onto him. Her lips closed around him. She could feel his muscles tensing. The power she held over him was heady.

When she removed her mouth from him, Flynn sprang into action. "Okay, I give. And now it's your turn again." Before she could react, Flynn slid out from under her and flipped Katie onto her back. He made quick work of her clothes, not taking the time for finesse. "Sorry, honey, but I'm about at the end of my control," he muttered.

"Do you see me complaining?"

Flynn looked down at Katie. She was wearing only her bra and matching panties, both a soft pink color that somehow didn't clash with her hair. She could feel the admiration in his gaze, and it pleased her. Flynn had a way of making her feel beautiful. Flynn palmed her panties, and she moved under his hand in encouragement. He undid the hook of her bra, allowing her breasts to spill out.

While he nipped one tightened bud, Flynn hooked a thumb under the strap of her panties. He yanked them down her thighs. Reaching for his pants, he grabbed a condom from his wallet. Katie glanced at him as he rolled the condom down his length.

She could feel her skin flushing everywhere. She smiled at him, an invitation for sure. "I want to feel you buried in me, Flynn."

"It's good that we want the same thing, Katie," were his last words as he edged her center with the tip of him. When she moved her hips to accommodate him, Flynn plunged all the way in. She wrapped her legs around his back to anchor herself even as she began to drift away.

He paused for a moment, staring at her as though trying to memorize every line of her face. Then he withdrew and plunged back in. Again and again. Perspiration clung to both, mingling with the other scents in the room. Flynn leaned down and captured her mouth, his tongue initiating a dance as old as time with hers. It was a mirror image of what the rest of them was doing.

Katie groaned into his mouth. The sound was one of complete satisfaction. With one last thrust, he took them both straight over the edge. Katie arched her back and cried out, falling with him.

Flynn collapsed on the floor next to her. Katie cradled his head to her breast, while she stroked one hand idly up and down his back. She lost herself in the moment. She had never felt a connection with any man as she did with Flynn. It had to mean something.

Chapter Eighteen

Katie reveled in the weight of Flynn's head on her breast. The warmth of his body pressed along the length of hers. She didn't know what this meant for them long term, and she didn't care. For this moment, she was happy.

"There's another way to burn off pizza," she quipped.

"Just as sweaty but much more fun than running," he answered.

The sensation of his mouth moving against her breast as he spoke sent zings through her. The aftershocks of her orgasm still rippled through her. "Speaking of sweaty, I could use a shower," she said. "Or a bath. I have a huge bathtub."

Flynn grinned against her breast. "Was that an invitation?" Without awaiting her reply, Flynn stood up and extended his hand to Katie. "What a great idea. Why don't you start the bath while I grab the wine?"

Katie took his hand, trying to not think about the fact that she was naked. She looked at him instead. Flynn was magnificent. Not overly muscular, which she had never cared for anyway, but lightly muscled in all the right places.

"You're probably a runner, right?" She sighed. It figured. She hated running.

Flynn shook his head. "I am. I prefer to swim."

"It's paying off for you," she murmured. She tried to not feel self-conscious, but it wasn't easy.

Flynn tipped her face up with a gentle finger under her chin. "You are beautiful. Never think anything else. I love your body, Katie. Every inch of it."

For the first time in a long time, the tension she felt around body image melted away. He was serious. And Flynn had never, not even once, made any sort of critical comment about her eating or weight.

"I'll keep that in mind," she murmured as she headed up the stairs. Katie headed straight into her master bathroom and turned on the tap in the garden tub. After making sure the temperature was right, she walked to the linen closet and grabbed two towels for them. Then she added a small amount of bath foam to the tub. She chose one with a light scent so that Flynn wouldn't object. She thought the bubbles would be fun.

Next, Katie lit a candle that sat in the corner ledge of the tub and turned on some soft music. With nothing left to do, she slid into the warm water and wondered what was keeping Flynn.

As the thought entered her mind, Katie heard him enter the room. He was carrying two filled glasses. "Sorry I took so long. I ducked into the downstairs bathroom to clean up." He held up an unused condom by the foil wrapper. "And then I grabbed another from my wallet. Just in case."

"Good thinking, boy scout. You're going to need that. And just for future reference, I have plenty." The look she gave him was pure sin.

Flynn placed the condom on the edge of the tub and stepped in, sliding down behind Katie. The water sloshed as he settled in. She snuggled up against his chest, her rear not so accidentally rubbing against him. But Flynn surprised her. He leaned back against the tub, bringing her with him until she was floating in the cocoon of his arms. She felt contentment. And peace.

She sighed and trailed her fingers along his arm that was draped across her abdomen. "I never pictured this happening, Flynn."

"I did," he murmured from behind her. "Maybe not this specific scene. But us together? Yes, I pictured that. From the very first time I saw you, Katie Fitzgerald. I knew there was something special about you. It may have been the way you fought so hard to save that patient's life. Or the care that you took with his family when you couldn't. There was a passion there that I couldn't ignore." He stroked his hand along the side of her face as a shudder ran through her body. "Does that scare you?"

She twisted to look at him. Her bright green eyes flashed at him. "No, Flynn, I was never scared of you. Just what you might do to my heart." A raw honesty reflected in her eyes. And a plea for him to not break her heart.

Flynn brushed a damp tendril back from her face. He returned her direct stare. "I would never hurt you on purpose. Never. I would sooner cut out my own heart."

She smiled at him. A tentative smile with the promise of something to come. "I'm beginning to understand that, Flynn."

He leaned back again, taking her with him. "Good. Now that we have that established, I have a question for you."

"Okay…" Sudden tension radiated through her muscles. There was something in his tone that alarmed her.

"My parents are celebrating their anniversary in December with a big party. A fancy one. Black tie. In Atlanta. Will you come with me?"

"As your date?"

"Uh, not as my sister. I already have enough of those."

Unease snaked through her. She wasn't ready for this. Everything was too new. Too up in the air. She wasn't ready to go public. Katie laughed, but the sound was brittle. "I'm not ready to meet your parents. That's a big step."

Flynn was silent for a long time. Katie's throat was dry and felt like she had swallowed broken glass. Things were going so well, and then he had to ask that of her. Why didn't he understand her reluctance? Katie got up so suddenly that water threatened to spill over the side of the tub. Stepping out and on to the bath mat, she turned her back to him and wrapped herself in a towel, as though it was a suit of armor. "Flynn. Say something."

He stayed in the tub. "What do you want me to say? I don't understand why this is such a big deal. I've already met your parents. Several times. And I'm friends with your brothers."

"Yes. But that happened before."

"Before what, Katie?"

Water streamed down her wet hair, but desperation came off her in waves. "Before this." Katie gestured with her hands.

"Before we had sex," he spat out bitterly. "Isn't that what you're trying to say?" Flynn rose from the tub and grabbed a nearby towel and dried off hastily. With a disdainful glance at the condom still sitting on the edge of the tub he muttered, "I guess we won't need that today." Flynn walked out of the bathroom without another word.

Katie pressed her fist to her mouth to keep from crying. She could hear him fumbling around downstairs, getting dressed. Katie grabbed the robe that lived on the back of her bathroom door. Ignoring the fact that she was damp at best, she threw it on and ran down the stairs.

"Flynn, wait," she cried out. She dashed into the living room, her chest heaving with the effort. Flynn's hand was on the doorknob when she caught up with him. "Please don't go."

Flynn stood there as though carved from stone. He didn't turn to face her. His hand remained on the knob. In a voice strained with emotion he asked, "What's the point, Katie?"

Her Irish temper, famous in the Fitzgerald family, was starting to rear its ugly head. "So, this is how it's going to go, Flynn? I disagree with you one time, and you leave in a snit?"

His hand fell from the knob. Flynn turned to face her. His normally warm blue eyes were icy. His voice wasn't any warmer. "This was not a disagreement, Katie. A disagreement is not wanting to see the same movie." He took a deep breath as if trying to calm himself. "You're a coward, Katie Fitzgerald. I wanted you to go with me to the party, as my *date*, because that's what you do when you're in a relationship. My family is very important to me. So are you. I wanted y'all to meet. I am not in a snit. I am disappointed." He turned back around as if to leave.

"Oh, no you don't, Flynn Reynolds." Katie closed the gap between them and grabbed his arm. "You started this. You knew how I felt about getting involved with you, knew about both of our issues with it, but you pushed anyway. I need time to adjust, Flynn. Why does this have to be all or nothing?" Her voice broke on the last word, but she wouldn't cry. She refused to give him that.

Anger or arrogance she could have handled. But everything about Flynn screamed hurt and disappointed. "You're right, Katie. I pushed you too hard. And probably too fast. All I wanted was to be with you, Katie. To be important to you. Not someone you called for a fun time. We've barely even been out in public." Flynn's voice was soft and full of hurt. "I can't blame you. I asked for too much. More than you were willing, or able, to give. I want you in my life, Katie. Not just in my bed. That's why I want you to meet my parents. I'm sorry that I put too much pressure on you."

This time when Flynn turned to leave, Katie didn't stop him. She was frozen to the spot. Both his tone and words were so final. Katie walked to the couch and sat down. Curling herself into the tiniest ball possible, she let go of all the tears she had been holding back.

*****

Flynn entered his darkened home, threw his keys on the counter and didn't bother with the lights. He grabbed a beer from the fridge and drank it at the kitchen table. He'd blown it with Katie. Plain and simple. He'd wanted too much, more than she was ready to give. He should have given her time. Been supportive. Instead, he'd rushed her into something she wasn't prepared for. Understanding his mistake, however, didn't make Flynn feel any better.

His cell rang, breaking his ruminations. Flynn's heart slammed against his ribs. With a bit of luck, Katie was calling to talk about how things had ended between them. He answered in a rush without looking to see who had called.

"Katie, I'm so glad you called." If it was possible to wear your heart on your sleeve, then Flynn was wearing his in his voice. He needed to fix things.

"Sorry, no, it's only Elizabeth," came the cautious reply. "Why would Katie be calling you?"

Disappointment stabbed through him. "Sorry, Elizabeth. I didn't look at the screen."

"Obviously," came the dry reply. "But that doesn't answer my question."

"I wouldn't know where to start. That's a story for another day. So, tell me all about Hawaii."

"If you open your front door, you can see the thousands of pictures I took."

Flynn hesitated, not excited for conversation with a happily married person. But the decision was taken out of his hands. Before he could even answer her, his front door opened. He ended the call and walked through the darkened house to greet her.

"There you are," Elizabeth exclaimed. She turned on a lamp as she made her way towards him. "That's the last time you'll give me a key so that I can let in the cable guy."

Flynn laughed. He couldn't help it. Elizabeth was a ray of sunshine in his life. Right after moving in, Flynn had driven to Atlanta to celebrate his grandmother's ninetieth birthday. Elizabeth had come over to let the cable guy in to install new service.

"Nah. I'd still be waiting for another appointment if it wasn't for you." He grabbed Elizabeth up in an exuberant hug, swinging her around before placing her back on her feet. He looked behind her. "Lose your new husband already?"

Elizabeth laughed. "No, Flynn. He and I are stuck with each other, for better or worse."

Flynn grinned from ear-to-ear; his first genuine one since the argument with Katie. "Not that either of you would have it any other way."

"Exactly," agreed Elizabeth. She grabbed him by the hand and led Flynn to the couch. "Enough about me. Tell me about Katie." She clapped her hands with delight. "I knew there was something brewing there."

The smile slid from Flynn's face. "If you had asked a few hours ago, I would have had a wonderful story to tell you."

Elizabeth's expression immediately sobered. "What did you do?"

Flynn would have taken affront to that. If she hadn't been right. "How do you know it was me that did something wrong?"

"Don't take this the wrong way. But you can be a bit impulsive. And then there's your sense of humor. I find you hysterical. Not sure everyone feels the same way."

"You had me at impulsive." He filled Elizabeth in on what occurred in her absence. She was silent as he talked, but Flynn knew she was paying attention. Being a gentleman, he left out the X-rated parts. When he finished, Flynn sagged against the back of his couch; all the fight had gone out of him.

Elizabeth took his hand in hers. "Oh, Flynn, I'm so very sorry. I know you're hurting. As is Katie. But surely you can fix this. You know how Katie can be. There's a price for that beautiful red hair of hers. Even when we were kids, she had a quick temper on her. But it was always quick to dissolve as well."

"It's not about anger, Elizabeth. It's about trust. And she doesn't have any. She was honest about that from the beginning." Flynn hung his head. His posture screamed defeat.

"I wouldn't give up yet, Flynn. Give her some time. I could tell last summer that there was something between you two. She lights up when you're around. Has a glow about her. She needs time to process."

He raised his head and looked at Elizabeth. "Do you really think so?" For the first time since leaving Katie, he felt the tiniest glimmer of hope.

"I do. But she needs time. Don't rush her. Now, let me show you those ten thousand pictures."

*****

The next morning, Katie sat in the hospital parking lot for as long as she could. Then she ended up running all the way to the building to avoid being late for the news interview. But that's how desperate she was to *not* see Flynn. She had spent a mostly sleepless night. Her face had paid the price. There was only so much makeup could do. It was blotchy and red after last night's crying jag.

The last thing Katie wanted to do was face Flynn this morning. But her career was all she had left. She would do this interview and anything else necessary to ensure the success of the event. Then she would get into the NP program of her choice and excel there as well. Somewhere along the way, she would learn to get over Flynn. At least that was her plan.

Katie spied the local news van as she approached the main lobby. The wood and copper façade was gorgeous. She rarely entered this way, usually taking the employee entrance in the back. Katie crossed her fingers as she walked through the doors. Please let this not be the most awkward thing ever. And please let the news person not be a size zero knockout. She didn't think she could handle some bimbo flirting with Flynn right now.

She slowed when she saw Flynn standing near the ornamental waterfall. His back was to her. The pristine white of his doctor coat did nothing to hide the expanse of his shoulders. She took a deep breath, releasing it slowly through her nose. You can do this, she told herself. He's just a man. If the situation was different, she would have laughed at the ridiculousness of that statement.

He wasn't any man. That was like saying Sean Connery was just an actor. Flynn was the man she loved. Katie gasped aloud, unable to stop it. She felt the color drain from her face as Flynn turned to see what was happening. *Loved*? When had that happened? No. She couldn't be in love with him.

The man in question approached her, his handsome face tight with concern. "Katie, are you okay?"

She nodded, afraid to speak. *Suck it up buttercup,* she told herself. She wasn't that woman; the one who threw away everything for a man. Not even for Flynn. She would do this and move on.

Forcing herself to smile, Katie approached the willowy blonde who had been standing behind Flynn. She immediately recognized Stacey Carmichael from the news. The universe really must hate her. Stacey was drop dead, in your face gorgeous. And most definitely a size zero. Great.

"Ms. Carmichael, I'm Katie Fitzgerald. Thank you so much for coming out today." Katie extended her hand and tried to not grimace as the stunning woman shook hers. The other woman's teeth were so bright, Katie suppressed a wince.

"Katie, please call me Stacey. Flynn was telling me how excited he is for Saturday's event."

Katie stiffened as she felt Flynn stand next to her. "Yes, Stacey, it is exciting. We take the health of our community very seriously."

Stacey was no longer looking at her. The news woman was paying rapt attention to Flynn. Naturally. What woman with a pulse wouldn't? Katie still wanted to punch her.

Stacey's laugh rang throughout the marble lobby. Her hand was resting possessively on Flynn's well-defined bicep. The blood red nails in stark contrast to his white coat.

A tall man carrying a very expensive looking camera approached. "Uh, Ms. Carmichael, are you ready?"

Stacey removed her hand from Flynn's arm and smoothed out imaginary wrinkles form her tight-fitting dress. Katie could have kissed the camera man. "Of course, Gill." She addressed Flynn. "Dr. Reynolds, we'll start with you. Maybe a bit about your background, etc."

Flynn smiled as he cut her off. "Ms. Carmichael, I know you care as much about the health of the community as we do, so let's keep this about the event. And Ms. Fitzgerald is the lead on this anyway. I'm just here to help."

Katie had to hand it to him. He was smooth. Flynn had redirected the focus in a way that the news woman couldn't balk at. She could have kissed him. Not that she ever needed an excuse for that.

Stacey's smile was a bit less bright as she turned to Katie. "Okay. I'll ask you some questions about the event in general. We can edit later." She snapped her fingers at poor Gill. "Let's do this."

After that, the interview was painless. Because Katie was passionate about community health, she forgot about the camera. The hardest part was standing next to Flynn without touching him. But that was crucial to her survival. Hands off. It was bad enough she had to breathe in his scent.

When they finished, Katie thanked the woman for coming and turned to leave. But not before she saw Stacey hand Flynn one of her business cards. And overhear that her *personal* cell number was on the back. Not that it mattered to her of course.

She walked out into the sunshine, ignoring Flynn as he called her name. Cowardly? Yes. Necessary? Absolutely. Katie didn't stop until she was at her car, winded from almost running in heels. She thought she was home free until she heard Flynn call her. His voice was impossibly close.

"Katie, why are you running from me? Can't we at least talk like civilized human beings?"

Katie whirled on him, but all the fight fled from her body when she saw him. Misery covered him like a cloak. Her heart squeezed. "I'm sorry, Flynn. I don't have anything to say." She slipped into her car without a backward glance. Katie wasn't sure she could keep her resolve if she did.

Over the next few hours, Katie called local churches and community agencies to remind them of Saturday's event. Around three, she slid into her bed, desperate for a nap before work. She fell into a boneless sleep, only waking when her alarm rang at six in the evening. That gave her just enough time to jump out of bed and get ready for her shift. Living close to work helped on days like this.

Katie settled in for her shift when she heard a woman say, "Excuse me." behind her. Thinking she was a patient's family member. Katie hurried over to help the attractive woman.

"Hi. How may I help you?"

The other woman smiled, displaying a dazzling array of gleaming white teeth. "I don't mean to bother you. I'm looking for Dr. Reynolds. Do you know where I can find him?"

Before Katie could answer, Flynn walked out of a patient room. The elegantly clad woman shrieked his first name and launched herself at him. Katie watched with a knot in her chest as Flynn picked her up and swung her around. The woman, damn her, threw her arms around his neck and gave him a smacking kiss. Katie's head spun as Flynn led the other woman off the unit.

Pam came up behind Katie and laid a sympathetic hand on her shoulder. "You don't know who she is, Katie. Best to not jump to conclusions."

Katie nodded, the lump in her throat preventing a response. All she had to do was make it through this night. And the next. And the one after that. She shook her head to clear it. She loved her job, and her patients needed her. They also needed her to be level headed and smart. Losing her heart, and mind, over a man wasn't going to help anyone.

The first half of the shift passed. Katie was in charge and only had one patient. Mr. Simmonds, "call me Billy Ray," had been admitted early this morning for new onset chest pain. He'd passed an uneventful day. If that remained true, Billy Ray would be transferred to a lower level of care tomorrow with aim for discharge soon after.

By eleven, he was sleeping and Katie had nothing more to do for him until morning. That left time to round on the other patients and entirely too much time to think. She couldn't get the image of that beautiful woman in Flynn's arms out of her head. Who was she? Old doubts plagued her.

But there was an air of familiarity, and affection, between the two. Maybe she was some Atlanta debutante that his mother had once sent his way. If he cared so much for her, why would Flynn have left her in Atlanta?

Ugh! Katie had become what she always hated in other women. Hooked on the thought of some guy. She stood up, stretched, and then stomped into the employee lounge. Time for some caffeine.

While she waited for it to brew, Katie thought about the last few days. Although they had generally sucked, one good thing had come of them. Katie had submitted all her graduate school applications. It was time to get serious about this. She also pored over her finances and monthly budget. She had always lived frugally and had a decent amount in savings. Unfortunately, she couldn't take advantage of the medical center's tuition reimbursement program. She needed to stay full time to quality.

As much as she didn't want to, the best option was to take on a roommate. The thought was less than pleasant. After living with David for a few years, she enjoyed her own space. But she had to be practical. School was expensive. And she had a mortgage plus other bills. Even with picking up shifts when she could, it was going to be tight. Having a house mate to share the expenses made sense. Katie sighed. Being an adult was exhausting. And not a lot of fun sometimes.

She clicked on her work email account when someone cleared their voice above her. Katie glanced up to see Dr. Slater, the "I-Know-it-All" second-year trauma resident. The superior look was gone from his face. She was surprised, even shocked, to see a humble one in its place.

"Dr. Slater, may I help you with something?"

He cleared his throat. "Uh, no, I wanted to apologize. You know. For the other week? I was being an..."

"Ass?" she suggested sweetly.

He had the grace to blush. "I was going to go with pompous idiot, but that works." The first genuine smile she had ever seen from him spread across his face. "I really am sorry that I was so rude to you and Pam."

Not about to let him off that easily, Katie asked, "And almost killed our patient?"

The muscles in his face tensed, and the smile faltered on his lips. "Yes, of course, that too."

Katie stood and walked around the counter that separated them. "My priority here will always be my patient, not your feelings. What I did that night, going over your head to the attending, wasn't meant as a slight to you, Dr. Slater. It was me, doing my job." She took a deep breath. *In for a penny,* as her dad always said. "Nurses spend way more time with these patients than doctors do. We know a lot about them and their conditions. You could learn something from us." Her tone was very gentle.

"Oh, don't worry. I am very aware of the importance nurses have in patient care." He grimaced as if remembering.

Katie chuckled. "I'm sure you are. Dr. Kilpatrick has always been one of our staunchest allies."

Dr. Slater blinked several times. "Dr. Kilpatrick? She had a few choice words for me, but I was talking about Dr. Reynolds."

It was Katie's turn to look confused. "Flynn? Uh, I mean Dr. Reynolds? What does he have to do with this?" She remembered Flynn physically restraining the resident when he thought Dr. Slater had threatened her. She assumed the incident ended there.

A dull red crept up the younger man's neck. "Later that night, after I got out of surgery, Dr. Reynolds and I had a 'chat.' He wanted to be sure that I understood how to treat nurses." He must have noticed the shock on her face. He rushed on to reassure her. "I do, Katie, I promise. Anyway, I haven't had a chance to talk with you since that night, and I wanted you to know how sorry I am."

"Well, I appreciate that, Dr. Slater. It means a lot to me. We need to work together not against each other. For our patients. Critical care is no place for personality clashes."

"Agreed. Is Pam working tonight? I'd like to apologize to her as well."

"She is. She has rooms nine through eleven. You can find her in one of those."

"Okay. Good. I'll go find her. Thanks again, Katie."

She shook her head. Never in her wildest imagination did she see that one coming. Dr. Slater apologizing. Wow! She had no idea what Flynn had said to the resident, but it had clearly made a lasting impression.

She went back to charting her patient's assessment, but the conversation stuck in her head. She had rather snottily told Flynn that she didn't need him defending her. And yet he had taken it upon himself to have a little chat with Dr. Slater. She wasn't sure if she was pleased or pissed. Probably a bit of both.

Chapter Nineteen

Katie leaned back in her chair for a moment and closed her eyes. Growing up with so many brothers had made her tough. Her sister Riley was the same way. Yet she knew that any of her brothers would have her back in an instant if she needed them. And while she always fussed when they did, she was also secretly pleased. So why was Flynn protecting her any different?

"It's too early for daydreaming, Katie."

She opened her eyes and smiled at Pam. "I wasn't daydreaming. More like wool gathering. What's going on?"

Pam plopped into the chair next to her. "I had a very interesting conversation with young Dr. Slater."

Katie grinned. "I did as well. He seemed sincere. We'll see."

"That wasn't the interesting part to which I was referring." Her grin sent a warning tingle down Katie's spine. "It would seem your Dr. Reynolds was the impetus behind the change in Dr. Slater. What do you have to say about that?"

Katie's lips clamped shut. She made a gesture of locking her lips and throwing away the key.

Pam rolled her chair right up to Katie's. "Come on now! You now I live vicariously through you young folks. Throw me a bone."

Katie laughed out loud. Pam might have almost thirty years on her, but she was one of the most energetic women she knew. "Nice try, Grandma," she commented.

"Okay, playing the senior card didn't work. I'll try for straight honesty. What's going on with you two?"

To Katie's horror, and Pam's shock, a single tear made its way down Katie's cheek. She brushed it away. "I wouldn't even know where to start, Pam." She gave Pam the highlights. When she was done, she waited for motherly advice. That's not what she got.

Pam shook her head. And not in a friendly way. "You're an idiot, my dear." Her gentle tone softened the harshness of her words.

Katie's jaw dropped. "Wow. Why don't you tell me what you really think, Pam?" As tough as she was, her friend's words hurt. A lot. Because Katie knew they were true.

"That's one advantage of my advanced age, Katie. I don't have to sugar coat things anymore."

"But Pam, that's not fair to me. You don't know the whole story."

Humor faded from Pam's eyes. "What don't I know, Katie? David hurt you when he left the way he did. It was unfair and horrible. And then along comes Flynn. Another doctor, true. But one who's charming, bright, wickedly sexy, and best of all crazy about you." She held her hand up when Katie would have protested. "And maybe he pushed a bit harder than he should have. And a bit quickly. But, he shouldn't pay for David's crime."

"It's not that simple," Katie protested weakly.

Pam placed a hand on Katie's shoulders and looked her square in the eye. "I'm sure it's not, Katie. But life is short. And men like Flynn Reynolds don't come along every day. Playing it safe doesn't keep your feet warm at night."

She got up and pushed in her chair. "It's a lot to think about, I know. Take your time, Katie. Think it through. Just don't overthink it." Pam squeezed Katie's shoulder and walked away, leaving Katie more confused than ever.

*****

Flynn dragged himself into the office the next morning, yawning all the way. Ally's impromptu visit last night had cost him many hours of sleep. He loved catching up with his sister but she had caught him off guard. Which was of course Ally's plan. That's what he gets for not returning her calls for several days. They had stayed up late, hashing it out, and he had nothing to show for it. Other than yet another woman telling him he screwed up.

"The coffee won't actually put itself into the machine," advised an amused Sebastian from the doorway.

Flynn snapped himself out of his reverie. He was standing in the middle of the staff lounge, with the Keurig pod in one hand and a mug in the other. He sighed. It was going to be a long day. He placed his mug and the pod in the machine and waited.

"Hey," he muttered in Sebastian's general direction. He smothered another gigantic yawn.

Sebastian laughed. "I know we didn't have any late admits in the ICU. Is there a good reason for you being so tired this morning?" He raised one eyebrow in question.

"Ally."

Sebastian grinned. "Hurricane Ally's here? In Windsor Falls? How'd you ever get her to leave Atlanta?"

Flynn smiled at his friend's nickname for her. It was spot on. "I didn't. She showed up. Without warning. In the ICU, last evening."

A knowing look settled in Sebastian's face. "What did you do this time?"

Flynn had the grace to look sheepish. He was getting used to being wrong. "I didn't return any of her calls. For three days in a row."

Sebastian laughed and stepped forward, clapping Flynn on the back. "Momma Bear has her claws out, does she? Who's she protecting you from this time?"

Flynn pulled his mug from the coffee maker and blew across the top. Steam swirled around it. "It's not like that this time. I screwed up. Big time."

Sebastian searched his friend's face. "Huh. Not sure what to say. You never make mistakes with women." He paused at his friend's snort of disbelief. "Well, at least not major ones that bring Ally running. What happened?"

Flynn shook his head and looked at the wall clock. "Not enough time. We'll catch up later."

*****

On Wednesday morning, Katie once again threw on some decent clothes and makeup. She'd be glad when this last interview was done. Katie couldn't wait for Saturday, but being "the face" of Windsor Memorial was a bit much. The segment on the evening news had gone very well, despite the reporter's fascination with Flynn. The director of community events called Katie this morning to tell her how calls about the event had boomed.

Katie was glad, and she would be even more so when this was over. Things had not changed between her and Flynn. In fact, she hadn't even seen him since the mystery woman had appeared on Monday. Her imagination had a field day with that in the middle of the night. When Katie should have been sleeping.

But they were in the home stretch now, and soon she would be able to relax. And Thanksgiving was next week. Always a family favorite, Katie was looking forward to spending time with them. She just had to get through this week.

"Hello, Katie."

She had been lost in thought hadn't seen Flynn coming. Apparently, her radar was off.

"Hey, Flynn." She nodded in his direction, desperate to not make eye contact. "Ready for this? Last one." She could feel the weight of his gaze on her and summoned the courage to meet his eyes. Mistake. His normally bright blue eyes were dulled. His smile only half-hearted. He looked like she felt. The sight of him hurt her heart.

"I am. All in the name of helping people, I guess."

She was saved from making small talk by a middle-aged man carrying a camera bag. "Katie Fitzgerald?"

She nodded. "You must be from The Gazette. I'm sorry. I don't know your name. They didn't tell me who they were sending."

"Doug Littlefield, ma'am."

"Thank you for coming, Doug." She introduced the two men before they filed into Flynn's office.

Doug looked around, nodding his head. "Yes, this will work." He pulled an expensive looking camera from his bag. "I'll take a few shots of you two in here while I ask you about the event. Shall we get started?"

After being interviewed by the ice princess on Monday, this should be a snap, Katie thought. Not much chance of Doug hitting on Flynn. Katie took a seat in front of Flynn's desk and relaxed.

The day of the big event finally arrived, bringing with it bright sun and chilly air, as mornings usually did in November. The local weather man promised temperatures in the mid-sixties later in the day. Katie yawned as she walked into De Luca's Bakery. The first of her many volunteers would be arriving by seven. She was picking up the breakfast items Mr. De Luca had so thoughtfully donated.

"Hey, Katie, right on time." Kat sprang from the back room with her usual enthusiasm. Because she knew Katie so well, she came bearing coffee.

Katie thanked her and cradled the to go cup in her hands as though it were the Holy Grail. This early, it just might be. She took a sip and sighed as hot caffeine hit her veins.

Mr. De Luca came from the back room, carrying two large boxes. "Hey, Katie! I have your stuff all ready for you. Come look."

Katie walked over to him, giving him a peck on the cheek. "You're the best, Mr. De Luca. I'm so thankful for your donation today. The volunteers will be as well." She peered into one box he was holding. Inside was a dozen heart-shaped donuts with red icing. Katie laughed and clapped her hands. "That's perfect, Mr. D."

Kat's father blushed at the attention. "Oh, go on. It's just my Valentine's special a few months early. And for such a worthy cause."

"Well, we appreciate it. And now I have to dash."

Kat helped her to carry the items to her car. "Is Flynn going to be there?"

Katie ignored the smug look on her friend's face. She closed the back of her small SUV. "You know he is, Kat. And it doesn't mean anything." She hugged her friend. "Now, I have to go."

Katie drove to the hospital and parked near the entrance to the medical arts building. Pam and Annie were walking up the sidewalk as she jumped out of her car. "Morning, ladies!" Katie walked to the back of her car. "Care to help me carry in breakfast?"

Annie ran up to the car and peered in the back. "Ooh, is that from De Luca's? Where do you want it?"

The two women each grabbed a box and headed inside. The normally busy medical office building was empty on this early Saturday morning. Katie and some of her helpers had been there until late last night, setting up what they would need for today.

The lobby was walled in glass and afforded a fabulous view of the mountains. The welcome area sat just inside the doors. There were several tables holding information about today's events and educational pamphlets people could take with them. Assistants from the hospital's volunteer department would man these, handing out pamphlets and guiding attendees to events.

Katie had arranged for use of several of the large conference rooms on the first floor. Each would host a different health screening. Visitors to the fair could have their weight and BMI, blood pressure, cholesterol, and blood sugar levels tested. Students from two local nursing schools would be running these stations, under close supervision from their instructors. Katie considered that a win-win situation. The hospital gained more volunteers, while the volunteers got a first-hand insight into community health.

Flynn, Sebastian, and several other physicians from the cardiology department would be on hand as well. Each had volunteered to lead discussions on various aspects of cardiac health. Katie hoped that Flynn and Sebastian would acquire new patients for their practice.

Other departments, such as nutrition and cardiac rehabilitation were sending employees as well. Katie had finalized plans with the director from each on Thursday. Nutritional counseling and lifestyle and exercise information would be available to anyone interested.

She had already had one almost disaster this week. The medical center had sprung for tee shirts for everyone working today's event. They had arrived on Tuesday. Seventy-five shirts. All in size adult *small*. She had nearly needed CPR when she opened the boxes. The company who printed them had acknowledged their mistake and sent new ones; this time in assorted sizes. The new shirts had arrived last night.

In the next hour, her volunteers arrived in twos and threes. Many nurses and other personnel from the hospital had stepped up to volunteer today. Each would be given specific tasks that had already been planned. Katie was grateful for each one of them. They were grateful for the pastries. The doors would be open to the public at nine with various events planned until four in the afternoon. Then there would be hours of breaking down equipment and cleaning up. A few of the guys from environmental services had kindly offered to come in at the end to help with that.

By thirty minutes prior to the start, every one of her volunteers was in place. She held a last-minute review of the day's events to ensure each person knew exactly where they would be going and what they would be doing. Katie thanked each one for their dedication. And punctuality. Now, all she needed was for the community to come.

And they did. Katie had not assigned any specific duties to herself. Ensuring that things ran smoothly would be task enough. By eleven, she was convinced that was her best decision yet. The initial rush had been huge, with people waiting to get in the door.

She was thankful but exhausted as the day progressed. Katie had seen Flynn, from a distance, as he walked in earlier with Sebastian. Their gazes connected, but she had been busy directing a group of the nursing students to their places. When she looked up again, he was gone. Probably better. The sight of Flynn was painful enough.

A local deli had donated lunch for the hungry staff. Katie had made sure that every helper got a chance to eat. By the end of the day, several thousand people had come through the doors, taking advantage of the day's offerings. The health fair had been a wild success. Katie was smiling ear to ear after speaking with the Director of Nursing. Ginny had personally congratulated her and promised to write a glowing letter of recommendation. Despite her fatigue, Katie practically danced with excitement.

Katie was the last to leave the building, only after ensuring every volunteer had gone and the medical office building was pristine. Sunset had already come and gone as she dragged herself to her car. She contemplated sleeping in it, except the temperature had dropped. All she wanted was a hot bath and her bed. What she got was Flynn, leaning up against her car.

"I hope you're half as proud of yourself as I am of you, Katie."

The words were her undoing. After all the anguish and sleepless nights, Katie finally lost it. She didn't even bother to hide the tears that rolled down her face.

"Yes, Flynn, I am," she answered in a toneless voice. The day had lost a bit of its shine. When would seeing him, talking to him, no longer be painful? "But more than anything, I'm exhausted. I just want to go home." She opened her doors remotely to prove her point.

Flynn stepped aside, graceful as a large jungle cat. "I'm not trying to make things harder for you, Katie. I wanted to say congratulations." He leaned in and kissed her cheek, his breath rustling her hair.

It took every bit of will power Katie didn't know she had to let him walk away. When he had disappeared into the night, she got into her car, leaned her head on the steering wheel, and sobbed.

Chapter Twenty

Katie awoke at dawn on Thanksgiving. She hadn't had a decent night sleep in two weeks thanks to Flynn. And her own fear. At least she had plenty of time to go for a walk before showering and heading to her parents' home. As much as she loved Thanksgiving, the thought of the long day made her tired. She really needed to sleep like a normal person.

Enough of those thoughts. Jumping out of bed, Katie dressed in warm layers. She pulled her hair into a ponytail. Makeup consisted of lip balm. Grabbing her keys, phone, and sunglasses, Katie set out.

The early morning air held a definite nip, so after stretching, Katie set out at a brisk pace. She would be shedding a layer soon enough. Thanksgiving was one of her favorite holidays. Always had been. Thanksgiving meant family. And lots of her mom's homemade cooking. Dinner rolls from De Luca's and a salad were her contribution. Neither involved Katie cooking.

She smiled as she greeted an older couple walking in the opposite direction. There were always others around when she walked. The natural beauty of her home town inspired people to be outdoors. The smile withered on her lips as she thought of Flynn. Nothing new there. She wondered what he was doing today. Was he in Atlanta with his family? She wondered if mystery woman would be joining him.

Katie quickened her stride, trying to outrun her thoughts. Things had not ended well with Flynn. The tension strained their working relationship. Exactly what she had feared all along. She had seen him several times since the parking lot. Each time was excruciatingly awkward. Partly her own fault, of course. Mostly. She had wanted to talk with him about everything that had happened, but the time was never right. And work wasn't the appropriate place.

She completed almost two miles before turning back towards the center of town and De Luca's Bakery. A fine sheen of sweat now covered her face. Katie removed her sweatshirt and tied it around her waist as she crossed the street to the bakery. She forced a smile. She wasn't in the mood for Kat's questioning.

Katie enjoyed the delicious aromas wafting out on the wind as she held the door for a departing customer. The scent of freshly baked bread set her stomach gurgling. She hadn't had much of an appetite since the issue with Flynn. She'd even lost a few pounds. Normally, she'd have been over the moon. Not this time.

"Hey, Katie. I have your order all ready to go," called Kat's father as she entered the bakery.

"Thanks Mr. De Luca. Happy Thanksgiving! How much do I owe you?"

A deep scowl marred his rugged face. "Like I would charge a member of the family. On a holiday, no less. For you, bella, a kiss." He came out from behind the counter as she approached.

Katie leaned up on her tip toes and placed a smacking kiss on his right cheek. Then another on his left. "Thank you, Mr. De Luca. That's very sweet of you." She grabbed the bag off the counter. "Besides, no one wants rolls I made."

Mr. De Luca laughed, as she had intended. Katie's lack of culinary skills was legendary in Windsor Falls. "One day, Katie, I will take you in the back and teach you the right way to bake. The Italian way, of course." His big belly shook with his laughter.

"I might take you up on that. Have a nice holiday. Tell Kat I'll call her later." Katie left the bakery and headed home. She needed to hurry. Being late for Thanksgiving Day prep was not allowed. Even though she didn't cook, there would be plenty of peeling and chopping for her to do.

After a quick shower and throwing on an outfit, Katie set out again. Today, as always, she was thankful that she hadn't moved far away. She wasn't sure how Elizabeth had lived in California for so long. Katie was thrilled to have her back home. She and Sam would be joining them later today for dinner.

As Katie turned on to her parents' block, disbelief overcame her. Parked at the curb was a shiny, black Mercedes. She only knew one person who drove that car. That answered the question of what Flynn would be doing for Thanksgiving.

She pulled into the driveway and parked. Her hands shook as she removed her keys from the ignition. Katie clenched them in her lap until the edges bit into her palm. Only then did she release her grip. And take a deep breath. She could do this. She didn't have a choice.

Katie got out of the car and went to the back to retrieve the dinner rolls and salad. Flynn was good friends with her brothers. Their poker nights were legendary. One of them must have mentioned to her mother that Flynn would be alone for Thanksgiving. Maggie would never allow that. But Katie had no idea why he was here so early, hours before dinner.

Katie's breathing was almost normal as she walked onto the porch. Very Zen of her. She would get through this day. All she had to do was stay busy. And not talk to Flynn. And not touch him. In any way. She was doomed. She hung her head in defeat rather than open the door, wondering if it was too late to run away. And so of course that's how Flynn found her. Standing on her own mother's front porch, contemplating retreat. The universe must really hate her.

"Katie, aren't you coming inside?" Flynn propped the storm door with his hip and took the salad from her nerveless hands. Their fingers brushed, and she stifled a gasp at the contact.

A false smile lit her face. If it didn't reach her eyes, there was nothing she could do about that. "Of course, I'm coming inside, Flynn. What a ridiculous question." She breezed through the door, sailing past him. Katie tossed out greetings to various family members, not stopping until she reached the safety of the kitchen.

The sight of her mother at the stove, wearing her ludicrous Thanksgiving apron, comforted her. This one sported a large cartoon turkey and read "I'm not pulling your leg. Happy Thanksgiving." The cartoon turkey's legs were mammoth and disproportionate to the rest of its body. "Nice one, Mom," she said, pointing to her mother's chest.

Maggie turned from the stove and hugged her daughter. "You like? It was a gift from your father. Other women get roses," she sighed dramatically. But Katie wasn't fooled for a bit. This was tradition. She'd never seen two people more in love than Joe and Maggie.

"He chose well. They keep getting funnier every year."

Flynn entered the kitchen carrying the salad Katie had made. "Good morning, Mrs. Fitzgerald. Where can I put this wonderful salad that Katie created?"

Maggie smiled. She bustled over to kiss him on the cheek. "I believe I already told you to call me Maggie. I'm sorry you won't be spending the holiday with your family. But I'm so pleased you can join us. If you don't mind, there's another fridge in the garage. We don't need that taking up room in here until dinnertime."

"No problem. And thank you again for inviting me. I was looking at a frozen turkey dinner all alone in my house before you were kind enough to include me."

Maggie made a distressed sound. Almost nothing bothered her as much as the thought of someone being alone on a holiday. Katie had to give Flynn credit. Throwing in the part about a frozen TV dinner was a nice touch.

"My goodness! We couldn't have that, Flynn. You're welcome here anytime."

Flynn smiled and left to take the salad to the garage. She would get through this, Katie reminded herself. "So, Mom, what can I do to help?"

Maggie laughed. "You can do what you always do, Katie. You can set the table. Take Flynn with you. You know where everything is. I'd say twelve to be safe. Plus, the kids of course." She turned back to the stove.

Katie had been setting holiday tables for years. She tended to get the non-culinary assignments. As for having Flynn help her, no thanks. She could do this in her sleep, and the last thing she needed was any more alone time with him. She went into the dining room to get started.

Unlike the kitchen, which was really the heart of this house, the dining room was reserved for holidays and other special occasions. The formal, Cherry table didn't bear the marks of six children as the kitchen table did. Katie's mother had polished the surface to a high sheen. The table sat eight without the leaves. Today, she would be adding them to meet the demands of a Fitzgerald family holiday. She noticed they were sitting in their box in the corner. Someone had brought them down from the attic, for which she was grateful. They were heavy, and the attic stairs were steep.

Katie had begun to wrestle the first out of the box, when another pair of hands appeared. "I'll get those," drawled Flynn.

Katie snatched her hands back. No touching Flynn today. "Thanks, but I'm fine. Wouldn't you rather be watching the parade with everyone?" She didn't want to be rude to him, but her own survival was more important.

"That's okay. Your mother sent me in to help you."

"I'm sure she did," Katie muttered under her breath.

A smile appeared on Flynn's handsome face. "It's just some help, Katie. I promise to keep my hands off you."

High spots of color appeared on her cheeks. Katie almost bit her tongue off to stop from answering. Because she wanted his hands on her. All over her. Exactly the kind of thoughts that got her in trouble. She crawled under the table to unhook the latch, allowing for the leaves to be added. When she came back up, she saw Flynn standing there with a peculiar smile on his face.

"What?"

"Oh, nothing. Just enjoying the view," he drawled.

"Very funny," she sputtered. Trying her best to ignore him, Katie walked to one end of the table and pulled. "This would go better if you pulled from your end, you know."

Flynn nodded and sauntered to the other end. He grabbed the table and pulled. Katie tried to not think about how those hands had felt on her body. She muttered a curse. Being around him was so much harder.

Flynn smirked. "Such language. Problems, Katie?"

"No." The last thing she needed was for Flynn to realize how much he still affected her. She pulled her end of the table out a little further and then walked over to grab the first of the leaves. But Flynn beat her to the punch, removing it from the box.

He held up a hand to stop her. "I know you can do this all by yourself. After all, you don't need me for anything. You've made that clear. But I was not raised that way." He placed both leaves in the table and left the room without a word.

Hollow victory. After she locked the table again, Katie found the appropriate table cloth. She smoothed it over the table and set a dozen places. She lovingly fingered the handle of a fork, thinking about the many relatives who had used it before her. It belonged to a set that her mother had received from her grandmother. Katie closed her eyes on the shaft of pain that pierced her heart. That's what she wanted; kids and grandkids to pass things along to.

*****

Flynn paused in the doorway, watching the pain that crossed Katie's face. The knowledge that he had created that pain cut him just as deeply. Katie was proud and wouldn't want him as a witness to this. He retreated from the room, not wanting to cause her anymore distress.

"Can I give you some advice on our Katie?"

Flynn startled, not knowing her mother was standing right behind him. He smiled down at her. Not knowing what to expect, Flynn lifted one shoulder.

"Come into the kitchen, dear. We'll have some tea."

He followed her into the kitchen and took a seat at the table. Watching Maggie bustle around the kitchen reminded him of Katie. Both had a purpose and efficiency to their movements.

When the water boiled, Maggie joined him at the table, pouring it into two mugs. She breathed in the scent of her fragrant tea, smiling as she did. "My mother thought this was the answer to all the world's problems." She took an experimental sip to check the temperature before sighing. "She may have had a point. Tell me what's wrong between you and my Katie."

Flynn had the urge to run a finger along the neck of his sweater, even though he was wearing a V-neck. Suddenly, there wasn't enough air to breathe. He replied cautiously. "That's not something I'm comfortable discussing with you." He gave her a wan smile by way of an apology.

"Good answer. As much as I want to know everything about my children's lives, I have to accept that somethings weren't meant for my ears." She patted Flynn on the hand, making him feel like a small child. "May I give you some advice, then?"

Flynn smiled. "Of course. She's a bit of an enigma."

"You know, of course, about David."

The vehemence with which she said his name, almost spat it really, made Flynn never want to be in that position. He nodded.

"That man was no good for her. Long before he left her the way he did. He didn't care about Katie, only himself. Always put himself first. But she thought she was in love with him." She sighed deeply. "It's hard to watch your children make mistakes. To get hurt. But that's what Joe and I had to do with Katie. To be honest, I was pleased when David left. But not with the way he broke her trust."

Flynn wondered if there was a point to this but nodded again.

"I'm telling you this to make you understand. Katie doesn't trust anymore. Especially handsome doctors. And, as we all know Flynn, you are a handsome doctor. You have your work cut out for you."

"That's it? 'You have your work cut out for you?' I thought you were going to give me some advice." He tamped down the bubbling frustration. Yelling at her mother was not a way to impress Katie.

Maggie smiled. "You're a smart man, Flynn. Figure it out. Just don't hurt her." A scary glint replaced the early benevolence in her eye. "My Joe's in the construction business. They'd never find your body."

Flynn sat in a stunned silence, his heart beating wildly in his chest. Then Maggie burst out laughing. "Gets them every time." She got up and left the kitchen.

He stayed where he was, sitting at the table, and drank some of his tea. Interesting family, he thought. Not for the first time.

*****

Katie managed to avoid Flynn for several hours. Not an easy task. But, then it was time for dinner. Katie volunteered to sit in the kitchen with the kids but was vetoed by her mother. Aidan got that job, much to his horror, because he didn't have a date with him. She knew better than to argue. With her mother. On a national holiday.

They all trooped into the dining room, each family member carrying various dishes. Flynn held her chair for her. Of course, since he was her date, she was expected to sit next to him. So much for avoiding him. Maybe dinner would be a quick affair, she thought. But Katie wasn't stupid. Just desperate.

Donovan said grace, and chaos broke out. Food passed in both directions for a few moments until everyone had what they wanted on their plates. Katie had skipped breakfast for the occasion. But one really needed to fast for a week to do her mother's holiday meal justice.

After a little while, she heard a distinct groan coming from her left. "Let me guess," she said not unkindly. "You ate breakfast."

Flynn wiped his mouth on the maroon linen napkin before answering. "I did. How'd you know?"

"Rookie mistake."

"Good to know for next time."

"What makes you so sure there will be a next time?" Katie turned and asked Riley a question about the latest book she was reading. That would keep her busy for at least ten minutes. Riley was the bookworm of the family.

But Katie only half listened, as she often did when Riley went off on a book tangent. It didn't help that Flynn's thigh pressed against hers. Whenever he shifted in his chair, his leg rubbed against hers. Katie didn't know if this was deliberate or not. Either way, it was distracting.

Thousands of calories later, dinner finally ended. Since she was working that night, Katie would be leaving soon. They had eaten a bit earlier than usual to allow her to take a nap before going into the hospital. The tryptophan would help with that. She carried her plate into the kitchen and rinsed it before placing it into the dishwasher.

She found her mother relaxing in the family room. It was tradition in the Fitzgerald home that whoever cooked didn't do any of the clean-up. Since she loved to cook but hated dishes, this worked in Maggie's favor. Katie leaned over her mother's chair and kissed her. "Thanks for such a wonderful meal, Mom. I've gotta go digest some of this before work."

"It's a shame you have to work tonight, Katie. Won't you take some pie with you?"

The thought of pie almost put her full stomach over the edge. "I couldn't eat another bite, Mom. But, don't worry. I'll be around this week-end. I'm sure they're will be some left."

Katie grabbed her purse and coat from the closet and slipped out the front door. Muffled sounds of laughter and conversation followed her into the street. She left before Flynn realized she was gone and felt a bit guilty but not enough to say goodbye. It was easier this way.

Chapter Twenty-One

The next week passed quickly. Katie had been fortunate enough to evade Flynn at work, for which she was grateful. She was a coward. But Flynn Reynolds was a hard man to get over. Seeing him poured salt in the wounds, even if she had been the one to break things off.

She still had no idea who the mystery woman was, not that she had asked him. Her identity was a major source of gossip at Windsor Falls Medical Center. Another reason to avoid a relationship with him. Katie didn't care to have her personal life on display. She wasn't going there again.

On Wednesday night, Katie reported for her third shift in a row. She was exhausted and cranky. She had not slept well since seeing Flynn on Thanksgiving. Having him at her family dinner had felt so right. Once you got past the awkwardness of trying to avoid him. Her brothers liked him. Poker buddies and all that. Her mother asked about him all the time. Not very subtle that one. As a result, she dreamed about him. Of them. And how they had been together. She missed him, something that hadn't happened since David's departure years before.

Disgusted with herself, Katie got to work and prayed for an easy night. So, of course, she got anything but that. The unit was full, and they were short staffed. There was a virus making its way around the hospital, decimating staff nurses. As a result, she had two patients plus being in charge, which was never good. Even worse when one tried his best, twice, to die on her. Katie almost wept with relief when day staff started coming in the next morning.

She handed off her two patients and discussed the unit with the oncoming charge nurse. She was about to make her escape when she heard someone call her name. Katie froze in place. She didn't need to turn around to know that David was standing on the other side of the desk.

She didn't know whether to laugh or throw something. She turned, without smiling, to face him. "David. This is a surprise. What are you doing here?" Screw her manners. She didn't care, and she knew her mother wouldn't be civil to him either.

"Why I came to see you of course, Katie. You always were the funny one."

That was odd. David had never found her funny before today. Feeling as though she were sleep walking, Katie rounded the desk and approached him. She stopped short of arm's reach. "I can't imagine why, David. After all, you made it very clear when you left that you were never coming back."

A megawatt smile brightened his face. He always had been a bit of a salesman. "I missed you, Katie."

She peered up into his gorgeous face. His thick hair was just as blonde. His teeth just as brightly white. He looked great. Yet she felt nothing other than anger. David assumed that he could just stroll back into her life as though nothing had happened. That thought alone made her blood boiling.

David, who could never read her on a good day, missed the flush on her face and tenseness of her muscles. Instead, he closed the gap between them, enfolding her in a hug.

Katie was acutely aware of everyone staring at them. She hated that more than anything. She struggled a bit to get free of his arms, backing up as she did. That's when she saw Flynn, standing inside the door of the unit.

He held her gaze for a moment. But it was long enough for her to see the pain in his eyes. The sadness etched into his features. Then he was gone.

"Flynn, wait." She yelled. But the unit door closed behind him.

She started to run in that direction, but David grabbed her arm. "Katie, I need to talk to you."

She whirled on him. "Really? What could you possibly have to say to me after almost three years?" Her chest heaved. "You're sorry? Tough. Too little, too late, David."

"You don't mean that, Katie."

His face bore the utter disbelief in his tone. And Katie laughed. Until she could hardly breathe. And suddenly she didn't care that everyone could see. "Oh, but I do, David. It took me a while to figure it out, but you did me a favor, leaving when you did. I was too blinded by you to see what you were, David. Not good for me."

He puffed out his chest and waved a hand at her. "Obviously that family of yours convinced you of that after I left, Katie. They never liked me."

And then she smiled for the first time since seeing David standing in her ICU. The first real smile. "No, David, they didn't. Because you weren't good enough for me. They were just too kind to say it to my face. I wish they had." She glanced at the closed doors of the unit. She needed to find Flynn.

Without even a backward glance to the man she had once thought she loved, Katie ran towards the elevator. She needed to talk with him. Now. She had so much to say, but it was all a jumble in her head. How could she ever make him understand that she had been afraid? But being away from him these past few weeks, and then seeing David again, had made everything clear.

She missed Flynn. In ways she had never missed David. Above and beyond the wild attraction she felt for Flynn, he was comfortable and easy to be around. He didn't try to change her. "Improve" her as David had called it when they were together. Even when she filled the house with smoke trying to make him dinner, he had laughed with her and ordered pizza. David would have never done that.

There weren't any guarantees in life. Except one. If she didn't take this chance with Flynn, didn't risk her heart, she would always regret it. He was a good man who cared about her deeply. She knew that now. All she had to do was tell him.

That thought drove her. Too impatient to wait, Katie took the stairs, running down to the second floor. She slowed to a walk across the pedestrian bridge that connected the medical center to the medical office building. And then she ran up two flights of stairs to his office. Sweat poured down her face. Her lungs burned. She really needed to start exercising. But that didn't stop her from bursting into the office. A startled receptionist looked like she might call security. Katie was too out of breath to even explain what she was doing there. Luckily, an amused Sebastian came in right behind her.

"Katie, what a surprise!" She gave him a wan smile, the best she could do while her heart beat wildly and she gasped for air.

Sebastian ushered Katie down the hallway to his office. Once inside, he shut the door. "We have about five minutes before my first patient. What's going on?"

"I need... to see ...Flynn. Is he here?" She leaned over, head between her knees, and blew out a long breath. Katie clenched her hands against the anxiety that flooded her system. Flynn seeing her with David was the last thing Katie had wanted. And she needed to tell him she wasn't afraid anymore. That she wanted to take a chance on love. With him.

But Sebastian was shaking his head and had a sad look on his face. Not what she needed at this point. "I'm sorry honey. You missed him."

Hysteria bubbled right below the surface, threatening to take over. "What?" Her voice was high pitched and piercing, but Katie didn't care. "Where is he?"

Sebastian handed her a bottle of water. She drank from it greedily as he explained. "He stopped in before leaving for Atlanta, Katie. I thought you knew. This weekend is his parents' anniversary party."

"But it's only Thursday morning. I thought he wouldn't leave until tomorrow."

Sebastian reached out and touched her shoulder. "Sorry. He's had this arranged for months. He's heading down today because his sisters are all coming in early to spend time together before the party. I'm covering the practice."

Katie slumped into the chair in front of Sebastian's desk. It seemed appropriate that this was where patients sat to hear news about their hearts. She was feeling pretty heart sick herself. She had blown it. Now Flynn was going away for a few days with the image in his head of her wrapped in David's arms. And nothing settled between them. How was she going to fix this?

Sebastian dropped into the chair next to her and took her hands in his. That was all it took. Big, fat tears slid down her face. Katie didn't even try to stop them. It was too much.

"None of that now, Katie. Anything but tears." He shuddered. "I hate it when women cry. What's wrong, honey?"

She sniffed and grabbed some tissues from the box perched on his desk. After blowing her nose loudly, Katie turned to Sebastian. "I love him. That's what's wrong."

"And the problem is?"

Katie fixed him a look that said he might not be all that bright. "The problem," she drawled, "is that you are not Flynn. I just said I love him, out loud, for the first time ever. And I told *you*." She shook her head and muttered something unflattering about men under her breath. "No offense."

"None taken." Sebastian got up and walked around his desk. Reaching into the center drawer, he pulled out a heavy vellum envelope in a lovely cream color. He came back around the desk, leaning against it, and handed the envelope to Katie. "Maybe this will help."

Her hands shook as she drew out the contents from the envelope. She held her breath as she read the invitation. Saturday evening, six o'clock for drinks to start. The Peachtree Country Club, Atlanta, Georgia. She looked up at Sebastian and tried to hand it back. "I can't take this. I can't go there alone."

"But you can go with me. And you can do this. What better way to show you care than to come to this? Meet his family? That smacks of commitment." He looked her up and down. "I might suggest a change of wardrobe first, though."

His words had their desired effect as Katie burst out laughing. "What?" She stood and struck a pose. "Wrinkled scrubs with a questionable stain won't make the dress code?"

"Probably not. But if Flynn is half as crazy about you as I think he is, I don't think it would matter what you wear." His face grew serious. Frown lines bunched between his eyes. "Please tell me that you like him for who he is. Not what he is. Or rather the bank account attached to him."

Katie's face flamed with color. She sputtered in her incense. "Sebastian Walker, what do you think I am? I couldn't care less about that. If you knew me better, you'd know that."

Sebastian chuckled, making her outrage grow. "Calm down, Katie, I had to check. He and I have both had that problem with women." He shrugged a shoulder as if it was an everyday occurrence.

"Oh. I guess I never thought about it." Her stomach filled with knots. "Is he that rich?"

Sebastian grinned. "Other than his education, I don't believe Flynn has ever touched a dime of his inheritance."

Katie chewed on her lower lip. "I guess I never thought about it. But that doesn't matter to me. I love him for who he is. Not who his family is."

Sebastian's grin split his face. "That's all I need to hear. So why don't you go buy yourself a dress, and I'll drive you there tomorrow. You can be my date."

Hope bloomed in her chest for the first time. "Are you sure?"

Sebastian nodded. "I can leave right after my last patient. How's two o'clock? My father keeps a suite at a hotel not far from the club for out of town guests and business dealings. You can stay there."

Suddenly emboldened by the idea, Katie agreed. "Okay then. Pick me up at two." She rattled off her address. Hugging him hard, Katie thanked him for everything.

On her way out the door, she waved to the still suspicious woman at the front desk. Her heart soared. She could do this. She loved him, and she was going to tell him. Apparently in front of a large audience. Being there with Flynn, at the anniversary party as he had wanted, was important to her. It would show Flynn how serious she was.

Katie texted Elizabeth to see where she was as she waited for the elevator. There was no way she could sleep now, not with adrenaline coursing through her.

Starting a shift. What's up? came Elizabeth's reply.

Are you busy? Have a moment? On my way out, Katie responded.

Elizabeth's answer was instantaneous. *Stop by.*

She would do that, Katie thought. She needed advice on what to wear. What to do with her hair. What to say. Basically everything. Elizabeth had recently overcome demons of her own to have the life she now enjoyed with Sam. Who better to help her?

*****

Flynn pushed the Mercedes engine as he sped down route eighty-five towards Atlanta. When the needle danced past a hundred, he took his foot off the gas and engaged cruise control at seventy-five. No need to die today.

His car may have settled, but he hadn't. Acid washed his stomach as he thought about Katie in the arms of that other man. Another nurse whispered the name David to her friend as they passed him in the entryway of the unit. That was all he needed to hear. Katie's ex. He thought that she was no longer in love with him, but the sight of her in his arms said otherwise. Not his problem, he told himself.

Thirty miles later, it was still his problem. He had fallen in love with her, and she was afraid of getting her heart broken. Again. Katie shied away from anything that smacked of commitment, which was why he was heading to his parents' anniversary party alone. He missed her. And he wanted her to meet his family. So, no, he wasn't worried so much about David as he was about Katie and her inability to commit.

Flynn's hands clenched the smooth leather of the steering wheel. It took everything in him to not turn around and head back to Windsor Falls to talk some sense into her thick head. But his family had been planning this for almost a year. As much as he wanted to see her right now, Flynn knew continuing to Atlanta was the right thing to do. He would head back as early Sunday as he could. One way or the other, he had to make her see that he wasn't going to hurt her. That he loved her. With a plan in place, Flynn tuned the radio to classic rock and tapped his fingers on the wheel, his heart lighter.

*****

Elizabeth greeted Katie with a warm hug and ushered her into the staff lounge. It was the only place to find any privacy. Katie appreciated the gesture. Tongues were already wagging upstairs. No reason to start them in the ED as well.

"So, what's going on?" Elizabeth asked as she filled her water bottle from the cooler.

Katie watched her friend drink from the bottle, suspicion growing in her mind. Elizabeth, like many healthcare professionals she knew, was a confirmed coffee addict. She gasped as the implication hit. "Are you pregnant?" she squealed.

Elizabeth's face flushed. "Shush," she commanded. "No one knows yet, and Sam and I want to keep it that way. It's still very new." She smiled beatifically. "A honeymoon baby." The corners of her mouth drooped. "I'm trying to not get too excited."

Katie wrapped her arms around her former sister-in-law. She knew that Elizabeth was thinking of the baby she had lost years ago when Connor died. Her heart ached for her. This had to be difficult.

Elizabeth stepped out of her embrace and wiped a single tear from her face. She laughed self-consciously. "I'm a mess already, and I haven't even seen an OB yet."

"But you know for sure?"

"Oh yes. Just like last time. My breasts are sensitive. As is my stomach." She frowned at the thought. "No more coffee. Or wine. And I've taken like a dozen home pregnancy tests. Just to be sure."

"And Sam? How's he?"

The beautiful smile returned to her face. "He's over the moon. But crazy. Wants me to quit my job and stay home. Wrapped in cotton." She laughed.

"I can see him saying that. He'll calm down. Don't you remember how nuts Donovan was through every one of Nora's pregnancies? Wouldn't let her lift anything heavier than a pencil. Wanted her to stop driving. Stop exercising. Ugh! It was a disaster."

Elizabeth held onto her side as she laughed hard. "Had he never met her? Nora is not exactly a push over."

"Exactly. Sam will calm down. You have a long way to go." Katie saw the anxiety creep back into her friend's eyes. "Elizabeth, this is different. You're healthy and Sam isn't going anywhere. You're going to do fine."

She took a deep breath. "I know you're right, Katie. Sam and I have talked about it. I have an appointment set up with Dr. Livingston in OB tomorrow for a consult. I'm eating well and exercising. I'm almost thirty-six, but there's nothing I can do about that. We're taking it one day at a time, for the next nine months." She squeezed Katie's hand. "And no one knows but the three of us now. I need to keep it that way until I pass twelve weeks. Then I'll feel better."

Katie returned the squeeze. "Absolutely. I understand, and I promise to not tell anyone. Doesn't mean I won't enjoy having a secret from my siblings."

She wiped the tears off her face. "Now, tell me why you were looking for me in the first place. This has something to do with a certain handsome cardiologist, if I'm not mistaken."

That shouldn't have surprised Katie, but it did. "How did you know?" Then the lightbulb turned on. "Oh, that's right. You two are buddies."

"Yes, that. And the fact that no one else exists when you two are together. Not to mention the sexual tension you can cut with a knife."

Katie felt her face flush but didn't care. Why deny it? She told Elizabeth what had happened between them. Then she mentioned this morning's events.

"Well, I wasn't here for the whole David fiasco, but I've heard enough to know I'm not a fan. Sebastian's plan is brilliant! And I have just the place for the dress.

Have you been to Lisa Warner's shop, Infatuation, in town? She has some stunning dresses. She was in my year in high school. Her maiden name was Babcock."

Recognition dawned on Katie. "Oh, on Poplar Street, around the corner from Kat's bakery. I've drooled from the sidewalk but never had the courage to go in." She glanced sown at her scrubs and shrugged. "I'm usually pretty casual."

"I get it. I'm the same way. But this occasion calls for a killer, yet classy, dress. Lisa will fix you up. And she has all the accessories you'll need as well." She stopped as she heard her name paged over the intercom. "And now, I have to get back to what's shaping up to be a busy morning."

Katie hugged her friend. "Thanks so much for listening. You are a loyal friend." She glanced down at Elizabeth's still flat stomach. "I'm so excited for both of you."

"Me too," Elizabeth replied as she walked back into the ER.

Chapter Twenty-Two

Sitting next to Sebastian in his stylish car, Katie wondered what she was doing for the thirty-seventh time. Sebastian turned into the lane leading to the country club, and Katie knew she only had seconds to change her mind. She clenched her hands on the silver clutch Lisa had insisted was perfect with the dress. And remembered to breathe.

Sebastian grinned at her. "Almost there."

"Yes," she murmured from between clenched teeth. "I can see that."

Get a grip, she ordered herself. Katie smoothed an imaginary wrinkle from the front of her gorgeous dress. Elizabeth had been right. Lisa was brilliant. The slim column of silk was navy blue, almost black. The color was an elegant foil for her bright red hair. Tiny, silver beads swirled in a pattern along the bottom and neckline. The front was modest, with a high neck that left her shoulders bare. The back revealed a tantalizing amount of skin without being too much. Lisa assured her it would be perfect for this crowd.

A pair of silver sandals and the matching clutch completed her look. The diamond bracelet and earrings that she had borrowed from Elizabeth were her only jewelry. The magician in the hotel salon had tamed her locks into an up do. Several curly tendrils framed her face on either side.

They reached the front of the valet line, and Katie had wrangled her nerves into some semblance of order. True, butterflies still floated through her stomach.

But that she could handle. She would feel better once she had spoken with Flynn. Gotten this whole thing settled. Then she would meet his family and finally enjoy the evening. At least that's what she hoped.

Sebastian came around to her side of the car as the valet slid in. "You look amazing, Katie. If you weren't ready to settle for my friend, I'd give him a run for his money." His wolfish smile made her laugh.

"Very funny, Sebastian. As you know, I am not 'settling.' But thanks for making me laugh. It helps with the butterflies."

"You have nothing to worry about, Katie." He kissed her hand lightly before tucking it in his elbow. "Shall we?"

She took a deep breath, willing the nerves away, and nodded.

Sebastian led the way through the front doors. He greeted many people along the way. Katie wasn't surprised. Sebastian looked completely at home here. They turned down a hallway, and he led her through the door of the grand ballroom. The room was decorated tastefully in black and gold, befitting for a fiftieth wedding anniversary. There were more than a hundred and fifty people milling about, most in small groups.

"How many of these people do you know?" she whispered to her companion.

Sebastian grinned at her. "Ninety percent. But there's only one that matters, and there he is."

Katie followed his finger to where he pointed out a man in black tie. Even with his back turned, Katie could tell it was Flynn. The tuxedo emphasized his long legs and the width of his shoulders. She remembered it from the wedding.

What she didn't expect was the raven-haired beauty clinging to his arm. It was the same woman from the ICU earlier this week. Only this time, she was even more stunning in a floor-length, emerald green gown that showed her curves to perfection.

Katie stopped dead in her tracks, not an easy feat in high heels. "I changed my mind," she whispered to Sebastian. Katie turned, trying to lead him back to the door. But when a man weighing at least fifty pounds more than you didn't go in that direction, you didn't either. She was still turned away from Flynn but the hairs were standing up on the back of her neck. It was too late. He was right behind her. Time to face the music.

Katie turned as she mustered the shreds of her dignity. At least getting this over with would allow for a quick escape. But when she faced him, the mystery woman was still attached to his arm. This was more than she could take.

"I'm sorry. This was a mistake." Sliding her arm from Sebastian's, she turned to leave but a hand grabbed her opposite wrist.

"Please, Katie, don't go. There's someone I'd like for you to meet."

Before he could perform the introductions, the mystery woman stepped forward. And to Katie's shock, hugged her. "I'm so happy to finally meet you, Katie. My brother has told me so much about you."

First shock then relief flooded through Katie as the other woman's words hit home. "Brother?" she parroted aloud.

Sebastian stepped in. "Since Flynn seems to have lost his social graces, allow me. Katie, this is Allison, Flynn's sister. Allison, this is Katie Fitzgerald from Windsor Falls."

"I saw you at the hospital the other night. I thought you were…" Katie stopped there, having already made a fool of herself.

Allison grinned and looped her arm through Katie's. "I can only imagine what you thought, Katie, and I'm so sorry. I came up to drop in on my brother unexpectedly, and I tracked him to the ICU. Please forgive me."

Katie would have forgiven the other woman anything now that she knew she was Flynn's sister. "No need for forgiveness." She smiled at Allison.

Flynn cleared his throat. "If we're done here, I'd like to take Katie to meet our parents. If I can find them, anyway."

Everyone laughed, and Sebastian took Allison by the arm. "Let me buy you a drink, Ally. Where's that husband of yours anyway?"

Katie didn't hear Allison's reply as Sebastian led Flynn's sister away. Suddenly, she was alone in a crowded room with Flynn. Her mouth was dry and her throat tightened. "I need to talk with you before you introduce me to anyone else. Please."

Flynn nodded and led her to an empty edge of dance floor. "Will this do?" he asked as he enfolded her in his strong arms.

Coherent thought was next to impossible, so she nodded. They swayed in time to a lovely old ballad. Katie tried to think of what she needed to say, but her thoughts floated away like notes of the music. Instead, she leaned into Flynn and inhaled his scent. Closing her eyes, she reveled in his touch. This was what she had missed. Being with him. *This* was worth risking her heart.

When the song ended, she stepped out of his arms but slid her hand into his. "We need to talk." Spying an empty corner, she led Flynn to it. Now or never, she thought.

"Katie, I have something to say as well."

She placed a finger against his lips. "Please, let me go first." He nodded and fell silent.

Katie swallowed, knowing the next few words out of her mouth held the power to change her life. "Flynn, David means nothing to me. Less than nothing. I need for you to know that."

He shook his head. "I do, Katie."

Relief flooded her. "Oh. Good. When you saw him with me the other day, I worried you thought something different."

He shook his head. "David doesn't scare me. But you do."

Katie took both of his hands in her own and met his gaze. The normally cobalt blue was almost black with emotion. "Flynn, I'm so sorry for pushing you away. You were trying to let me into your life, and I panicked." She took a breath and let it out. "I was so afraid you'd break my heart that I got scared. I ended up hurting myself. And you. I shut you out. I've missed you, Flynn. More than I've ever missed anyone." Emotion choked her, and Katie couldn't say another word.

That's when Flynn stepped in. "No, Katie. If anyone should apologize, it should be me. I pushed you too far and too fast when you warned me not to. I'm sorry for that. Maybe we could slow things down a bit and start over?"

Katie shook her head no, and his face fell. She smiled into his eyes. "No, Flynn, I'm afraid I can't do that." She placed her hand along the curve of his cheek. "I love you, Flynn. I don't want to slow down. I want to move forward. I want to take a chance. With you."

Happiness and love shone in his eyes. "Yes, Katie, of course. That's what I want too. I was planning on heading back early tomorrow to try and convince you to take a chance on me."

"And how exactly would you do that?"

He laughed, a rich sound coming from deep within him. "Well, I'd show you now, but there's about two hundred too many people here." He leaned down and branded her with a hot kiss that left Katie weak in the knees. She clung to him for support. Flynn lifted his head. "In case you haven't already guessed, I love you too."

Katie smiled at Flynn, her love for him glowing from every inch of her body. "I know, Flynn. You are so worth taking a chance on," she whispered before touching her lips to his.

The End

Acknowledgments

I'm delighted to report that it did not take me fifteen years to publish this novel. Unlike my first novel, *Coming Home*. *Taking Chances* was, however, just as much a labor of love. Only this time, I have assembled an army of helpers. Once again, as with *Coming Home*, I was swept away by the characters and the endless beauty of the Blue Ridge Mountains. I hope you enjoy reading *Taking Chances* as much as I did writing it.

Thank you to the extraordinary Lauren Plude. Lauren is so much more than my editor. She has been my sounding board and rock. While I am so excited for this next chapter in her life, I'm more than a little sad to be losing her. Good luck with the new job and city, Lauren.

Julie Cupp, Head Fairy at Marie Force's Formatting Fairies is a woman with seemingly unlimited patience. And I appreciate that. She saw me through copy-editing and formatting. I only hope this second time was a bit easier for her...

Rebecca Pau, of The Final Wrap, is the most amazing graphic artist ever. I continued to be both impressed with and humbled by her talent. This time, I just told her "Mountains again, and it's Fall." Thank you for this second, beautiful cover. I tell everyone about your mad skills!

Kate Burns, Eleanor Boyle and Denise Gatton are my beta readers. I so appreciate their time and effort, although they are far too kind. Thank you, ladies!

Writing while also working full time is never easy. Thank you to my husband and children for understanding and being, mostly, patient with me. I try to not miss a single soccer game or band concert while juggling these chainsaws. Same goes for my friends, both here in North Carolina and up north. I love you all!!

Wondering who will fall in love next? Read an excerpt from the next Windsor Falls novel, *Second Chances*, by Kimberley O'Malley. Keep in mind this is a work in progress and is therefore subject to change. *Second Chances* will be available in the fall.

Charlie Avery ran as though her life depended upon it. Sometimes, she thought it might. Running had always been a favorite past time of hers, and it had served many purposes. As a child, she had run while playing soccer and basketball for her school teams. In college, she continued running for the physical benefits. During her four years of medical school, running was an escape from the grind of reading and studying. But she had always been blessed with a high metabolism, so running was never just about keeping fit. These days, sadly, she could only jog. And lightly at that. And it was more for her mental health.

Her heart rate kicked up just at the thought of what she had done, and seen, over the past months. Volunteering for Doctors without Borders had been a dream of hers. Last year, after several years of practice as an emergency medicine physician, Charlie had felt ready. The large urban medical center in Chicago had been an excellent place to hone her skills as an emergency physician, but the city was not meant to be her permanent home. Charlotte Grace Avery was a southern girl at heart, born and raised in Charleston, South Carolina. Chicago had just been another in a long series of ways to piss off her mother. Africa had taken the cake.

Charlie raised her head and looked around the quiet streets of Windsor Falls, North Carolina. Her best friend, Elizabeth, someone she had met and instantly bonded with in residency, had returned to her hometown last year after ten years away. Considering the tragedy that had befallen Elizabeth, Charlie wasn't surprised her friend had left here. Coming home, and deciding to stay, had taken great courage. Elizabeth had rekindled her relationship with her childhood friend, Sam, and a great love blossomed. Elizabeth and Sam were married just last October. Sadly, Charlie was already in Africa. She hated to miss the wedding of her best friend.

But she was here now, thousands of miles from the horror and misery she had left behind. Her heart beat erratically in her chest at the thought of those days in Africa. Charlie took a series of deep breaths and slowed to a walk. Remembered to feel the warmth of the spring sun on her bare arms. She was safe here. She glanced at the scenery as she walked. Lovely homes with well-manicured lawns flanked both sides of the street. There weren't any babies dying from hunger and disease. Nor were there rebel soldiers, sun glinting off their deadly guns. She was safe here, she reminded herself.

Charlie turned the corner and slowed further. Time to warm down. She had already put in two miles, which was nothing compared to what she used to be able to do. But that was before Africa and everything that had happened. No need to push it and risk her recovery. The growling of her stomach reminded her that she had skipped breakfast this morning. There were some amazing scents coming from the kitchen of the B&B this morning. Charlie had gotten to town late last night and hadn't even seen Elizabeth yet. She had come in a day early when even one more day with her mother might have resulted in murder. And not hers.

Charlie sighed at thoughts of her family. Just as quickly, she pushed aside those thoughts. She was in Windsor Falls, not Charleston. No one had expectations of her here. She could be herself. Whatever that was.

After two months with her parents, during which she was supposed to be resting and healing, Charlie had almost lost her mind. Which explained her early arrival in Windsor Falls. She had quit her position in Chicago and shipped her few belongings to South Carolina prior to taking off for Africa. Now she was back and essentially homeless. The last few weeks had proven that Charleston was no longer home for Charlie.

Elizabeth's mention of a position at her ER, here in Windsor Falls, had been a lifeline. She had an interview on Friday. Hopefully, her experience and a good word from Elizabeth would suffice. The opportunity couldn't have come at a better time.

Thoughts of seeing her old friend again lowered her pulse rate. She and Elizabeth had met on day one of their emergency medicine residency in Los Angeles. Theirs had been an instant friendship made stronger by the shared hell of residency. Despite the long and often crazy hours, the two found time to hang out and help each other through. Charlie was the first person that Elizabeth ever told about her doomed marriage and miscarriage back in North Carolina. In turn, Charlie had regaled her with painful stories of her childhood, fraught with her mother's endless attempts to "fix" Charlie.

Even after Elizabeth stayed in Los Angeles and Charlie elected to go to Chicago, the two had remained close. They would see each other when their scheduled allowed and talked several times per week. Elizabeth had always spoken so highly of her hometown, that Charlie wasn't surprised when she decided to stay after her mom had become ill. Seeing it for the first time, Charlie could understand why.

She slowed to a halt, clutching her abdomen and breathing heavily. Most days, Charlie felt fine. Almost normal. The jogging may have been a bit much. The sounds of children's laughter drifted on the breeze. Charlie glanced up and saw a small, neighborhood park. A dozen or more small children climbed on a jungle gym while others shrieked on the swings. She watched them with a touch of envy. Charlie had always loved the feel of the wind in her hair as she sailed through the sky.

Because she was focused on that spot, she saw a small, blonde child dart out into the road after an errant soccer ball. The little girl was just a blur. As was the car speeding down the street from the opposite direction. Charlie had mere seconds to react. She sprinted towards the girl, diving for her just seconds before the car would have made contact. The momentum sent both rolling across the hard pavement.